Grand Opening:
A Family Business Novel

Grand Opening:
A Family Business Novel

Carl Weber

with

Eric Pete

www.urbanbooks.net

Urban Books, LLC
97 N18th Street
Wyandanch, NY 11798

Grand Opening: A Family Business Novel
Copyright © 2015 Carl Weber
Copyright © 2015 Eric Pete

ISBN 13: 978-1-62286-911-4
ISBN 10: 1-62286-911-7

First Hardcover Printing September 2015
Printed in the United States of America

10 9 8 7 6 5 4 3 2 1

This is a work of fiction. Any references or similarities to actual events, real people, living or dead, or to real locales are intended to give the novel a sense of reality. Any similarity in other names, characters, places, and incidents is entirely coincidental.

Distributed by Kensington Publishing Corp.
Submit Orders to:
Customer Service
400 Hahn Road
Westminster, MD 21157-4627
Phone: 1-800-733-3000
Fax: 1-800-659-2436

Grand Opening:
A Family Business Novel

Carl Weber

with

Eric Pete

Other Family Business Novels

The Family Business with Eric Pete
The Family Business 2 with Treasure Hernandez
The Family Business 3 with Treasure Hernandez
To Paris with Love with Eric Pete
The Man in 3B

Other Novels by Carl Weber

Lookin' for Luv
Baby Momma Drama
Player Haters
The Preacher's Son
So You Call Yourself a Man
The First Lady
Something on the Side
Up to No Good
Big Girls Do Cry
Torn Between Two Lovers
The Choir Director
She Ain't the One with Mary B. Morrison

Dedication

This book is dedicated to Johnny and Minnie Walker, my great-grandparents from Waycross, Georgia. If it wasn't for you, I would have never known about Oak Street, and this story probably never would have been written.

Dear Readers,

I sincerely hope that you enjoy this addition to the Family Business saga. I'm extremely proud of this new work, and can't wait for you to read it. During my travels, people have been asking me about my decision to write in this genre. The question has come up over and over again at book signings, speaking engagements, and book club appearances, to the point where I knew I had to write this letter. Over the years my books have covered church characters, big girls, con men, and gangsters. This time, I wanted to do something with more of a period piece, a prequel to the Family Business that had my voice and the drama that I always bring.

Once I made the decision to try something new, I got in my car, where I do my best thinking, and drove around L.A., where I was working on my latest film project. Before I reached the ocean, I came up with the story and shared it with Eric. I think you're really going to love the new characters, like Larry, Levi, Big Shirley, and of course my favorite, NeeNee.

So, I'm really hoping you'll take a chance and read my newest book, Grand Opening. I promise you that it will become one of your favorite Carl Weber books, and yes, I'm already thinking about a part two.

Best,

Carl Weber

Acknowledgments

To Edna Mae, thank you for a mother's love. Even though you're no longer here physically, I see your smile every day. Though you're missed by so many here, Heaven is no longer missing an angel.

Family and friends, I thank you for your belief in me and support during the roughest time in my life. I don't think my motto ever applied more than then.

To Carl Weber, my co-author, thanks for allowing me to share in creating the Duncans and The Family Business world. It has truly been an experience.

Portia Cannon, blessings to you for your patience and diligence.

To all the readers out there, I am forever grateful that you've found the time and room in your life and hearts for my works over the years.

We ain't done yet.

Can't stop. Won't stop. Believe that.

Eric

Prologue

1975

The breeze kept flapping the pages of the book I was reading, so I held onto it for dear life as I sat in the passenger seat. I was looking out for police as Sam sped the Cadillac convertible down the rural roads of Georgia, going God knows where. Down here in the South, police didn't take too kindly to seeing uppity niggas in fancy cars they couldn't afford. Things were going well for us, so the last thing we needed was to get acquainted with anybody's jail cell. I knew better than to tell Sam to slow down, though, because I was responsible for making us late for his big meeting in the first place. I'm sorry, but when the lovin' was that good, I wanted it morning, noon, and night.

"Sam, baby, this is so nice. I think I want to see the whole country in this car." I snuggled up next to him and stared up at his face. Sam had to be the prettiest man I'd ever met. Sometimes I didn't understand what he saw in me, but whatever it was, I didn't want it to stop. Maybe, just maybe, God finally decided that I had suffered enough—that after all the beatings, rapes, and verbal abuse I had endured, it was my turn to be happy.

"We make it to this meeting and things go right, to hell with the country. I'm going to take you to see the world," he assured me, leaning over for a kiss. I found myself wishing I was a genie, like in the story of Aladdin, and I could grant Sam's every wish. How could one man make any woman so happy?

Sam and I had met a week ago outside the Savannah, Georgia bus station, where I was crying and hungry after someone had stolen my pocketbook, along with my bus ticket. I'd run away from a sexually abusive stepfather and an alcoholic and physically abusive mother, so I had absolutely no one in my life who I could count on. I was not sure why Sam took me in that rainy night, feeding me and sharing his hotel room with me, but I was sure he'd saved my life. I was smitten by his good looks and his fancy clothes right away, and I was impressed by what a gentleman he was. Given the way I'd been used and abused in the past, it was an unexpected surprise that he didn't even try anything in the hotel room that night.

He took me to the beauty parlor the next day so I could get my hair blown out natural. Then he treated me to lunch and took me over to JC Penney, where he bought me three halter tops, some matching hot pants, and my first pair of platform shoes. I put on some sunshades, and when I walked out of that store, I looked so good my own momma wouldn't have recognized me.

I wasn't sure where Sam came from, but that night I took matters into my own hands to make sure he wouldn't go anywhere, and we'd been together ever since.

My eyes lit up when I saw a sign that read: WELCOME TO JACKSONVILLE.

"Wow!" I swooned, placing my hand over my heart. "We are actually in Florida."

For the next twenty minutes, we drove through the city of Jacksonville. On both sides of the street, people black and white stopped to stare at the Negros in the fancy Caddy. I felt like a queen.

"We're here!" Sam's voice boomed excitedly as he pulled up in front of what I can only describe as a resort.

"This is soooo pretty," I sang.

I was mesmerized. It had to be the fanciest place I had ever seen in my life. This was the kind of luxury hotel I read about in books. In the lobby, I stared up at the crystal chandelier as Sam led me to the elevator, where a black man in a uniform pushed the button for us. The elevator operator kept sneaking glances at me, so I held onto Sam, keeping my head high because, after all, that man was just the help. We stepped off the elevator and walked down the plush-carpeted hallway, arm in arm, to room 1120. Sam knocked on the door.

He turned to me and said, "I love you, and I'd do anything for you."

I'd never had anyone tell me they loved me before, and to be honest, it was a bit overwhelming, but I knew I felt the same. "I love you too, Sam, and—"

Before I could finish my sentence, the door opened and a tall, olive-skinned man with straight, combed-back hair answered the door. He was wearing all white from head to toe. I couldn't be sure if he was mixed because of his olive skin, but he reminded me of that guy Al Pacino, who played in the movie *The Godfather*. Next to Sam, he had to be the handsomest man I'd ever met in person.

He and Sam clasped hands like old friends, although Sam kept it very professional. "My man Alejandro!"

"Sam Bradford," the man replied in a heavy Latin accent. He stepped aside to allow us to enter the hotel room, which looked more like an elaborate apartment. I could feel his eyes lingering on me as I passed. I glanced at Sam, and I was sure he noticed the way Alejandro was watching me too. I just hoped it wasn't going to affect whatever business the two had, because this meeting was important to Sam.

"Can I offer you a drink?"

"Yeah. Why don't you hook us up with a couple of rum and Cokes?"

Alejandro walked over to the lavish bar while Sam took in his place.

"Man, I've got to give it to you, Alejandro. This is one bad motherfucking hotel room," Sam said as Alejandro handed him two glasses. "Business must be good."

Alejandro glanced at me then looked back at Sam. "And who is this woman?"

I suddenly felt so out of place. He might have been checking me out when I came through the door, but this man sure didn't look like he trusted me all of a sudden.

Sam came to my defense. "Oh, her. That's my girl, Charlotte. She's cool. She's just here to party."

I detected a hint of nervousness in Sam's voice, something I hadn't heard before. Whoever Alejandro was, he put some type of fear in Sam, and that made me uneasy.

"Baby, why don't you take a seat over there?" Sam said. "Let us men talk."

I did what I was told, sitting down on a sofa that was more comfortable than most beds. I didn't much like the way Alejandro gawked at me, but I did like his style.

"Look, man, I don't mean to put business before pleasure, but I got quite a few customers back home looking for what you've got," Sam said. Once again, Alejandro glanced at me, taking a long sip of his drink. "I just need to know if you've got that package I ordered."

"Yes, I've got it. You have my money?" Despite his accent, Alejandro's words were as clear and cold as ice.

Sam removed a wad of cash from his pocket and handed it over. "It's all there, and plenty more where that came from."

Alejandro opened it and flipped through the cash, quickly counting it. He nodded when he finished.

"All right. You got your cash. Now where's my shit?"

Alejandro handed him a set of car keys. "It's in the trunk of the red T-Bird parked outside." He turned his attention to me. "So, is she for me?"

Sam's answer was nothing like what I had expected him to say. "She sure is. Young and fresh, just the way you like 'em."

"Yes, she'll do," Alejandro said in a firm voice.

I turned to Sam, feeling tears well up in my eyes. "What is this? What is he talking about?"

"Alejandro, my man, do you mind letting me speak to my lady here for a second in private? It'll just take a minute."

"No, not at all. I'll be in the bedroom. When she's ready, I'll start with a blow job. I like her lips." The bastard had the nerve to smirk as he got up and walked toward the bedroom. Like me sucking his dick was a forgone conclusion. Visions of my stepfather passed through my mind, and suddenly I felt anger rising in me. How the hell could I have run away from one bad situation only to find myself here in the presence of another son of a bitch who wanted to use me as his sex toy?

"What the fuck is he talking about, Sam?" I raged as soon as Alejandro left us alone.

"It's not what he's talking about. It's what you're talking about. I thought you said you loved me and that you'd do anything for me."

"I do love you," I replied, feeling confused.

He shook his head violently. "No, you don't! If you loved me, you wouldn't be trying to ruin this deal for me. You have to trust me. Trust that I would never do anything to hurt you."

"I do, but . . ."

"But what? I thought you said you wanted to go to Orlando, to Disney World. Well, what that man has in that car outside is going to get us to Orlando tomorrow morning. By this time tomorrow you could be having lunch with Mickey, but it ain't going to happen if he don't get what he wants."

A single tear escaped and rolled down my cheek. I felt trapped. If I didn't do this, I could ruin Sam's business deal, but if I did it, I could ruin our budding relationship. "You're not going to want me if I do that," I cried.

He wiped away my tears. "I'm going to want you more. Our bodies are just vessels. It's what's in our hearts that count. What man wouldn't want a woman who would do anything to make him happy? I'm in this for the long haul, baby. It's time you made up your mind if you're willing to do the same. So, are you going to Disney World tomorrow, or back to that bus station in Savannah?"

I stared at him for a moment as I considered the situation. I'd just had the most fantastic week of my life, and it all boiled down to this: I'd done a lot of shitty things on the street after I ran away from home, with a lot of shittier people than the man sitting in the other room now. If I was willing to do those things just to get bus fare, would it be so bad to do it to make Sam happy? I picked up my drink and guzzled it. "Go get your package, baby, 'cause we're going to Disney World."

A huge smile spread across Sam's face. "I never had a doubt."

Lavernius "LC"

1

Five weeks later

Kool and the Gang's "Jungle Boogie" was on the radio and just getting to my favorite part. You know, where the horns first kick in. Too bad one of the speakers in the old tow truck was crackling with static, or else I would have been in seventh heaven. I lifted my ass off the ripped up pleather seats like they were a hundred degrees, only it wasn't the seats that had me moving around like a Mexican jumping bean, it was—

"What was that?" my fiancée, Donna, asked, raising her head from my lap. She nervously peered over the cracked dashboard like a gazelle looking out for lions.

"Nothing," my moaning quickly changed to a whining in less than three seconds flat.

"I thought I heard something. Is someone coming?" Her head swiveled back and forth on her neck like a bobblehead doll.

"Nah, you're good. Can't nobody see us way over here," I replied, anxiously trying my best to coax her head back into my lap without being disrespectful. "Now please, please, go on and finish what you were doing. It was just starting to feel good. And we ain't got that much time, baby," I pleaded. I knew I sounded like a desperate little punk, but that's what I was at that moment. Shit, what she was doing felt so good that I would have said or done anything to get her to continue.

"Don't you do your business in my mouth, LC Duncan," she warned.

"I won't. I promise." I flashed her a smile. "I got a tissue for that." I showed her the tissue then sighed thankfully when she finally lowered her head.

I was supposed to drop Donna off at home after we finished studying at the library. Then I was going to come down here to the Trailways and pick up my older brother, Lou, who'd been out of town for almost a month. However, once Donna found out I was going to meet Lou, her nosy behind promised that if I let her tag along, she would give me a blow job, something respectable girls like her rarely did. Sure, I knew Lou was gonna be sore when he saw her, but the thought of her warm lips wrapped around my Johnson for the first time wasn't something I could pass up, so I just resigned myself to the fact that I would have to deal with my brother's attitude.

Donna was nothing like the girls from our side of the tracks. For one, she was classy and came from money. Her father was a big time doctor who came from three generations of college-educated Negros. Truth was I didn't know what Donna saw in me, even if I was enrolled in South Georgia State College. My people were just common Georgia farmers. Well, my brothers had also developed a rep as hustlers.

As Donna's lips did their thing, I closed my eyes, gently cradling her head in my hands. It wouldn't be long now, and I was trying to savor the moment, locking the memory in my mind so that I could retrieve it on one of those lonely nights when she was nowhere to be found and I needed relief. I'll tell you something, though: If I didn't trust her so much, I would have sworn this wasn't her first time giving a blow job, 'cause she was working her lips and tongue like a pro. All I could do was lift my hips, lean back, and moan, "Oh, got damn!" The more I moaned, the harder she worked. I was trying to get her attention with the tissue when I got close, but she was so into what she was doing she didn't even pause for a second.

Knock! Knock! Knock! "What you doing in there, boy?"

Donna might not have been paying attention to me, but she damn sure paid attention to the voice and the knock, stopping abruptly.

I wanted to scream, "No! No! Shit! Don't stop! I was almost there!" at the top of my lungs, but instead I opened my eyes to deal with the reality of the situation. Through the windshield I saw the Trailways bus pulling out from the station about fifty yards away.

Knock! Knock! Knock!

Then I turned toward the knocking and was greeted by the pearly white smile of my brother Lou, laughing at a horrified Donna with my Johnson hanging out of her mouth.

"Oh my God, this is not happening," Donna said, scrambling to sit up. I tucked my pecker back in my pants, glancing over at my mortified girlfriend.

"You okay?" I reached for her and she pulled away.

Knock! Knock! Knock! I turned to Lou then back to Donna.

"Open the door, LC," he demanded.

There was no need for both of them to be mad at me, so I reached past Donna and flicked open the passenger-side lock. Donna buried her head into my shoulder to hide her shame from Lou, who strutted around to the passenger side of the truck like Super Fly. Despite the awkwardness of the situation, I couldn't help but notice how clean my brother was in his bell bottom pants, red polyester shirt, and brand new patent leather shoes. I swear, no matter where we went, he was always sharp as a tack. Lou was the type who would spend his last dollar on his appearance because he always wanted to look good.

Lou tossed his huge blue Samsonite suitcase into the back of the truck but held on to the duffle bag he was carrying as he slipped into the passenger seat beside Donna, who continued to hide her face as she sobbed. I wrapped my arm around her, trying to comfort her, but it didn't seem to be working.

"What's wrong with her? It's not like I ain't ever seen somebody get they dick sucked before." He let out a raucous laugh.

Donna squealed and tried to move her body as far away from him as possible in the confined space of the truck. I turned to my brother, giving him the stink eye.

"Lou, leave it alone, okay?"

"A'ight, a'ight. Shit, I didn't know she was so sensitive. Any other time, you can't get her high-siditty ass to shut the fuck up."

"Lou!"

"A'ight, drop me off over on Oak Street. I got some business with Sam needs to be taken care of." When Lou said business, he really meant trouble, 'cause trouble was the only thing he was going to find on Oak Street—but that was none of my business. All I wanted to do now was drop him off, calm Donna down so she could finish what she'd started, and get the tow truck back to my boss.

"Okay, so how was New York?" I pulled the truck out of the lot. Despite her embarrassment, I could feel Donna's nosy self turn her ear to hear. Half the reason she'd wanted to come with me was to hear about Lou's trip to New York. We'd been talking about going to New York for almost a year. "What'd you do?"

"Man, LC, NYC is *baaaad*. First thing I did was go down to Delancey Street and pick me up some threads. I got me some of those gabardine suits and polyester shirts and got you and the boys a couple of them authentic African dashikis you was asking about."

I smiled. "Thanks, Lou."

"So after Delancey I hit up Sylvia's soul food restaurant in Harlem, and you not gonna believe this, but I ran into James Brown when he came up to the spot. He said I was the second baddest dresser in there. No fuckin' joke. And you know me, LC. Your big brother was big-timing it." Lou sparked up a Pall Mall cigarette. "Then I took in a movie in Times Square with a couple of sweet thangs who saw me hanging with the Godfather of Soul, and I bedded them both. I tell ya, man, there's just so much opportunity up there in New York for black folk. Not like here. Got me ready to move up there." He took a drag of his cigarette. "Man, I ain't never had so much fun in my life. I even hooked up with this *I-tal-yan* cat who put me on to a quick five thousand–dollar job. Five big ones!"

"Italian ain't nothing but another name for a white, Lou, and you know what Daddy told us about them white cats. You can't trust 'em."

"Man, I ain't never, never met a white boy like this cat Sal Dash before, and neither had Dad, 'cause this was the blackest cracker I've ever met. I mean, this was one cool motherfucker—and he got a brother paid." He pulled out a knot of cash.

"You got that from working with him?" I was surprised, because all the white boys I'd met were either racist rednecks or straight-up white trash. Then again, except for going down to Jacksonville two or three times, I'd never left the state of Georgia.

"Sure did. That's the coolest white boy I ever met, and he introduced me to some of the finest women I've ever seen. Oh, and check this out: this dude loves him some sisters, and he ain't afraid to show them off in public." I could feel Donna stirring. Like me, she was probably wondering if she'd heard Lou correctly.

"What'd you mean he loves him some sisters? He's into black women?" I asked. The only white men around here who would admit that they liked black women were not the types you wanted your daughter around.

Lou chuckled. "Is he? That white boy loves big asses and nappy-headed pussy more than me. He got a black girlfriend in every borough of New York City, including this place they call Long Island. And he treats 'em like queens."

That made Donna lift her head. She stared at Lou until she realized what she was doing and buried her face back in my shoulder.

"Get the heck outta here."

"Little brother, I'm telling you, you got to come up north with me next time." He glanced over at Donna. "It'll make you see this backwards place for what it really is and what it really has to offer in a totally different light."

"Just let me know so I can get off work. I always wanted to see New York," I replied.

"Not without me, you're not." Donna chimed in without lifting her head. She was not about to let me go to New York or anywhere else outside of Ware County without her if she had anything to do with it, especially if it had to do with my catting brother. "I'm not letting you go to New York without me. Not with this man."

"We'll talk about this later," I said, wishing like hell she wasn't in the truck at that moment.

"You can talk until you're blue in the face, but you're not going anywhere without me."

Lou let loose a bellowing laugh. "Man, this skirt got you henpecked like a motherfucker. Maybe you should switch seats so you can suck her dick."

His words hurt my pride so much that I shouted, "Fuck you, Lou!" I gave him the finger as I turned down Oak Street. Lou just laughed at me.

I pulled in front of Big Sam's, which was situated right in the middle of a two-block strip of stores. Most people considered this area the seediest part of my hometown of Waycross, Georgia. I was sure Donna's father would have killed me if he knew I ever brought his daughter to this part of town, let alone to the doorstep of Big Sam's.

"Can we go in and have a drink, LC? Please?" Donna asked with pleading eyes. "I always wanted to see the inside of this place."

I glanced over at Lou, who shook his head. "No, this ain't no place for you," I said.

"Why? Lou goes in there and so do you. Why can't I go in there?"

Big Sam's wasn't your ordinary bar or club. Sure, they served liquor, mostly watered down if you asked me, but it was the other vices, like the gambling room in the back and the readily available supply of drugs and whores, that made Big Sam's special.

"Because the only women in there are whores, and despite all the fucked up things you might be, you ain't no whore," Lou spat as he stepped out of the truck, leaving Donna dumbfounded.

I got out and walked around to say good-bye to my brother. He left the Samsonite behind, but he was holding the duffle bag. I could only imagine what was in it.

"Thanks, big bro," I said.

"I didn't do it for you. I did it because I didn't want her daddy finding out and having his politician friends shut Sam's place down. That's where I make my money."

"Well, thanks anyway."

He grinned, slapping me five before he handed me a set of keys. "Bring my deuce and a quarter over here when you get off work and we'll talk about New York." He reached into his pocket and pulled out the knot of cash he'd shown me earlier. Peeling off two twenties, he handed them to me. "Here. Take that little uppity broad of yours out to eat. Some shrimps and fries should help her forget I saw your dick in her mouth." He chuckled. "Oh, and when you come back, bring Levi with you."

I raised an eyebrow. "You sure about that?"

"Yeah, I'm sure. I'm home now. Can't keep him locked up forever. Know what I mean? Besides, Larry's supposed to meet us over here around ten. Time to remind folks who the fuck we are."

Larry

2

I sat in my '73 Plymouth Duster, peering over my sunglasses as Quincy Wilson slopped his fat ass in the back door of the Oak Plaza Lounge, a half-ass bar in the sharecropping town of Blackshear, Georgia, about five miles outside of Waycross. The Oak Plaza Lounge didn't have much going for it, except on Friday night when a few local high rollers crowded around a table in the back room to talk shit and play Tonk. Wasn't nobody going to get rich playin' in the game, but there was usually five or six hundred dollars on the table, which might as well have been a million to these poor folks. Good old Quincy was a regular in the game, but like most degenerate gamblers, he usually came out a loser.

I waited for a few hours, and then I saw Quincy coming out of the lounge whistling and singing as he counted his money like it had been his lucky day. Just goes to show you how wrong a stupid motherfucker can be. He was so busy feeling good about winning that his dumb ass didn't bother to look up until I was almost on him.

"Remember me?"

"Oh, shit. Larry!" Quincy's eyes got big.

"That's right. Larry. Where you been hiding, Quincy?" I hit him square in the nose with the butt of my sawed-off shotgun, and blood squirted everywhere as he crumbled to the ground. I kicked him in the side for good measure then quickly stripped him of the .38 he was carrying. It took him a moment to get his bearings, but when he did, he looked like he was going to shit himself.

"Man, Larry, I been looking all over for you."

"You lying"—swift kick to the ribs—"piece of'"—another kick to the ribs—"shit!" Hard stomp to the face. "Everyone in Waycross knows where to find me." He wasn't moving, so I had to stop for a second to make sure he was still breathing. "Wake up, you son of a bitch."

He finally moved, looking up at me with pure terror in his eyes. "Larry, I'm sorry, man."

"You really fucked up, Quincy. Lou don't like people borrowing money and not paying it back, and neither do I. Makes us look like punks. Do I look like a punk to you?" I pointed the shotgun at his bloody face.

He started shaking his head rapidly. "Tell Lou I just need a little more time. It's not like I ain't good for it. I've always paid you back. I was just going through a little dry spell is all, but I'm out of it now. Look." He reached for his pocket and I almost blew him away.

"What the hell are you doing?"

"Don't shoot me, man. I'm just giving you my winnings." I allowed him to reach in his pocket. He pulled out a small wad of money and handed it to me. "It's almost three hundred dollars."

I reached down, grabbing him by the throat and slamming his head against his car. "Three hundred ain't gonna do it, Quincy. You owe us two grand."

"I know, I know, but this should buy me some more time, right?"

I laughed, shaking my head at how funny he sounded. This dude was acting like his ass had only borrowed some sugar.

"C'mon, Larry, you know I'm good for it. One month, that's all I'm asking for. Please, please, Larry, killing me ain't gonna get your money back." He was pleading, but it was too little too late for that now. It was time to send a message to all the deadbeats out there: the Duncan brothers weren't anyone to play with.

"You know, Quincy, if you had come to me like a man and asked for some more time, I would have given it to you. But you been running from me and Lou for over two months. I bet your bitch ass won't run no more." I raised the shotgun and pulled the trigger. *BOOM!* The sound of the shot was followed by a blood-curdling scream.

"You shot me! You son of a bitch, you shot me!"

"I shot your foot. Next time I'll aim at your fucking head. Now remember that shit! You got one week to get my money, and instead of two thousand, now it's twenty-five hundred. I suggest you sell that fancy car of yours. And don't even think about making me come look for you again," I threatened, although it wasn't like he could run anywhere, at least not with half of his toes blown off.

By the time I pulled the car into Big Sam's, I had calmed down and was ready to get to drinking. Sitting behind the wheel in the parking lot, I pulled the money out of my pocket and counted it. I couldn't put it past a guy like Quincy to short me, even on this little bit of money.

I opened the door to get out, and before my foot even hit the pavement, a bunch of whores came at me, sniffing around and acting all horny like they smelled my money.

"Hey, Larry. Wanna come upstairs with me?" A whore with short hair and a gap in her teeth tried to flirt with me and even had the nerve to grab onto my arm, like I wanted some used pussy when I could get better than what she had for free.

"Haven't you figured it out yet?" I snapped. "I don't pay for nobody to suck on my dick. You bitches need to pay me for the privilege." I pushed past them without bothering to listen to nothing they were saying.

I went inside the bar and announced, "Gimme some Jack," as I slapped my hand down on the bar.

"Larry, Lou's upstairs." The nosy-ass bartender smiled at me like we were old buddies—which we weren't.

"Did I say I was looking for my brother? Shit, he's a grown man, and if he wants to spend his time fucking cheap-ass tramps then that's up to him. I came in here for a drink."

He turned and took the bottle of Jack off the shelf, set it on the counter, then picked up a glass and filled it with ice. Every move he made seemed to be in slow motion, which just riled me up even more. This guy always took so long to do something so easy.

"Here's your drink," he said, setting a finger of bourbon, probably watered down, and a whole lot of ice in front of me. I reached in my pocket and tossed a bunch of bills next to the pitiful excuse for a drink.

"Nah," I snorted. "Bring me the whole goddamn bottle over here." I slammed my fist down on the bar and dared him to disobey me.

Chippy

3

Six of us girls, led by Big Shirley, had sneaked out to the side of the building to smoke some reefer. After patiently waiting my turn, I finally got the joint from Little Momma just as an old, beat-up tow truck pulled up in front. Despite the fact that it looked and sounded like it was on its last leg, all five girls started grinning like they had hit the number when this tall, brown-skinned brother stepped out of the passenger side. He wasn't all that, if you ask me, but they were swooning like he was Fred Williamson or something.

"He's back, Big Shirley. Oh my God, Lou's back," one of the star struck women mumbled, clutching her hands like a school girl who'd just been asked to the prom.

"Mm-hmm, I can see that." Shirley grinned. "And he's handsome as ever."

Shirley headed toward the man with a purpose, her over-sized ass swaying like two huge watermelons under her skimpy dress. She was followed giddily by three of the other girls. Only Little Momma's pothead ass remained with me, but her eyes never left the man. She reached for the joint and took a long pull.

"Who's that?" I asked.

"Who, him?" she replied in her heavy country accent. "Girl, that right there is Sweet Lou Duncan. He's what we call a ho's best friend." She was grinning like something real good had slipped down her skirt.

"A ho's best friend?" I laughed, rolling my eyes skeptically. "And here I am thinking it was money."

"Not when Lou's around," Little Momma replied. "Lou's special. He's the type of man that could take a girl away from a place like this."

I glanced over at Lou, watching the girls openly fawn over him. "He's dressed nice, I'll give him that, but he must be one hell of a trick to have Big Shirley acting like that."

Little Momma passed me the joint then bent down to wipe the dirt from her shoe. She was so short that she didn't have far to go to reach it. Funny thing is, she wasn't actually called Little Momma because of her four foot seven stature, but because she'd had six kids by the time she was twenty. "He ain't just some trick, baby girl. Don't you ever get that mixed up, you hear me? He and his brothers are about as tough as they come in these parts. He is nobody to be fucked with. Shit, truth be told, they're the only ones Sam has any respect for in this town."

"Oh, I see, so he's a pimp like Big Sam? No wonder he's dressed so fancy."

"No, he ain't no pimp. Lou's just sweet, a real gentleman, unless you piss him off. Oh, and he's got the biggest dick on the planet and knows how to use it." She headed toward Lou and the other girls, waving her hand. "Come on. I'll introduce you."

"Nah, you go on. I'm gonna smoke a cigarette before I go back in."

"Suit yourself. Just remember, Sam don't like us being out here but so long."

I took one last hit of the reefer, putting out what was left of the joint on the side of the building before searching my bag for my Newports. I lit a cigarette as I watched Big Shirley and KeKe, a tall, jet black beauty with a dynamite shape escort Lou into the building. The other girls, including Little Momma, were trailing close behind, chattering excitedly.

With the girls inside, I made my way to the front porch, leaning against the pole that held up the awning. As I stared up at the stars, I started daydreaming of being anywhere but Waycross, Georgia.

I still couldn't believe I had ended up here, turning tricks for Sam. When I slept with Alejandro for him, I had thought it was a one-time thing. The next day, Sam took me to Disney Land and treated me like a queen. I swear I had never felt so special in my life. My night with Alejandro felt like nothing more than a bad dream—until the end of the day at Disney, when Sam admitted to me that he was broke. He also told me that there were some very bad men after him, who would kill him if he didn't pay the money he owed them. Before I knew it, I had let him convince me that if we wanted to be together, I had no choice but to help him out by selling my body. He also promised that once his debts were paid, we would leave that life behind and see the world together. I had visions of us traveling, with every day feeling as special as our day at Disney World had. The hope of that future was what kept me going when he brought me back to Waycross and introduced me to the rest of his girls. By the time I figured out he was a pimp, I was already deeply in love with Sam. Part of me wanted to start walking and never look back, but the truth was that Sam was all I had, so I would just have to be satisfied with these stars, this cigarette, and my high, until Sam said we could get out of this life.

"Bitch, did I say you could come out here and sit on your ass?" Big Sam scared the shit out of me as he stuck his head out the door and yelled at me. I wasn't surprised though. I'd already made my quota for the night, but Big Sam wasn't one to let his girls spend idle time at his establishment. I hadn't really expected my smoke break to last very long. "How many times I gotta tell you time is money? Now, get yo' yella ass in here. These dicks ain't gonna suck themselves."

"Coming, baby." I never liked to displease Sam, so I quickly gathered my Newports and my lighter and scurried back inside. By the time I entered the club, however, Sam had already forgotten about me. He'd probably retired to his smoke-filled private office at the back end of the club.

"Move, bitch," this heifer Sandra said, knowing she could have gone around me with her john. About half her size, the man looked like he was stone cold in love before he had even gone for a test ride.

"I'll move when I damn well please," I growled at her. She ignored me with a smack of her lips and a switch of her ample hips as they disappeared behind the beaded curtain.

Meanwhile, I saw Lou sitting at a table with about ten of the girls surrounding him like he was a rock star. Curiosity got the best of me, and I moved closer to see what the commotion was all about. He was reaching into a duffle bag on the table and handing each of the girls some type of gift, most of which were I LOVE NEW YORK T-shirts and small statues of the Empire State Building or the Statue of Liberty. From the way the girls were reacting, you would have thought they were gold coins.

"Well, well, well, what do we have here?" He'd just finished handing out his little trinkets, and I guess he noticed my hands were empty. He looked me up and down, smiling with his pearly white teeth as he undressed me with his eyes. "What's your name, Red?"

"My name's not Red," I snapped at him. I hated being called Red. It was such a cliché.

"We call her Chippy," Little Momma jumped in, trying to clean things up for me.

Chippy was what they had begun calling me when I started working there last month, just to get under my skin. They said it was because I acted like a stuck up bitch when I arrived—like I had a chip on my shoulder. Truth be told, it was because most of them were jealous of how much Sam loved me. So, rather than fighting it, I claimed it. At least it wasn't what I was called back home; then again, nothing could be as bad as what they did to me back home. I took some solace in the fact that I had a room of my own and decent food. Even more importantly, I had Sam, who loved and protected me, and I wasn't nobody's victim anymore. I knew exactly what I was doing . . . despite the fact that everyone kept calling me naive.

"Okay, okay, Chippy it is, then." He reached in his duffle bag and pulled out a red T-shirt. "How about we fix you up with a Big Apple T-shirt."

I shook my head firmly. "No, thank you. I'll get my own when Sam and I travel to New York."

Lou sat back in his chair and pulled Little Momma into his lap. "Oh, well, excuse me." Little Momma wrapped one arm around his neck while she massaged the growing imprint in his pants. Lou laughed at me, and so did all the other girls. "Sam's taking you to New York, huh?"

I lifted my head proudly. "Sam's taking me to a lot of places: Paris, London, New York, Vegas. We're going to travel the world."

"Shiiiittt, you ain't been past Main Street since you got here, so you might as well take that fantasy shit somewhere else," Big Shirley teased. "Your ass ain't going nowhere but on your back like the rest of us hoes."

I liked Big Shirley, but she was starting to piss me off. "Don't tell me what I'm going to do, Shirley. I was on my way to Vegas when my purse got stole with my ticket in it. And as soon as I get enough money, me and Sam are getting the hell out of this one horse town."

"You and Sam?" Big Shirley let out a big, infectious laugh and soon it seemed like everyone in the group was laughing at me, including Lou. "Bitch, you got to be the dumbest ho I've ever met. You been here over a month and you still drinking Sam's Kool-Aid. Let me pull your coat to something: You might be Big Sam's little queen right now, but we all been there at one point or the other. You ain't nothing but the flavor of the month, baby girl, and trust me, next month there will be a new flavor, and you'll be just like the rest of us hoes."

LC

4

After pleading with Donna to finish what we'd started in the Trailways parking lot, I was eventually sent home with blue balls. It turned out that in her eyes, Lou's untimely interruption was just God's way of reminding her that she wasn't that type of girl. I didn't care what she had to say. It sure felt like she was that type of girl when she had her lips wrapped around my dick—although I wasn't about tell her that. Frustrated and uncomfortable, I dropped off my boss's tow truck then headed home to take a cold shower.

After my shower, I made my way back to Big Sam's with Levi to drop off my brother's car. I might even stay for a while, I decided. Hell, I'd earned a good time after what Donna had just put me through.

You know what they say about time heals old wounds? Well, it must be true, because by the time I found a parking space on Oak Street, which was packed because of the Friday night crowd, I'd almost forgotten about my sexual frustration with Donna. It may have also had something to do with the fact that I'd completely fallen in love with my brother's car. I'd always been a car nut, but Lou's Buick Electra 225 was like nothing I'd ever driven before. It was like a Caddy and a sports car all rolled into one.

"Man, I got to get me one of these one day," I said to my brother Levi as we stepped out of the car. I turned to admire the car, but Levi barely paid attention to me or the car. His mind was on one thing.

"Wh—wh—where's Lou?" Levi stuttered.

I looked up at my hulk-like brother, who at 6 foot 8 towered over my meager six foot frame. Levi was so big he barely fit through most doorways without turning sideways. Despite his size, my brother was really nothing more than a big teddy bear who spent most of his time at the house tending to his animals. The only time you had to worry about him was when he thought you might do some harm to one of our family members. Yep, ol' Levi had a good soul, but to be quite frank, he was what some people called slow.

"We're going to see him at Big Sam's."

The door of the club opened and the sound of music and laughter poured out into the parking lot, putting a smile on Levi's face. He and Sam were real close, and as he eloquently put it, "I–I–I like Ba–ba–big Sam's."

As Levi and I went into Big Sam's, I swear it was like a scene from a movie when the record stops playing. The entire place became silent as everyone watched us—or at least Levi—enter. It wasn't every day you see someone his size.

"L–look at all the pu–pu–pu–pussy, LC," Levi said excitedly, his eyes wandering from one scantily clad woman to the next. "Y–y–you th–th–th–think I'm g–g–gonna get some pu–pu–pu–pussy tonight?"

Levi might not have been the brightest bulb in the box, but he was all man, and he loved him some women ever since Lou had paid Mimi Knotts to give him some on his sixteenth birthday. "Yeah, big man, I'm sure you're going to get some tonight. You know Lou wouldn't have me bring you all the way here if he wasn't going to get you some."

"LC, Levi." I turned toward the voice to see Sam Bradford, the forty-something-year-old owner of Big Sam's and the closest thing Waycross had to an HNIC. Big Sam was one of those tall, light-skinned pretty boys with green eyes that black woman always seemed to fawn over. Being a dark-skinned brother, I'd always hated those type of guys, not just because they were usually arrogant fucks, but because they were always the ones with the girls I wanted to be with.

"What's happening, Sam?" despite my personal dislike for the man, I offered my hand in politeness. He slapped me five.

"Nothin' much," he said, patting the sides of his head like I actually gave a shit about his five-inch fro. "You know how it goes, baby. Another day, another dollar. Making these bitches work so I can get rich."

"I heard that. You seen my brother?"

"Which one? Lou's upstairs trying to put two of my best hoes out of commission, and Larry's over there nursing a bottle." He gestured toward a table in the corner, where my older brother Larry was sitting alone. "One of the girls tried to holla at him, but man, that's one ornery son of a bitch. What's his problem anyway? He hate the world, or just pussy?"

"I like pu–pu–pussy," Levi stuttered, causing Sam and I to laugh.

"We know you do, big man," I said to my brother then turned to answer Sam. "Nah, that's just Larry. I don't think my momma hugged him enough as a child," I replied half-heartedly.

"You know, that makes sense. Lou always said you were the smart one." Sam chuckled, waving over a half-naked cocktail waitress. "Look, what you cats drinking? The first one's on me."

"I'll take a rum and Coke," I said

"I'll take a Sh–sh–shirley T–t–temple, but I'mmmm not really th–th–thirsty," Levi sputtered, shaking his head. "I–I just want some pu–pu–pussy."

"Let me talk to Lou and see what I can do, big man," Sam replied. He walked away, and I followed him with my eyes as he whispered in the ear of a cute, light-skinned woman. She glanced over at us then climbed the stairs. Meanwhile, Levi and I headed toward Larry's table.

"Well, well, well, if it isn't my two younger brothers, the college boy and the simpleton." Larry picked up the half empty bottle of liquor and put it to his lips. "I heard the playboy's back in town. Where is he? Wait, let me guess. He's upstairs fucking one of Sam's two-bit whores."

Lou

5

"Ohhhhh, Lou, that's right, honey. Fuck me with that big ol' dick!" Little Momma shouted loud enough for everyone downstairs in Big Sam's to hear. Not that I could blame her. I was fucking her real good, while Big Shirley lay next to us, rubbing a piece of ice on her sore pussy from the beating I'd just put on it. It didn't matter how big her ass was; Shirley's tight-ass pussy wasn't meant for what I was packing. No matter how hard she tried, she always needed a ton of lube. Now, Little Momma was a different story. She'd had so many babies her stretched out twat was perfect for my baseball bat–sized cock.

I heard a knock at the door. I didn't miss a stroke as I continued to pump Little Momma, but I did lock eyes with Big Shirley. "Who the fuck is that?" I asked.

She shrugged. "I don't know."

"Well, go find out. Can't you see I'm fucking?" I turned my attention back to the velvety wet goodness of Little Momma.

"Ooooh, shit. I'm about to come," Little Momma moaned, shaking her ass like a vibrator.

I slammed my hips against her to go deeper as I felt myself ready to explode. "Urrrgh!" I growled, damn near lifting Little Momma off the bed with my last orgasmic thrust.

It took me a minute to regain my composure, but when I slid my semi hard dick out of Little Momma, I was face to face with Sam's newest whore, the girl they called Chippy. Her red ass sure was fine, standing there gawking at my pride and joy. "Like what you see?"

"I told you that shit was big," Little Momma said with a laugh.

"Ummm, yes you did." Chippy nodded, her eyes still glued to my dick. "Damn!"

"So . . ." I snapped, breaking her trance. "You come here to join us, or you here for some other reason?"

"Oh, yeah," she muttered, finally looking up at my face. "Big Sam said to tell you he's in his office and that your brothers are here, and one of them is running up a tab."

"That's probably Larry's drink ass," Big Shirley added.

I shot her a look of displeasure. I hated when anyone talked about my brothers, although she was probably right. Neither Levi nor LC were big drinkers, but Larry was a drunk.

"Tell Sam I'll be right down."

Chippy nodded her head and then she was out the door, giving me a glimpse of her fine figure and very shapely ass. "Hey, Red!" I yelled after her. "Maybe I'll bring you back up here after I handle my business with Sam."

She stopped, turned, thought about it for a second while she stared at my Johnson, then shook her head. "No, thanks. I'm woman enough to know when I'm outmatched. That thing you packing isn't even human. I know horses who'd be jealous of a dick like that."

I laughed, nodding my head. Shit, I had to respect her, but I couldn't lie and say I didn't want her. There was something about her that made her different from the rest of the girls. "A'ight, but if you ever get the urge to test out Space Mountain,"—I grabbed my Johnson, pointing him at her—"we're always here."

Ten minutes later, I had cleaned myself up and dismissed Little Momma and Big Shirley. I walked up to the table my brothers were sitting at.

"L–L–Lou!" Levi shouted excitedly as I walked over to him. I placed my arm around his massive shoulder and pointed to the women.

"There's a lot of pussy running around here. Which one you want?" I asked my younger brother, who looked like he was gonna bust a gut.

"Th–that w–w–one." Levi pointed at a slightly heavy yella girl named Sandy, who had the biggest pair of titties I'd ever seen. I'd played hide the sausage with her on a few occasions, so I knew she'd treat Levi right. Plus she was big enough so he wouldn't break her.

"Hey, Sandy," I addressed the girl, crooking my finger for her to join us. "Come here for a minute." She couldn't get there fast enough, wrapping her arms around my neck then kissing my cheek. Man, the women sure loved Sweet Lou.

"What can I do for you, Lou?" She purred sexily, rubbing those massive titties up against my chest.

I gestured toward Levi. "Why don't you take my brother upstairs and show him a good time. I'll take care of you later." I slapped her ass playfully.

"Sure, Lou. Come on, Levi. You ready to have some fun?"

Levi didn't speak. He just nodded his head happily. Sandy took his hand and led him up the stairs. I turned my attention to LC, who tossed me the keys to my deuce and a quarter. "She's parked down the block in front of the liquor store. I'll tell you, Lou, that's one fine ride."

"You like that, huh, little brother? Well, next time I go out of town I'll leave you the keys." LC smiled like a little boy. I think he loved cars more than Levi loved pussy.

"Man, enough with the BS chit-chat," Larry chimed in. "I don't care about your car. What I care about is in that duffle bag you carrying and how much we gonna get for it."

"You see I came back in one piece. Italians wanna move more product in the South, and that's where little ole me ingratiated myself to them. Gonna make some moves with Big Sam. Water the garden and watch it bear fruit. Pretty soon we'll have a fruit stand."

"I don't trust Big Sam," LC coolly admitted. He normally kept his opinions to himself, but as he aged, he was becoming more vocal. The boy had a good head on his shoulders, and to be honest, a lot of that shit he was bringing home from school made sense.

"That's because you're smart," Larry chimed in with a chuckle.

"Most folks in this world are dumb as fuck. Sam makes a living off them. I got this, li'l bro. I understand not how the world *should* work, but how it *does*."

"And I wouldn't know about that, right?" LC came back at me.

"You got time, boy. And as long as I'm around, I'll make sure you don't make my mistakes. Come on. Let me show you how it's done."

I gestured for them to follow me, praying Larry's rebellious ass wouldn't balk, because there was serious business to attend to, and we Duncans needed to at least pretend to be on the same wave length. Thankfully, by the time I knocked on Sam's door, Larry was standing next to me. I handed him the duffle bag.

Larry

6

We walked into the office, taking seats in front of Sam's fake-ass mahogany desk. Half the shit on it was thrown to one side, which told me he'd just finished screwing the yellow whore standing next to him. She was trying to adjust her clothes, and she didn't look very happy about the interruption. Personally, I didn't give a fuck. I had hated whores ever since I had one give me the clap in 'Nam.

"Go on and make ole Sam some money, baby, while I talk to these gentlemen." He squeezed her ass playfully. "We'll finish this up later on tonight. Oh, and tell the twins to come in here, will you?" She kissed him on the lips before making a quick retreat from the room.

Sam then turned his attention to us, catching Lou slobbering over the whore like he was about slap money down to fuck the bitch.

"What's Red's story? She's got a little more sass than these other girls," Lou said.

"Same as the rest. Found her at the Trailways up in Savannah. Bitch came down from North Cackalacky, where her daddy was fucking her and her momma was beating her ass so bad she ran away." He chuckled while faking to shed a tear. "Anyway, the bitch was talking about killing herself when I scooped her up. I wined and dined her for a few days, made her feel like a human being again, then turned her out. She's taken to this shit like a pro."

"She any good?" Lou's horny ass asked. "I'm thinking about taking her for a test drive."

"Best dick sucker I got, and she's hopelessly romantic." Big Sam laughed, brushing the lint off his suede coat. "She actually thinks we're going to get married soon as I pay off my debts to my connect. She works so hard; I had to check under her skirt and see if she had an assembly line attached to the pussy." We all got a good laugh on that, except for LC, who just sat there taking it all in. He always was the most serious of my brothers.

"Really, though," Sam continued, "she brings in twice what the other girls do."

"That's because she's in love and has a true purpose. I saw the way she looked at you, Sam. A woman like her will do anything for you, but when she finds out you been playing her, I wouldn't want to be you. If I were you, I'd tread lightly," LC spoke up. Why the fuck he did that I don't know, but it sure as hell made me laugh.

Sam sure didn't find that shit funny, though. He turned to LC angrily, and I knew that if it had been anyone but a Duncan brother, Sam would have knocked him on his ass. "Boy, I been turning bitches out since I was thirteen years old. My first ho was my own damn sister, and don't nobody love you like family. So don't tell me about love or pimping, 'cause I was making bitches fall in love when you was sucking on your momma's tit."

Sam turned to Lou. "Man, where'd you get this nigga from? Does he know who the fuck I am, or I should turn out that little doctor's bitch he's halfway fucking to prove it? I thought you said he was smart."

I glanced at Lou, who lowered his head, probably wondering why the fuck he'd invited our little brother to this meeting in the first place. "Now, Sam, take it easy. The boy's only giving you his opinion. Everyone knows your track record with women," Lou said, trying to massage Sam's inflated ego. If you asked me, he sounded like a little bitch.

I wasn't the one to play these type of games, trying to make people feel comfortable with me. Hell, I liked when people were scared of me or on edge. It gave me an advantage when I decided to slit their fucking throats.

"Yeah, well, he'll know it for sure when I turn out that little bitch of his," Sam snapped back. "Then he'll be paying me to fuck her ass."

I knew Sam had taken it too far, but before I could even react, LC was rising from his seat.

"I find your ass anywhere near my g—"

Lou cut him off just as he was about to get started. Meanwhile, I was watching Sam to make sure he didn't go for that little .38 he always carried. If he did, it was going to be the last thing he ever went for.

"LC, why don't you go check on Levi?" Lou made it sound like a suggestion, but the way he was pushing LC to the door, he was actually making a command. That was one thing I could say for the kid: he had a temper, but he was cool under pressure.

"So, now that we got rid of the twerp maybe we can get down to business!" Sam's voice mocked as Lou returned to his seat. Two of Sam's thugs—who we called Twin One and Twin Two because one had one gold tooth and the other had two—entered the room and stood behind their boss.

"I wouldn't taunt my little brother like that, Sam. He's still a Duncan, and unlike Levi, he's got a mind of his own. I can't control him." Lou chuckled, taking out one of those cheap-ass cigars he liked so much.

Truth was, Lou was right about LC. He may have been the youngest and the mildest mannered of us Duncans, but he had a memory like an elephant and a subdued temper that could explode at any minute if provoked. I didn't particularly like the way Sam was talking about LC, and Lou didn't have a clue, which meant I was going to have to make it my business to keep my little brother and Big Sam away from each other.

"Please, Lou, I was just fucking with the little twerp. I ain't worried about him. He's your problem. Best you don't make him mine. Now, you ready to get down to business?" Sam rubbed his big, meaty hands together in anticipation of some good shit coming his way. "What you got for me?"

Lou motioned for me to hand over the black duffle bag I'd carried into the room, so I placed it on the desk. Sam stared at the bag, his lips slowly spreading into a smile as he unzipped it. He reached in and pulled out a brick of marijuana. Raising the brick up to his nose, he inhaled real hard. His eyes became wide, and then his grin spread into a huge smile.

"So?" Lou asked, wanting to know what he thought.

"If it's as good as it smells, we're in business."

"I got a new connect up in New York with the best reefer in the city, and plenty of it to keep you in business. Wait till you get a real taste."

"Well, ain't that a coincidence, 'cause while you were gone, I got me a new connect for that good Colombian cocaine," Sam bragged, taking another whiff of the merchandise. He reached down into his drawer, pulled out an envelope, and tossed it to Lou.

Lou thumbed through the contents. "This seems a little light. I think you're mistaken about our agreement." Lou had a hardness to his voice that put me on alert.

"No, I understand exactly what we agreed upon. I just figured I'd change things up a little." Sam looked at my brother like he was his bitch. Made me want to slap off the little bit of black he had, but I knew Lou would get mad if I did that, so I held my ground.

"Sam, you know I don't like games. I want my money just like we agreed." Lou was about two seconds from jumping across the table himself.

I took a couple of steps closer to my brother, pulling back my coat so Sam could see what I was packing. This caused the twins to take a step up to back up their boss.

Sam raised his hands submissively. "Hey! Lou, this is me, baby boy. You don't have to sic your attack dog on me. We all friends here. Ain't nobody here to screw you." Sam turned to the twins. "You boys hang back and relax. We all good here." The twins stepped back, but I didn't move a muscle.

Sam gingerly opened his desk drawer, pulling out a manila envelope. He handed it to Lou, who spilled the contents on the desk—thirty or forty small clear bags filled with white powder. "Look, baby boy, I owe you two grand, dig, and right there is four thousand dollars' worth of grade-A coke, already packaged to sell. I figured two shrewd brothers like yourselves wouldn't mind putting in a little hard work to double your money. Am I right?"

He was right, but I couldn't stand when that motherfucker 'ked to us using that seedy-ass pimp voice, like we were a 'ch of bitches he was trying to turn out.

Lou glanced at me for approval, and I nodded my head. We weren't really into drugs other than muling a pound or two of weed, but getting rid of the coke wouldn't be a problem as long as it was quality shit.

"A'ight, Sam, we'll take the package," Lou said, scooping the coke back in the envelope.

"Well, there's another piece of business I'd like to discuss with you brothers." Sam leaned over his desk and lit Lou's cigar.

"What's on your mind, Sam?" Lou and I sat back down in our chairs, my brother puffing and smiling at Sam like they were best damn friends again. Sam placed another envelope on the desk, pointing at it.

"That right there is identical to the package in your hands." He pushed it across the desk until it was inches from Lou. "If you don't mind knocking a few country-ass crackers in the head over in Valdosta, it's all yours."

Lou glanced over at me, and I smiled, speaking up for the first time. "Sure. We'll do it. Everybody knows knocking crackers in the head is my favorite pastime."

That caused Sam to cackle. He stood up. "Shit, if I had known that, I would have given you half."

Lou picked up the package before Sam could change his mind.

Chippy

7

After a busy night, things at Big Sam's were finally winding down, so I came out onto the porch to have a moment to myself. I ain't gonna lie; parts of me were so sore there wasn't much else I could do except lean against the railing, letting the sunrise warm my face as I read my book. I'd been trying to finish it all day, but it seemed like every time I was about to get to the good part, I had to stop because some new john wanted his dick sucked.

Gales of laughter and chatter from inside drifted out to me. Most of the girls were sitting around the tables, eating fried chicken and having their last drink before going to bed, but I wasn't hungry. I'd much rather lose myself within the pages of Sidney Sheldon with hopes that Sam would keep his promise and call me to his bed when he turned in for the night.

I heard the door behind me open then slam shut, but I didn't pay any attention to who came out until I heard a man's voice.

"Is that a good book?"

"Yeah," I replied, turning to see two men headed toward the street. I'd seen both of them in Sam's office with Lou earlier, but kept my distance. No way did I want Lou, or that baseball bat he was packing, anywhere near me. "Sidney Sheldon is my favorite."

"I'm a little more partial to Robert Ludlum, but I've read a few of his books." The one who had spoken was close to my age, but I'd never seen him before today. I wasn't really attracted to dark-skinned men, but he had this regal look about him that reminded me of Richard Roundtree in *Shaft*. I'd seen the other man before. He was much lighter, although clearly related to the Roundtree lookalike. I didn't like the weird way the lighter one looked at me, and I damn sure didn't like that creepy-ass laugh of his that seemed to come out of nowhere. I gave him a wide berth until I realized what the fuck he was laughing at.

"This whore ain't read that book, LC," the man slurred, stepping toward me and reaching for my book. "Not unless it's got pictures."

"Yes, I did," I protested, taking a step toward him so that we were face to face. I hated when people lied about me or underestimated me. It was half the reason they called me Chippy, because I would not back down in a situation like that. "What? You ain't never seen a whore read a book before?"

"I ain't never seen a whore do anything other than lie on her back and occasionally get on her knees. Gimme that shit." He snatched my book from my hand. I reached for the straight razor Sam had given me in case one of the johns got out of hand. I was about to slice his ass up. Lucky for him, the Roundtree lookalike stepped in between us, grabbing the book from him.

"Cut it out, Larry. She ain't do nothing to you." He grabbed the man by the shoulders.

"She's a damn whore!" Of course I knew what people called me, but the way he said it made it sound even worse than it already did.

"That doesn't change the fact that she's not bothering you. Now come on. It's time for you to go home. I'm sure Nee's waiting up for you."

As the two of them stared each other down for a moment, I held my straight razor close, because that Larry guy didn't give me the impression that he was the type to relent. He finally backed down by taking a step back.

"You're lucky you're my brother and I love you," Larry told him, pulling the other guy close and kissing him on the cheek.

"Love you too, bro. Now go home and sleep it off."

Larry hesitated for a minute, giving one last unfriendly look, then he began to walk away. We watched him disappear around the corner of Big Sam's.

When he was out of sight, the dark-skinned brother turned and handed me my book. "Sorry about that," he said. "He's a little drunk."

"That's like being a little pregnant. He's lucky I didn't cut his ass." I showed him my straight razor, letting him know I wasn't playing.

He glanced at my razor then shook his head. "No, you're lucky you didn't cut him," he replied with a seriousness to his tone that made me take notice. "If you had cut him with that, you'd be dead right now."

I stared back at him defiantly. "I'm not some pushover."

"I'm not saying you are, but my brother's a killer. He spent five years in Vietnam as an Army ranger. They taught him to kill people." He sounded very calm and nonchalant, but I could tell by his eyes that he meant what he was saying. "It never left him when he came home. It's who he is. He's a killer and he can't get rid of it, so he would have had no problem going through me to kill you, believe that."

Faced with the thought that I had come close to being killed, I reached into my pocket to pull out a cigarette for my nerves.

He held out a lighter as I fumbled to find a match. "Here, let me get that for you." He lit my cigarette and I took a long pull. "By the way, I'm LC. LC Duncan." He reached out his hand to shake mine all proper. I wasn't used to that—at least not around Waycross.

"They call me Chippy."

"Chippy. What kind of name is that?"

"What kind of name is LC?"

"It's short for Lavernius Charles, and before you go asking what kind of name is Lavernius, I have no clue. It was my great-grandfather's name, and he was a slave." He laughed, and I joined in, probably too loud.

"So you're one of the Duncans. I heard the Duncan brothers were not to be fucked with in this town. You're the town hellraisers?" I asked, hoping to verify the rumors that seemed to be coming up about his family all the time.

"We're not going to let anything happen to one another, if that's what you mean." His smile dropped from his face and he grew serious. "Between you and me, it's a lot to try and live down. Truth is, I'm a lover, not a fighter."

I couldn't help but roll my eyes. "So you're like your brother Lou? I'll have to ask around and see if you measure up."

He shook his head adamantly. "Ask all you want. I got a girlfriend and we're going to be married. I don't mess with them nasty—" He stopped himself, probably realizing who he was talking to. "No offense."

"None taken. I don't plan on making a career out of this."

"I hope you mean that, 'cause some of those girls in there have been around as long as I can remember. Hell, Big Shirley took my virginity when I was fifteen, and that was seven years ago."

"Well, that's not going to be me. I plan on seeing the world." I took a drag of my cigarette, deciding to change the subject. "So it must be nice to work with family."

He shrugged. "I wouldn't know. I work at Byrd's gas station over by the Piggly Wiggly in the evenings, and I go to South Georgia College during the day for business."

I didn't try to conceal my surprise. "Wow, college. That's really impressive." We didn't exactly get too many educated brothers hanging around Big Sam's.

"Yeah, I'm trying to break the cycle. My daddy was a farmer, but he made most of his money as a loan shark like my brothers. I'm not gonna lie; once in a while I'll do a favor for them, but nothing . . . you know, physical."

"Yeah, I know. Probably safer that way," I told him. He seemed like a good guy.

We both jumped when the door was flung open. A wobbly Lou stumbled out, followed by another brother who looked like two football players put together. He had a giddy, shit-eating expression all over his face but didn't bother to speak. Lou staggered right behind him.

"Hey, Red. Sam's looking for you." Lou threw his arm around LC. "C'mon, little brother, let's go get us some real grub at the Huddle House."

LC turned to me. "It was nice meeting you, Miss Chippy. I'll see you around."

"It was nice talking you too, LC." I walked away with a smile, thinking that he was the kind of guy I would have loved to meet when I was in high school.

Juan

8

At the intersection of FM 1405 and East McKinney, we waited for the steady stream of big trucks to pass by. All of this activity was because of the US Steel plant. A lot of hungry mouths being fed because of oil pipelines in Alaska or something. The A/C wasn't blowing cold enough for me in the back seat, and the car's stationary position didn't make it any better. The shipments of large pipes and valves rolled out of the gate toward parts unknown, shaking the Chevy Nova we were in. The rumble didn't seem to bother the two men seated in front, but the silence in the car led me to nervously check my watch. Today was to be a big day, and I didn't want to mess up on account of being late.

Once the trucks were gone, we were again on our way. A mile down the road, we turned into the next open gate on the right and proceeded toward a large warehouse complex big enough to hide anyone or anything.

"We're here, Juan," Manny said as he stopped the Nova in the parking lot of one of the warehouses. He had been chattier last weekend at the club in Houston, when he drank too may brews and asked me if I wanted more work. Apparently I'd caught the eye of some smart folks. I wasn't at this warehouse for a pipeline job though. I was here for a promotion. If Manny wasn't lying, this was my chance to move up and make lots of money.

Miguel and the man he called his cousin led me from the car, sandwiching me in the middle of them like I was somebody important. His cousin wore his black cowboy hat tilted low over his face, with equally dark sunglasses hiding his eyes like he was afraid of the sun. Normally I'd be worried, but if they wanted to kill me, they didn't have to drive this far to do it.

After a double knock by Manny, we entered the office door. Inside, a bunch of men who looked like they belonged on a farm or ranch stood idly by, joking amiably, although they were wielding shotguns. Their arms weren't for handling cattle, and whatever crops they "managed" paid more than corn or soy beans. I was sure there were several more of them outside that I didn't see.

One look at Manny's cousin and they motioned the three of us through an interior door, leading deeper inside the warehouse. There was no turning back now.

Dead center was where all the action took place. Behind large sheets of plastic that doubled as makeshift walls, elderly men and women who looked as if they had lived hard lives were carefully loading several cars and vans. In my mind, I began counting the armed men around us and memorizing their positions. Just in case. Around Houston, I liked to carry myself like a million bucks, but inside these walls, I knew that I needed to act humble.

A muscled older man, no more than five foot five, with long black hair and a thick moustache, looked to be in charge. As he clipped the end a fresh cigar, he turned to acknowledge us.

"Juan!" he belted out as if we were friends. "Please. Have a seat." He directed me to a single chair that was waiting behind him. Talk about a hot seat. He was military and very formal when he spoke, probably educated up North. Even while being polite, his voice held a hint of a threat, like he was not used to being questioned. Those with questions probably asked them no more.

I listened and sat my ass down, knowing how to play the game.

"That bumbling idiot Gerald Ford is President now," the man in charge said, obviously having no love for him. He went so far as to imitate the President's fall down the stairs of Air Force One, which we'd all seen on the television. "But this DEA that Nixon started has us concerned. We don't know if they're serious about drugs like they were about alcohol during the Prohibition Era, but perhaps that is good for what we do. Just a few years ago we were worried that marijuana might be legalized, but of course it wasn't. Nevertheless, we must always plan for the future, and that involves expansion and forging new alliances."

From my seat, I listened to his history lesson, nodding like it was the only thing that mattered; but I also watched a team of younger men busy switching out license plates on several cars as if on an assembly line. I saw the New Jersey plate on the car closest to me and smiled. They must've known I could drive—and fast.

"Do you know why you're here?" he asked, seeing what really held my attention.

"No," I replied, feigning ignorance as I repositioned myself in the chair. I suddenly hoped I wasn't there as a lesson myself.

"You represent the new breed who can blend in. That is an asset, Juan," he lectured, stopping to chuckle. The other men followed his lead and laughed even harder at my expense.

They could laugh at me all they wanted. Unimportant, jealous fools was all they were to me. I was the one being given the opportunity to run with the wolves, to prove I deserved more than just peddling joints in night clubs and bars.

I focused on the shiny new Gran Torino I was about to have all to myself. I imagined the highways opening wide for me, like the actor Steve McQueen in *Bullitt*, doling out justice from behind the wheel. Except that was a Mustang Steve McQueen drove. Well, I could have one of those one day, too, but for now the Gran Torino would do. If they let me keep it, who knows how much pussy I could get around there.

"You want me to drive the Torino for you, no?" I asked as I dared to stand up. Because of my sudden move, I heard one of his men chamber a shell into his shotgun. My employer motioned to them that it was okay and then smiled wildly at me.

"Oh. That's not what you will be driving," he stated. He had his men pull the plastic down from around another car. This one had a Jersey license plate too, but it was quite different.

"A Country Squire," I muttered aloud as I grimaced over at what I was being shown. It was an old station wagon. Not a new Gran Torino, but a fucking station wagon, complete with wood panels along the sides. It was like something you'd see on *The Brady Bunch* for all those fuckin' California kids and their stupid dog, although even theirs looked better than this monstrosity.

"That. That is what you will be driving for us," he cackled gleefully as he blew a puff of cigar smoke into my face. "It's good, no?"

"But . . . I don't understand, sir," I began as respectfully as I could. This had to be a joke. "It's a station wagon. I will look like a fool."

"What? You thought we would let you go out there in a flashy racecar? You are already too flashy with your pretty hair and gold chains. We're sending you to deal with the Puerto Ricans, but not in a car that will attract the attention of the police or this new DEA."

"What do you mean, sending me?" I questioned, no longer hiding my annoyance. Reckless, I know. "I thought I was making a normal run."

"Oh, you are, Juan. We're delivering a healthy sample of our best crop to New York. You will be in charge of getting the shipment to Carlos Rodrigues, a low-level lieutenant with their families as an overture for future cooperation."

"Why me?" I asked, genuinely stunned by the responsibility I was being given. Neither Manny nor his cousin had said a thing since we arrived. Instead they stood off to the side as if deaf. I guess they knew better than to give me a heads up.

"We've been watching you, Juan," he answered, motioning for me to sit back down. I quickly complied. "We've seen you in the discos and we see how easily you can blend in with any group. Manny says you are a charmer, so you can bullshit your way out of certain situations. But mainly because you're expendable."

"What do you mean?" I questioned, suddenly angered by his gall.

"The Mafia families in New York don't know about our venture. These are delicate times as we try to branch into the Northeast, which they control. And if the Italians or Asians discover us encroaching on their territory, it will be unfortunate—for you. Understand?"

"I don't know about this," I mumbled, no longer as confident about my latest job opportunity as I had been when I strutted in here. But could I realistically decline and walk out of the warehouse alive? Maybe I could ditch the shitty station wagon on the edge of town and disappear.

As if in response to my thoughts, Manny's stoic cousin approached the man with the cigar and produced photos from his front shirt pocket. For the first time, the cousin grinned at me as he resumed his place next to Manny.

They were pictures of a woman and two girls. I recognized them as my mother and two sisters back in Nueva Laredo as the boss man leaned over, holding them close to my face. It was another fucking test, which took all I had not to reveal the anger and fear that gripped me equally. Manny was never my friend, and the man beside him probably wasn't really his cousin.

Mother of God.

"Your mother and your sisters?" my unnamed employer questioned, already knowing the answer. It was more like a taunt, daring me to deviate from their plans. I was running with the wolves, and they had very sharp teeth indeed. He continued, "You don't return with our money, we will torture them slowly before we kill them," he said as he held the end of the cigar against my mother's face, burning a hole through her photograph. Bile rose into my throat. I wanted to kill him, to rip his eyes from his head. "Maybe even have some fun with your little sisters. They're never too young, Juan. We could even pass them around to work off your debt. Make them wish they were dead. Understand?"

"Yes," I replied in defeat as my shoulders slumped.

"And from now on your name is John, not Juan." He handed me a fake driver's license and sent me on my way.

Chippy

9

"How you like that, baby?" I cooed into Big Sam's ear

I had him laid out on his stomach with his head buried into a pillow, about as relaxed as a man could get without having his dick sucked or fucked. I was sure we'd get to that later, but for now I was content to feel his body relax under the newfound skill of my fingers. I'd been secretly reading about giving massages in a book I'd borrowed from the library. I really loved the way it turned him from an aggressive tiger into a meek kitten. It certainly made up for how he treated me in front of other girls sometimes because he didn't want them to think he played favorites.

"Mmmm, like it? I love it. Your magic hands just about had me falling asleep. I like the way they working right now," he told me as I started to slide my hands down his body, closer to his biggest muscle. "Girl, I ain't never gonna let you go."

Of course I couldn't stop grinning from ear to ear. Sam wasn't in the habit of doling out complements like some of these tricks who told a string of lies because they thought that was the way to get a woman wet. He was way too straightforward for that. So, when he did give me a compliment, I knew he really meant it, and it made me feel special.

Sam knew how to make me feel good, but what he really did was show me how to trust him. Other men got to have my body as long as they met my price, but the rest of me belonged to Sam, and that was just the way I wanted it to be.

I rolled Sam onto his back, massaging his dick with both hands until it was standing at attention. I stared at it for a few seconds, Just the sight of its throbbing mushroom head made me moist. It had to be the prettiest ugly thing I'd ever seen. I climbed on top of Sam, sliding down on his rock hard member. As I rocked back and forth, I couldn't help thinking that it felt as if we were one.

Unfortunately, our special moment was interrupted. I hadn't slid down on his pole three times before the door flew open, crashing against the wall. "Sam, you motherfucker!"

"What the hell?" Sam shouted, damn near throwing me off of him. We both turned to the door, where Big Shirley was standing there looking pissed off. She was holding a beer bottle in one hand and some papers in the other.

"Shirley, you know got damn well you're not supposed to come into this room unless you invited. I'm busy!"

Shirley just stared at him, her chest heaving up and down. I didn't know what her problem was, but it was evident she'd been crying.

"You ain't shit, Sam Bradford, you half-white bastard," she fumed, waving that piece of paper around like it meant something.

"Sam, look out!" I screamed just as the beer bottle came flying across the room. It barely missed my head as it smashed against the wall above Sam.

"Bitch, have you lost your mind? You better get outta here! You hear me?" Sam rose up and stood to his full height—intimidating even naked—but Shirley didn't back down. She just looked for something else to throw. She had the nerve to cut her eyes at me like she had the power to scare me. Wasn't no secret she was a loose cannon, but now I was thinking she was truly nuts.

"Eighteen years, eighteen fucking years I've been loyal to you. I didn't even care when you stopped fucking me for the younger girls. I just kept sucking dick to put money in your pockets so you could ride around in a fancy Cadillac." She was crying again and mascara was running down her face. I didn't know what the hell was going on, but I was starting to feel sorry for her.

When I had first got there a month ago, Big Shirley was the boss bitch and took every opportunity to let me know her position. She was mean as a rabid dog and she took sick pleasure in getting girls in trouble so that Sam would beat their asses. For some reason, though, she never fucked with me. She barely spoke to me, other than to make a joke.

"I can't even count how many times I went to the clinic for yeast infections, crabs, chlamydia, and gonorrhea, and I don't even wanna think about how many abortions I had," she continued. "And all I asked was for one thing, one lousy thing in eighteen years, and you fucked me."

"What are you talking about?" The expression on Sam's face told me that he genuinely had no idea.

"My momma, you bastard!" She handed him the piece of paper and he started to read. "The only thing I ever asked you to do was give me the money to go see my momma before she died of cancer. You promised me that, but you never came through. Now she's dead. Do you hear me? She's dead!"

Sam's face showed real remorse. "Shirley, I'm sorry."

"No, you're not. You're not capable of being sorry." Her voice sounded shaky as she started ranting and raving. Sam had his eyes locked on hers, but I noticed what she was doing with her hands. In one quick motion, she reached for Sam's dick with one hand and into the waistband of her skirt with the other, pulling out a butcher knife. Before Sam knew what was happening, it was too late. He was already in big trouble.

"I swear you make one fucking move and they'll be calling you Little Sam," she spat.

"Hey Shirley, baby, you don't want to do that. Look, I'm sorry, I fucked up. Come on. Whatever it is, we can work it out." He spoke pretty calmly considering the position he was in, but it didn't matter. I knew she was way too crazy to be reasonable. This ho had lost her mind.

"Hey, Shirley, let's go downstairs and get us a drink," I suggested. As soon as I saw the way she tightened up her grip on Sam's dick, causing him to stand straight up on his tippy-toes, I knew I should just shut up.

Some of the girls had entered the room to see what was happening. I was hoping they might help.

"Take a good look, girls, 'cause this is the last time you're gonna see Big Sam's precious dick!" She started jerking her hand like she was going to cut it off. Poor Sam just squeezed his eyes shut like he was waiting for the first slice of the blade.

"Shirley, baby, I'm sorry about your momma. Why don't we ride on up to Macon for the funeral. Just me and you, like old times," he said with his eyes still closed.

"I ain't going nowhere with you, Sam," she shouted, pressing the blade against the base of his penis.

"Jesus Christ, will somebody do something?" Sam screamed, but none of the girls so much as twitched.

"I wish one of you bitches would, 'cause I'll cut your asses too," Shirley threatened, turning to them and pointing the knife.

I'd heard just about all I could stand. I grabbed an E and J bottle off of the night table and ran at her blindly, smashing it against her head. I was still holding the neck of the bottle as Big Shirley crumpled to the floor with her face cut up in a bloody mess.

"You all right, baby?" I asked. Sam was holding his Johnson like a long lost friend and staring down at Shirley.

"I should kill you, bitch!" he shouted, kicking her before turning to the other girls in the room. "I should kill all of you bitches. Now get this heifer out my room!" Big Sam kicked her again for good measure.

We both watched as she struggled to get up off the floor and hobble out of Sam's room like the mangy old mutt she was. Before she left, she turned back, and I swear the look she gave was so pitiful I gasped.

"Damn, baby, you one bad-ass bitch." Big Sam came over and wrapped his arms around me. "She's gonna look like a jigsaw puzzle the rest of her life."

"That's what she deserved for trying to hurt you. I don't know what I would have done if something happened to you," I told him and I meant it. Hell, I might not be the biggest and loudest girl in this house, but I loved my man, and I wouldn't let nobody touch him.

"You saved my life," Sam whispered in my ear. "Fuck theses bitches. I can't wait to marry you."

LC

10

I glanced left then right to see if anyone was around before I grabbed Donna by the waist, pulled her close, and kissed her passionately. My hands began to roam her body, and she didn't seem to mind, until they slid under her dress. That's when she abruptly broke the kiss, looking down the row of bookshelves in a panic. I tried to kiss her again, but this time she put up her arm to block me.

"What are you doing?" she whispered, straightening out her skirt.

"Kissing you," I replied.

"Not like that you weren't. That was not just a kiss. That was a . . ." She walked angrily back to the table where we'd been studying.

"Oh, no? Then what was it?" I asked her as I sat down next to her. "It sure felt like a kiss to me."

"You don't kiss with your hands, LC Duncan. This is the library, not the back seat of a car."

"Then let's go get in the back seat of your car," I suggested. "It's been, like, two weeks, baby. Your man needs some loving."

I could see from her face that she knew where this was going. It seemed like we had these conversations on the regular, because I was horny as hell and she made me work hard for even the slightest bit of action.

"My man needs to study," she shot back. "Did you forget you have a finance final tomorrow?"

"You're right, but I sure can't concentrate with this." I took her hand and placed it in my lap. She pulled it back quickly when she felt the hardness of dick.

"Oh my goodness." She gave me a naughty smile. "We're definitely going to have to take care of that this weekend when we go to the show."

"This weekend?" I did nothing to conceal my disappointment. "This needs to be taken care of now. We can go over to my place."

"Unh-uh. No way," she said, her naughty look replaced with an adamant frown. "I'm not going back to your house. Your brother Lou might be there."

"So?"

"What do you mean, so? He saw me with your thing in my mouth," she said. "I don't think you understand how embarrassing that was."

"I do, but you don't understand how much I want you." I came up with a compromise. "Why don't we just go somewhere and park before you have to go home, then I'll come back and study?"

"I can't." She pulled out her final argument: the Daddy card. "Daddy's having company and I promised my mother I'd help get everything together." Donna popped up and began to gather her things.

I took her hand. "Donna, please. I really need this." This was getting old. I hated the fact that I was begging the woman I loved to be intimate with me when other women who I didn't give a shit about would damn near throw themselves at me.

"LC, let's just wait until this weekend when you get paid. We can have dinner, go see the show, then go to a hotel. It'll be fun. I promise." She picked up her books and kissed me on the cheek. I couldn't believe that once again she was going to leave me high and dry. I tried to think of what Lou would do in a time like this. Lou was a master at using reverse psychology to guilt women into sleeping with him.

"Promises, promises," I mumbled under my breath. "What I shoulda done was take Missy Wilkens up on her offer."

"And what offer was that?" Donna snapped with attitude, placing a hand on her hip.

There was no doubt I had her attention. Now all I had to do was execute the plan.

"Huh? Oh, nothin'," I replied coyly, lowering my head. Donna couldn't stand Missy and I knew it. She'd caught Missy cheating with her last boyfriend.

"LC Duncan, if you don't tell me what that slut Missy said, so help me . . ."

"She ain't say nothing, Donna. Just forget about it. I'll see you later." I opened my textbook and pretended to read.

She grabbed me by the ear and started to squeeze, threatening me with, "If you don't stop lying to me, so help me I will rip your ear off."

"All right, all right," I said, pulling her hand off my ear. She was digging her nails in and that shit was starting to hurt for real. It didn't stop me from telling her another lie, though. "Missy said that when I'm finished messing with little girls and ready for a real woman, I should give her a call."

"Oh, she did, did she?" She let go of my ear, staring me like she'd just caught me in the act. "So is that what you think, that I'm not a real woman?"

"I didn't say tha—"

She cut me off. "You didn't have to, LC. I know how men think. All y'all want is to get your little dick sucked. But that's not what relationships are all about. Did you at least tell her we were engaged?"

I shrugged my shoulders. "No. Was I supposed to?"

Her eyes welled up with tears. "What do you think?" She stomped off toward the exit.

It took me a moment to realize that this whole thing had just blown up in my face. I jumped up and gave chase, damn near running over a woman on my way out the library door. When I saw my brother Lou, I might just punch him in the face. Reverse psychology my ass.

By the time I caught up to her, Donna was getting in her car. "Donna, wait. Please."

She stood there gawking at me as if there she wanted to ask something but was afraid of the answer. Finally she whispered, "Did you sleep with her? Did you sleep with Missy?"

"No, I swear."

I could see the relief in her eyes as she shot off another question. "Did you think about it? Did you think about sleeping with her?" The answer was no, but I'd hesitated for a split second longer than I should have, and by then it was too late. Donna had already jumped to her own conclusion. "Well, then you need to call her."

"But—but Donna, I didn't." She stepped in her car without another word, locking the door as I reached for the handle. I watched her put the car in gear.

"Donna, dammit, don't leave. Donna, please . . . Fuck!" She barely looked at me as she sped off, leaving me standing in her dust. I stood there in disbelief for almost five minutes, waiting for her to return. She didn't.

I walked back in the library and sat down at the table where I'd left my books. I wanted to go home and wallow in self-pity, but despite my girlfriend problems, I still had an exam the next day and I had to study. I opened my economics book.

Ten minutes into my studying, I looked up to see that someone was sitting at the other end of the table. I'd been so lost in the complicated theories on the page that I hadn't noticed her come to the table, but now that I saw her, I had to do a double take.

"Chippy?" I said tentatively. She had on a head scarf and wasn't wearing quite as much makeup as when we first met, but it was her. "Is that you?"

"Oh, so now it's all right for you to notice me in public?" I didn't know it was possible to whisper with attitude, but she managed to do it. I chose to ignore her tone and stay friendly. I'd already had one conversation with a female blow up in my face, so I would keep this one peaceful if I could help it.

"My apologies. I didn't see you sitting there," I said, hoping my smile would soften her up.

"I'm not talking about now. I'm talking about twenty minutes ago when you damn near ran me over running after that girl. What'd she do, rob you or something?"

"Oh, that was you. I'm so sorry." I realized how whipped I must have looked running behind Donna's ass like a puppy. "I was chasing after my girlfriend. We had a little fight."

"From the way you chased her down and she sped away, I'd say it was more than a little fight."

"I didn't think you saw all that." I felt my face burning from embarrassment.

"This is a small town. You've got to get your entertainment where you can find it." She giggled, and for the first time I saw her as a woman and not a—

"So what are you doing *here*?" I blurted out. I just couldn't keep the surprise out of my voice. My eyes traveled down to the books piled in front of her. Judging from the titles, it looked like she was studying geography.

"As opposed to what, lying on my back or getting on my knees? I do both, you know," she snapped in a voice loud enough for heads to swivel in our direction. When I glanced back to her, she was giving me a look to let me know that I deserved that.

"That's not what I meant."

"Yes it was. It was all over your face," Chippy replied, looking me up and down like she was finally figuring me out. She moved like she was about to stand up and leave, but I spoke up fast, hoping to stop her.

"What I meant was I've never seen you here. And no, you just don't seem like the type that spends your free time around a bunch of bookworms like me. However, I'm sorry. Considering I'm a Duncan, I should be the last to judge a book by its cover."

"Good recovery." She picked up a book from the pile in front of her like she was dismissing me. Instead of leaving her alone, I began to shuffle through her choices.

"*The Treasures of London, Rome on a Budget, Paris is for Lovers? The Architecture of New York City*?" I said, reading the titles out loud. She was a mystery to me before, but the more I learned about this woman, the less I knew.

"What?" she answered without looking at up from the book she was reading. I thought I understood why she was doing that. Her lack of eye contact kept up a wall between us. One of the things I'd been good at since I was little was reading folks, but this Chippy didn't make that easy.

"You going someplace?" I asked, prying for more information about this mysterious woman.

"I'm planning on it, when Sam and I get enough money. Did you think I work at Big Sam's because I like it?" She finally made eye contact. "Paris, London, Rome, New York . . . ever since I was a little girl I dreamed of running away and seeing the world. Now I'm gonna do it."

Normally I would have just ended the conversation with a woman like this who carried herself with such an attitude, but I felt no desire to leave now. In spite of the fact that she sold her body for a living, I wanted to get to know this woman's mind. Something about her intrigued me.

"Well, it sounds like you have a plan," I said, hoping she would continue the conversation.

"I'm sure someone smart like you has plans to see the world too."

"Nope. All I ever wanted to do was to get my degree in business and go to New York. My brother Lou goes all the time on business, but I don't want to just visit. I wanna live there."

"To do what?" she asked, closing her book and no longer trying to avoid eye contact.

"I've got this thing for cars. One day I wanna go there and open up a big-time car dealership like those guys on the *Black Enterprise 100* list."

She nodded and said, "After John Johnson, those auto dealers are always near the top of the list."

I almost fell out of my chair. She was the first woman I'd ever met who knew what the *BE 100* list was, let alone who was on it.

"Well, if you ever need a part-time secretary or bookkeeper, let me know. I was the best typist in my school before I dropped out."

I stared at her, wondering if I could ask the question I really wanted to ask without her slapping my face.

Chippy

11

"Chippy, why do you sell your body? You're better than that."

It was the same question I'd asked myself a million times, and here I was, sitting across the table from LC Duncan as he stared at me, waiting for a response.

Sam had given me the afternoon off after I saved him from Big Shirley and her big-ass knife. It wasn't like there was a whole lot to do with my free time in Waycross, so I strolled over to the library, where I knew I could get some peace and quiet. That's when I saw LC. At first he brushed past me, chasing behind some woman who looked pretty pissed off. When he came back into the library, the woman was nowhere in sight, and LC was so preoccupied that it took him ten minutes to even notice me.

The conversation between us was a little tense at first, but I'll admit that some of that was because of the chip on my shoulder. Most men I met weren't interested in conversing with me, so needless to say, I didn't trust them much. LC was persistent, though, and his conversation was so friendly and non-threatening that I found myself loosening up pretty quickly. And then he took it to the one place I didn't want to go.

The look on his face was one of confusion, not judgment, as he waited for me to answer his question. I stared back at him, wondering why in the world I would even consider explaining my choices to a man I barely knew. Then I realized why: I could use a friend, and unlike everyone else I'd met in Waycross, LC seemed to genuinely give a fuck.

I glanced around and realized that the library had started to get crowded. Even if I'd decided to open up to LC, I didn't want the whole world knowing my business. "You mind if we take a walk?"

He nodded, and I stood up, leaving my books on the table. LC and I walked out of the library and headed down Lee Street, a pretty, tree-lined block.

"Love," I said with a sigh when we were about halfway down the block.

"Excuse me?" He stopped walking and turned to face me.

"You asked me why I'm a whore, and the answer is love. I'm doing it for love."

I braced myself for his laughter, but he surprised me when he nodded and said, "I kind of figured that."

"You did?"

"First time I saw you was in Sam's office. The way you looked at him made me jealous."

I raised an eyebrow. He was confusing me. "Jealous? Why?"

"Because the only thing I ever wanted was for my girl Donna to look at me that way."

"Oh." It was all I could say, because I didn't have the heart to tell him that based on what I'd seen earlier in the library, I didn't think he was going to get much tenderness from her anytime soon.

"So, here's what I don't understand," he said. "How do you love a man who makes you sell your body for him?"

I felt my temper rising a little. Who was this guy to question Sam's motives or his love for me? Sure, what we had was a little unconventional, but what did LC with his perfect little stuck-up girlfriend know about real life? Some people had to make tough choices for love.

"That's all I have to give him," I said defensively. "I'm a whore because that's what I can do to help him for now."

"But you're worth so much more than that. Doesn't it bother you that he's got all those other girls around?" he asked.

I sucked my teeth, trying to conceal the truth, which was that I felt a stab of jealousy every time Sam touched one of the other girls. I told LC the same thing I told myself all the time: "What I have with Sam is completely different from what they have with him."

"Oh, really?"

"Yes, really." I felt myself getting fired up. Why was LC pushing this issue? "Look, the only reason I'm doing this job is for my man, so that we can make enough money to get the hell out this place."

I guess there was enough attitude in my voice to let LC know it was time for him to change the topic. "So that's why you reading all those travel books?"

"Yeah, Sam and I are going to travel the world together one day. See Bora Bora and the Eiffel tower. Hell, we might even take ourselves to the Great Wall of China." I laughed at the idea of Sam and me with all those Chinese people.

LC wasn't laughing with me. He had a serious look on his face, and he stayed quiet for a minute as we turned around and started walking back toward the library.

Back at our table in the library, we opened our books and started reading again, but the silence between us didn't last too long. He leaned across the table and whispered, "Aren't you worried that he's taking advantage of your love for him?"

I shook my head emphatically. "Don't many people know Sam the way that I do. He's not as tough as he seems. He's had a hard life, and most of the women he's loved, including his own momma, have disappointed him. I'm not going to be one of those. You know how in church they say to give your life over to God? Well, I found something better to give my life to. I committed my life to the church of Big Sam, and he's the one I plan to worship for the rest of my life." Maybe my devotion sounded extreme, but if LC was going to keep questioning my man, I was going to leave no doubt how I felt about Sam.

"That's deep. So you'd do anything for him?" LC asked me.

"Isn't that obvious? I already am, and I don't care what anybody thinks. When you love somebody, you can't sit on the fence deciding you'll do X for them but not Y. You have to be down with them in their corner like every day is a war between the two of you and the rest of the world. I'm either going to give you everything and call that love, or I'll give you nothing and you can fuck off." I glanced around the room to see if anyone had heard my salty language, but the people around us had their faces buried in books, and they were paying us no mind. I continued, whispering fiercely, "So, yeah, I love Sam, and there is nothing I wouldn't do to support him. Anybody got a problem with that can kiss my black ass."

LC put his hands together and briefly applauded after my little speech. At first I thought he was mocking me, but he actually had a smile on his face. "If I had a woman like you, I'd probably run the world."

"Probably," I said with a laugh, enjoying the attention and his compliment.

"Big Sam is a lucky man. I hope he knows it."

I could hear a touch of skepticism, but I ignored it. Other than Sam, LC was the nicest man I'd met since I left home. He was definitely the first one who wasn't trying to get into my panties.

"Well, that Donna isn't doing too bad for herself neither," I told him.

He scrunched up his face. "Why can't she see that?" he asked. "She just isn't in my corner like you are with Sam—and I'm ready to marry that woman."

His statement made me think of all those snooty girls back home with their legs zipped shut until their wedding day then doling out sex to their husbands like it was a reward. I hated the games women played, especially when they were lucky enough to land a good man. That's why their men ended up in places like Big Sam's every chance they got. Maybe someday I'd have a chance to talk to Donna to make her understand how to keep the good man she had.

"Wanna go get some food?" I asked. "I'm hungry."

He hesitated for a quick second, and I realized that it was stupid of me to even have asked. LC was friendly and all, but he was a college boy, and I was sure he didn't really want to be seen in public with me. What if someone spotted us and told his girlfriend?

I was about to rescind my stupid offer when he surprised me by saying, "Sure, why not. It's not like I can concentrate on this test anyway. I know a great spot for some fried chicken and biscuits."

"Sounds good to me." I started to gather my books to return them to the librarian.

"What sounds good?" We both looked toward the harsh voice that belonged to his fiancée. This sister was standing there, arms folded across her chest, looking completely bent out of shape.

LC looked like he was about to pass out, although I doubt she noticed, because she was busy boring holes into me with her harsh stare. Whereas before I was thinking about giving her some friendly advice about keeping her man, now I had nothing but contempt for this snooty heifer.

"Donna, you came back," LC said weakly.

She turned her attention to him, and the scowl fell off her face. "I thought about it, and my mother's dinner party can wait," she cooed in this overly dramatic voice she must have picked up from one of those corny-ass white movie stars. If she had to use that shit in real life at a place like Big Sams, she'd probably starve to death. "It's time I reminded you why I'm the only real woman in your life." She shot a glance in my direction.

The smile on his face lit that brother up like a Christmas tree. I'm sorry, but I had to laugh.

"Yeah," I interrupted, "if you were a real woman you wouldn't have to remind him of shit, 'cause you'd be putting it on his ass every night. But of course I wouldn't have to tell you that, would I?"

Her eyebrows shot up like I'd hit a nerve. She looked at LC like she was waiting for him to come to her aid as I put her in her place, but he stood there silently. I'll give it to her, though. At least she held her own and didn't shrink away from me. She gave attitude right back. "And who are you, might I ask?"

The look on LC's face told me he was silently begging me not to start any shit with his girl, and because he had showed me kindness, I decided to back off. "Oh, sorry," I said sweetly. "I didn't mean to be rude. I'm Chippy. I'm a friend of his brother Lou's." I extended my hand. Boy, did LC look relieved.

Donna looked me up and down like she was sizing up the competition. She didn't bother to take my hand.

"Who isn't a friend of Lou's?" she sneered with a nasty little laugh. "After all, he is a real ladies' man. He probably doesn't remember anybody's name after he . . . shall we say, meets them?"

"Oh, he remembers my name. Every man I know remembers my name and everything about me. That's 'cause I'm a real woman too," I added, knocking that smugness off of her face.

"Well, it was nice seeing you again, Chippy. I'll bring those books by sometime next week." LC shot me a look of gratitude as he took Donna's hand.

"Thanks, LC. You two lovebirds have fun."

"We will," Donna answered for him. "More fun than he's ever had."

As I watched them walk away, I thought, *Boy, he could do so much better.*

LC

12

"So, LC, how are your studies coming?" Donna's father drilled me as his wife smiled politely across the dinner table. Despite the fact that I had been dating her for almost a year, this was the first time Donna's parents had invited me to dinner. Donna, who sat to my right, was beaming like a lightbulb.

"Well, Dr. Washington, it's going great. I just finished finals, as you know, and I'll probably end up on the dean's list. I'm real excited about this history course I'm taking next semester on capitalism in the Renaissance. It's fascinating how they made sure that all the lower classes had to depend on the rulers for their basic survival. As far back as history can go, the power dynamic doesn't shift." This was the kind of thing I could talk about all day.

"So exactly what kind of employment are you planning to procure with an interest in Renaissance history?" Donna's father asked, his voice barely disguising his disdain for my choice of academic classes.

"Daddy, he's not getting a degree in history, but he's taking classes that interest him. How can you have a problem with that? You always said that knowledge is power," Donna shot back at her father, smiling while she spoke so she didn't appear disrespectful.

"Yes, dear. After all, it's only his undergraduate education," Mrs. Washington chimed in. No matter how many times I'd met them, something about Dr. and Mrs. Washington always made me nervous. After all, they were like royalty in our small town.

"I realize your family doesn't have much education, but—"

"Daddy!"

Dr. Washington glanced at his daughter, but her protest did nothing to deter him from lecturing me. "All I'm saying is that if I were paying for your education, I would never approve of nonsense like that. Graduate schools want to know that you are taking rigorous classes that are commensurate with your continuing education. I mean, how do you expect to apply to medical or law school with classes in Renaissance history?" As he spoke, the housekeeper appeared, placing the roast been on the table. He continued, "Boy, you need to take your education seriously," and his voice boomed so loudly that it caused the housekeeper to quickly retreat back to the safety of the kitchen. Hell, I wished I could have gone with her.

"Dr. Washington, history is only one of my interests." I turned to smile at Donna, and I guess that sent the wrong message to her father.

"Oh, really?" he barked. That's when I realized he thought I was referring to his daughter as my "other interests."

I rushed to clean it up. "Well, you know Bryd's gas station where I work?"

"Yes," he said arrogantly, "and I can still see the oil still stuck under your fingernails. Seems like they don't get clean even for Sunday dinner."

"Daddy!" Donna chastised as I curled my fingers into fists to hide my fingernails. I knew my hands were clean, but all the scrubbing in the world didn't remove the grease under my nails.

"No, that's all right. He's just telling the truth," I assured Donna. She reached out to stroke the side of my face, and her father cleared his throat loudly to register his disapproval.

"Donna, do not disrespect your father with public displays of affection. People like us don't engage in that sort of thing." Mrs. Washington instructed.

Sensing my discomfort, Donna touched her leg against mine under the table. Damn if that didn't make me more nervous, because it sent my mind running straight into the gutter, which was exactly where it didn't need to be. Not in front of her parents. It felt like they could read my mind, and man, if they knew the things we had already done and how I had corrupted their daughter, they would have tossed me out for good.

I took the conversation back to the place I had been trying to go before the subject of my dirty fingernails came up. "Dr. and Mrs. Washington," I said then stopped to make sure that I had their full attention. "You both should know that I love your daughter." I turned and glanced at Donna, who nodded for me to continue. "And I want you to know that one day soon I'm going to own my own business."

"And what kind of business is that, young man?" he asked, making no effort to conceal his doubt. "'Cause I done heard about that family of yours." I could have said something to defend my family, but this was my first time being invited to dinner, and I didn't want it to be my last.

"Byrd's. Old Man Byrd offered to let me buy him out when he retires, which will be soon. That way when I graduate, I will already be set up financially, and then Donna and I—"

He cut me off. "A gas station? You think I am going to allow my daughter to settle for a man whose entire future is fixing cars and Lord knows what else?" He was glaring at me. I locked my eyes on his, clenching my jaw to keep from flipping on his ass. He kept pushing, trying to antagonize me. Maybe he hoped that if he pushed hard enough I would leave his daughter alone.

"Oh, you think I don't know who you are?" he said. "This is a small town, and the Duncan family is legendary for being lowlife criminals. You got one brother can't stay out of jail, another I heard is too dumb to think for himself, and then you have that pimp working at Big Sam's, selling girls."

"Now, you wait one minute, Dr. Washington. Don't you ever talk about my brothers or where I come from." My voice thundered. I had tried to remain respectful to Donna's parents, but this man needed to know that there were some conversations off limits for the rest of his life, and my family was at the top of that list.

He stood up from the table. "I will not be disrespected in my own house. How dare you use that tone and threaten me?"

I took Donna's hand, working hard to calm myself before things got physical. After all, even if I didn't want him to talk about my family, much of what he said was true. The Duncans were not soft, and if he kept pushing me, he might find out just how much of that Duncan blood flowed through my veins.

Donna squeezed my hand, though, and that little reminder from the woman I loved was enough to make my rage subside a bit. I decided to talk rather than start swinging.

"Dr. Washington, I am going to marry your daughter with or without your approval, and that means that one day you will be the grandfather of my children. I suggest you be careful about how you talk to the man who will be responsible for siring your heirs," I informed him before I got up to leave. "Thank you for the invitation to dinner, but I seem to have lost my appetite."

"LC, don't go," Donna pleaded.

"Let him go," her father insisted, waving his hand like he was swatting away an irritating insect.

I looked dead in his eye and said, "I love your daughter, so I will be back." I leaned down and gave Donna a long kiss before walking out of the house with my head held high.

Lou

13

I woke up to one of Levi's roosters crowing outside my window around nine o'clock in the morning. I usually stayed in bed until noon, but I was drawn to the kitchen by the smell of freshly cooked bacon and biscuits. NeeNee Simpson, a shapely brown-skinned sister, was standing in front of the stove, wearing only a head wrap and a shirt that looked like it belonged to Larry. I'd known NeeNee most of my life; she was like family. She was also the closest thing Larry ever had to a steady woman, probably because she was the only one who would put up with his shit.

"Good morning, Lou. You want some cheese eggs and grits?" NeeNee held a spatula in her hand as she pointed me toward the coffee on the kitchen table.

"Mornin', Nee. Yeah, eggs and grits would be nice. Thanks." One thing I never did was refuse NeeNee's cooking, because the girl had a gift. She could make a piece of shit taste good, so you could just imagine what she could do with some eggs and grits.

I sat down next to Larry, who had on a stocking cap, wife beater, and his boxers, with a lit cigarette hanging out of his mouth. He was cleaning his .45 at the table. I poured a cup of coffee, adding cream and sugar. "Y'all hear about Big Shirley?"

Larry chuckled. Of course his morbid ass would find that shit funny. "I heard she was going to cut Sam's pecker off, and that new whore carved her up like a turkey on Thanksgiving."

"She'll be all right. Even with scars, Shirley's got some of the best pussy in Waycross." I took a sip of my coffee. "Speaking of Sam, we got that job in Valdosta to do today."

"Yeah, I know. What we gonna do about Jeffery Peterson? Weren't you supposed to go out there today?"

"Damn. Guess we're gonna have to send LC."

"Send me where?" LC walked in the back door, wearing his Byrd's garage overalls like he'd been working all night.

"Gonna need you to take care of something this afternoon," I said.

"Can't. I gotta work this afternoon," he protested.

"Figure it out. This'll only take an hour or two of your time," I told him firmly. "I need you, man, and I'll make it worth your while. You got my word."

LC sucked his teeth but didn't say anything.

"Well, here's something worth your while." Larry slid a folded newspaper across the table. I unfolded it, revealing a small stack of money. It had to be four or five hundred dollars.

"Matt Jones?" I smirked.

"Yep. Brought it by this morning. He sold his car after he heard what happened to fat-ass Quincy's foot."

"Quincy still owes us three grand, I might add."

"Don't worry about Quincy. I'll take care of him," Larry stated.

NeeNee placed two plates of eggs, grits, bacon, and biscuits in front of us then sat on Larry's knee as we started to eat. LC sat down across from me, carrying his own plate. For the next five minutes, we ate silently—until LC dropped the bomb on us.

"Old Man Walker died last night," LC said out of nowhere, shocking the shit out of us.

We all turned to face him. Mr. Walker ran the numbers rackets in Waycross and all of Ware County, which was a pretty lucrative business.

"What the fuck do you mean, he died?" Larry snapped, stabbing a biscuit with his fork. "How did he die?" Larry and Ray Jr., Mr. Walker's only son, were real close. In fact, he was so close to the family that he used to do number pick-ups for Mr. Walker before he went into the army. "You know, Lou, I wouldn't put it past Sam to have Mr. Walker killed, just like he did Ray Jr."

Rumor had it that Ray Jr. caught Sam messing with his old lady Sandra, and Sam ended up killing him. They never found Ray's body, but Sandra ended up working at Sam's a few weeks later, so you could just imagine what the rest of Waycross was thinking.

NeeNee said exactly what I was thinking. "Mm-hmm, everyone knows Sam wanted Mr. Walker's business."

Sam had been trying to get Mr. Walker to sell him the numbers business for a long time, but Mr. Walker refused.

"Sam didn't kill Mr. Walker. He died in a car accident over there on US1 this morning," LC clarified, and it was a relief for me. "Me and Mr. Byrd just pulled his car out of a ditch for the state police. They said he musta fell asleep at the wheel."

"Yeah, but you can bet your ass he'll still own Mr. Walker's business by the end of the month," Larry said with assurance, lighting a cigarette. "Damn shame, too. I know that old man didn't want Sam to have his business."

"I wouldn't worry about that. Ms. Walker's not gonna sell her husband's policy bank to Big Sam," NeeNee said, starting to clear off the table.

I shook my head. "If she don't, he'll just start up fresh. The Walkers don't have the muscle to stand up to Big Sam. Not with Mr. Walker and Ray dead."

"No, God dammit!" LC spoke up, slamming his hand on the table. He had that same shit eating grin he wore whenever he had a good hand in spades. "The Walkers don't have the muscle, but you and Larry do. Y'all should buy it from Mrs. Walker before Big Sam does."

I turned and looked at LC like he had two heads. Although the idea was sweet, the boy had no idea what he was suggesting. "What are you trying to do, get us all killed? Sam wants that business, LC. You don't go up against a nigga like Big Sam Bradford on something like this."

"Why not?"

"Because things don't work that way." I turned to Larry, who was sucking on what was left of his cigarette, listening intently. "Will you talk some sense into this boy?"

"I don't know, Lou. The kid's got a point. We've got the money, and I do know the business. I'm sure Mrs. Walker would sell us the customer list and give us her blessing."

I shook my head furiously. "Oh my God! Do you two hear yourselves? Do you fucking hear yourself? What about Sam?"

"What about him!" Larry exploded. "All I keep hearing about is Sam this and Sam that. You need to stop being his bitch, Lou. What's he going to do if we buy it?" Larry picked up his gun. "I'll tell you what—nothin'. That's what he's going to do, except maybe cut you off from getting free pussy."

"I don't fucking believe this shit. Y'all have lost your minds." I turned to LC and pointed. "You're going to get us killed with all your big dreams of grandeur, college boy. You don't understand how shit works. This is life, not some fucking college textbook or a rundown gas station you want to buy someday."

"I know it's life, Lou. What I don't understand is why my big brothers, who I look up to, aren't taking advantage of an opportunity to stand on their own," LC said confidently.

"Cause that opportunity could get us all killed," I replied.

"That opportunity could make us rich," Larry added.

I glanced back and forth between my brothers. What the fuck were they trying to get me into?

Larry continued, "I don't know about you, Lou, but I'm sick of being under that pimp's thumb."

LC got out of his chair, waving his hands around wildly as he talked. "It's simple, Lou. Are you going to be the man or the man next to the man? Make up your mind, because opportunity knocks, and whichever play you decide, I'll back you, and so will Larry and Levi."

14

First thing I noticed when I stopped the car in front of Big Sam's was how quiet the place appeared to be for two in the afternoon. Like somebody had replaced the normal revelry with an almost churchlike atmosphere. There wasn't one girl with her robe coming undone, requiring her to make a big show of retying it in order to reel in a customer. To say I was relived would be putting it mildly. Last thing I needed was for Donna to catch a glimpse of what really went on in this place. It was one thing to know, and an entirely different thing to see it with your own eyes.

"I'ma go with you," Donna insisted, staring up at the neon sign that read BIG SAM'S. Hell, it was bad enough that I was behind the wheel of her father's brand new convertible Chrysler K car. If her pops found out she'd let me drive and then I'd taken her and his car over to Oak Street, I don't know how crazy he'd get. It would be all the excuse he needed to get me away from his daughter for good, and I wasn't about to let that happen.

"Nah, you stay in the car." I picked up the pile of books that were in the back seat. "I'm just gonna run these in here and get something from Lou. I'll be back in a flash."

"But I want to go." Donna pouted, batting her eyelashes at me.

"Sorry, babe. Big Sam's is no place for you." I gave her a quick peck on the cheek then headed toward the door before she could make a fuss.

The quiet made me wonder if the cops had finally raided the place. As soon as I opened the front door, I could see how mistaken I had been. The party was in full force, with more happy, hard-dick drunk men than I'd seen in a long time on a weekday. They were being seduced by half naked girls who planned on emptying their wallets.

"Well, hello, Mr. Duncan." I looked up and saw Chippy in a black teddy, wearing a black cowboy hat and boots. A far cry from what she looked like at the library the other day, she took the phrase *Ride 'em, cowgirl* to a whole new level. She smiled at me, but unlike the other half naked women in the joint, her smile was genuine and not laced with any bullshit ulterior motives.

"Hey, just the woman I was looking for. How's it going?"

"Better now that I finished reading that book you suggested. The library had two copies. It must be really popular."

"Yeah, it was required reading for this psychology class I was taking."

"After reading what Viktor Frankl went through, it's been making me look at things a lot differently."

"We all go through stuff, but ultimately it's to get to the same place. Before I read *Man's Search for Meaning* I kept trying to make sense of things that didn't make sense, and then it just made everything clear." Despite the teddy, it was so hard to see her as one of Big Sam's girls as I stood here discussing literature with her.

"Exactly. When he says that suffering is in . . . in . . . Ugh!" She let out a frustrated sigh.

"Inevitable," I said, helping her. I liked how excited she was getting about that book. Most people read it because they had to.

"Yeah, inevitable. It just made sense, you know? We're not alone, and if he can live through a concentration camp and still remain positive, then we should be able to get through whatever challenges we have, too, without becoming bitter. Right?" She looked up at me, her face bright with hope.

"Yeah, you got it."

"So what else you got for me? You said you were going to suggest some books by black authors."

I handed her the books I was holding, and she looked like she was going to cry. "Are these for me?"

"Yeah, I brought you *Man Child in the Promised Land*, *The Autobiography of Malcolm X*, and my personal favorite, J.A. Rodgers' *Superman to Man*. These are books every black person should read. I was gonna bring you *The Spook Who Sat by the Door* by Sam Greenlee, but I think my brother Larry stole it."

She was grinning from ear to ear—until a toothless old man grabbed her around the waist and yelled, "Hey, cowgirl, I wanna go for a ride."

If you ask me, the man was just straight up disgusting, and Chippy obviously thought so too. She wrenched herself away from him, but he wasn't taking no for an answer.

"Girl, I just got my SSI check, and I got money to burn."

"Maybe later, Richie," she said. "I'm talking to someone." She turned back to me, but dude kept on going.

"I want to fuck you from the back while you wear that hat." He was starting to get belligerent. My first instinct was to step in and give him the ass whooping he deserved, but then I remembered that despite the friendship Chippy and I were developing, this wasn't my world and she wasn't my woman.

"What, you not working?" the old man shouted. His breath was so bad I could smell it from where I was standing, so I was sure it was killing Chippy, as close as he was to her. That was the final straw for me. I was about to make him back up off Chippy when her boss came over, reminding us all of where we were and what Chippy's purpose was in that place.

"Damn right she's working! Chippy, get your ass upstairs. This man's a paying customer!" Big Sam's voice boomed. He grabbed her by the arm and shoved her and the snaggle-tooth man toward the stairs. She still had the books in her hand as she followed the smelly guy up the stairs, looking totally turned off.

"Hey, young buck," Big Sam said. "Sorry I had to interrupt your little conversation, but I already know you ain't paying for a taste."

"No, not me. I'm looking for Lou."

Big Sam bared his teeth. He was trying to show me a friendly smile, but he always managed to look slightly menacing.

"Ask one of the girls. I'm sure he's in here someplace," Sam said. "Him and Larry got a job to do for me today." With that, he hustled off to God knows where. I didn't know what it was, but I genuinely disliked that man.

"You looking for Lou? He just went upstairs with Ebony." One of Sam's girls pointed me to the back staircase. "It's easier to go that way. It's the first door on your right."

I glanced over to where Chippy and the man had headed, but they were gone. Too much time had passed since I entered, which meant Donna would be getting annoyed at being kept waiting. I raced up the back staircase and knocked on the door. A minute later, a pretty dark chocolate girl wrapped in a towel, her breasts spilling out of it, opened the door.

"Hey, sorry to interrupt. I'm looking for my brother Lou."

She nodded and closed the door. A few seconds later, Lou came out, buck naked and grinning.

"LC, you have got to have the world's worst timing. What is it?"

I glanced past the woman staring at us from behind Lou. "You still want me to do that, you know, errand for you?"

It took Lou a second, then his eyes opened wide. "Oh, fuck yeah. Damn, I almost forgot about that shit. Baby, hand me my pants." He motioned to the ebony sister who had let the towel fall all the way off. Damn, did she have a hell of a body, but it still didn't compare to the image Chippy had installed in my brain with that hat and boots. The woman handed over the pants, and Lou pulled out his billfold, handing me some money and then a small .22 caliber handgun. "You know what to do, right?"

I tucked the gun in one pocket and the money in the other. "Yeah, Lou, I know what to do. I just hope this don't take too long. I can't be late for work again."

"You ain't gonna be late, and if you are, I'll go talk to Old Man Byrd myself."

"I'm gonna hold you to that."

"I don't know why you care so much about that two bit gas station job. Me and Larry will pay you ten times what you make there, and after a while we'll make you our partner like Daddy wanted."

"That two bit gas station could be a gold mine if he'd run it correctly," I said. "Besides, I like working on cars. You know that."

He patted me on the back. "Yeah, I know that. Now get out of here, kid. I got something waiting on me in there, and you're not gonna use me as an excuse for being late."

I hurried back down the stairs and out the door. My stomach turned into knots, and I felt like I was going to pass out when I opened the door and saw Big Sam leaning against the car, whispering in Donna's ear. She had her head thrown back in laughter like whatever he was saying was the funniest shit she'd ever heard.

"Yo, what the fuck are you doing? Stay the fuck away from my girl!"

Big Sam stepped away from the car with his hands in the air and an expression on his face that said he was trying to look innocent.

"What's the problem, young buck? I was just talking to the young lady is all, keeping her company while you left her waiting out here alone in the hot sun. With all those girls in there looking to give pleasure, who knew how long it would be before you even remembered this beautiful young thang? I was only doing my gentlemanly duty." We both knew he was full of shit. The only one who didn't know was Donna's grinning ass. Just seeing them together had me so hot I almost pulled out the .22 and blew his ass away.

"Everything all right, boss?" one of Sam's goons asked from the porch behind me. I was sure he would have shot me in the back if I tried anything, so I walked around to the driver's side.

"Everything's fine. Isn't that right, young buck?" Sam lowered his hands.

"Just stay the fuck away from my girl." I hopped into the driver's seat and sped away.

"What the fuck were you talking to him about?" I snapped at Donna, who didn't look the least bit concerned about how I felt. In fact, she snapped back.

"Don't talk to me like that, LC. I am not a child."

"Do you know who that man was?" I asked.

"No, but whoever he was, there was no reason for you to embarrass me like that. He was just telling me a joke." Donna shook her head, giving me a disapproving look.

"Well, then the joke's on you, because that was Big Sam Bradford, the pimp."

"That's Big Sam? Well, I guess the rumors are true. He's not bad on the eyes at all."

"What?" I swiveled my neck around to glare at her.

She tried to clean it up, but the damage had already been done. "That is, if you like handsome, light-skinned, green-eyed men, but I'm a chocolate-lovin' girl all the way." She leaned her head on my shoulder, reaching for my crotch.

Chippy

15

I sat at the bar, smoking a cigarette while reading the autobiography of Malcom X that LC had given me. I'd never been big on non-fiction, but this book had me hooked from the very first page. I was trying to get as far into it as I could, because in about twenty minutes, the after work crowd would start to come in. Since the incident with Big Shirley, Sam had been sweet as pie, showering me with gifts and stopping by my room every night for some loving. I liked the way things were, and I did not want to miss any chance to make money, which would piss him off.

"Heads up," Little Momma whispered, walking past me then sitting two seats down at the bar. "You got trouble coming down the stairs."

I glanced in the direction of the stairs, where Big Shirley was making her way to the main floor. She'd had about sixty stitches put in on the right side of her face, but she was on her back three days later, doing tricks for half the price of the rest of us to make sure she made her quota. Despite everything that had happened last week, she and Sam were back on speaking terms, although the fat bitch still seemed to have a problem with me. I was sure Sam didn't care as long as she made her quota. Plus, I think he felt sorry for her in some way I'd never understand.

Shirley eyed me maliciously the whole way down the stairs, only taking her eyes off me to speak to one of Sam's thugs. I slipped my hand nonchalantly under my book, opening my straight razor just in case she had a relapse in judgment and tried to get some type of revenge. Thankfully, when she finished her conversation, she headed toward the door.

The second Shirley hit the door, Little Momma slid into the seat next to me, picking up my cigarette and taking a long, slow drag. "Girl, did you see the way she was looking at you? Sooner or later she's coming for your ass. I hope you ready."

I lifted my book so she could see the weapon. "Let her come. I'll make the left side of her face match the right."

"Bitch, you just as crazy as her." Little Momma laughed until the front door reopened. Instead of turning around, we both looked in the bar mirror, expecting to see Shirley coming through the door. Instead, I was surprised to see LC. He'd been by a few hours earlier to see Lou and bring me a couple books. He stopped by the door to talk to one of the girls.

"Ain't that your little friend who be bringing you those books?" Little Momma asked, staring at LC through the mirror like he owed her money.

"Mm-hmm, that's him." I took back my cigarette.

"He's Lou's brother, isn't he?" I nodded, and she said, "You know, he's kinda fine with his chocolate self."

"Yeah, he's cute," I said nonchalantly.

Little Momma gave me a sideways look. "Girl, puppies and kittens are cute. That nigga is fine. What I wanna know is what kind of equipment he's working with. Is he as big as his brother?"

If there ever was a woman who was born for this business, it was Little Momma. I don't think I've ever met a woman who loved to fuck as much as she did.

I shrugged. "I wouldn't know. We're just friends."

"Oh, please. Friends, my ass." She almost sounded jealous. "Hoes don't have friends, Chippy. Hoes have tricks and hoes have pimps, but never friends."

I smiled. "Well, I do." At least I wanted to think I did.

"What does Big Sam think about this friend?"

Truth was I didn't know what Sam would say. I really hadn't given it any thought. "What Big Sam doesn't know won't hurt him as long as his money's right. He knows I love him."

"I heard that. You mind if I bed your *friend* to beef up my quota?" She knew damn well she was going to do it with or without my blessing, so I didn't even know why she opened up her mouth. I didn't know how I felt about that, but I damn sure couldn't say no.

"Go right ahead, but he's got a girlfriend and he's loyal. He's not like most of these guys."

"I guess you didn't know I'm a boyfriend's best kept secret," she said with a smirk. "'Cause I'll do what his girlfriend won't do."

LC walked up on us, but if he'd heard what Little Momma said, he must not have known it was about him, because he didn't react at all. In fact, he didn't look like his normal self. He looked stressed. Probably had another fight with that uppity girlfriend of his.

"Hey, Chippy. You seen Lou?" He didn't sound like himself either.

"Nah, not since earlier. He left with Larry about fifteen minutes after you."

"It fucking figures." He slapped his hand on the bar and slumped down onto a stool. "I feel like my life is falling apart."

"What's wrong?"

"Lou needed me to do something, so I was late for work." He took a deep breath and I could feel his sorrow. "And Mr. Byrd fired me."

"Damn, that's fucked up," I said.

it. "And because of the two of you, Big Sam is about to take things to the next level."

Lou and I glanced at each other, communicating that neither of us was really sure what the hell he was talking about.

"Fellas, let me introduce you to my new business partner, Ms. Wilma Steward." Sam gestured to the old woman. "Wilma and her girls work out of a house in Valdosta, and she was about to close down, until I sent you boys to handle that little redneck problem she was having."

Wilma stood up, walked over to us, and hugged each of us before gesturing to the girls, who stood up and approached me and Lou. "If there's anything I can ever do for you boys, and I mean anything, please don't hesitate to ask."

Lou wrapped his arms around the pretty Puerto Rican girl, pulling her down on his knee, while the blond-haired white girl stood in front of me. She posed a few times, trying to look enticing, and I rolled my eyes.

"Don't worry about him, baby girl. Sweet Lou's got enough to handle you both." Lou pulled her down on his other knee.

"Yeah, Larry's not too much for pussy, but he loves his scotch." Sam reached in a bag behind him and pulled out a bottle of twenty-year-old scotch. "Here you go, Larry. This is for you. Don't drink it all in one sitting. That shit cost a fortune," he boasted.

He handed the scotch to me. I didn't know what to say other than, "Thanks, Sam." Maybe this guy wasn't so bad after all.

"Don't mention it. You deserve it." Sam smiled then turned his attention back to Lou. He reached back on the other side of his desk and then handed my brother a wooden box. "Lou, man, I know how you love your cigars, brother, but it's time you stepped up your game from those cheap things you been smoking. I had these smuggled in special for you."

Lou opened the box, and when he saw what was inside, he almost knocked the whores off his lap he was so ecstatic. "Are these fucking Cubans?" He pulled a big-ass cigar out of the box, sliding it under his nose to take in the aroma.

"You bet your ass they are. Straight from Havana," Sam said, handing him a cigar cutter. Lou cut the tip then shoved it in his mouth. Sam leaned over and lit it for him. Lou had

Larry

16

It was a little after midnight when Lou and I returned from Valdosta, walked into Big Sam's, and headed straight toward the bar. We hadn't made it halfway there when that whore Chippy approached us, rolling her eyes and giving us shit about LC getting fired from that gas station. I didn't really a give a damn what the whore had to say, because it was none of her fucking business, but I did feel bad for LC considering he really liked working at that dump. Thankfully we didn't have to listen to her very long, because our conversation was interrupted by the twins, who explained that Sam wanted to speak to us in his office.

Neither of us hesitated to get up and go. The good thing about going to Sam's office was that it usually meant we were going to make some money. Lou knocked on the door then opened it. Sam was standing in front of his desk all smiles, holding a bottle of champagne and some glasses. Off to the left was an older woman, probably forty-five or fifty. She was dressed up like a whore, although I couldn't imagine anyone paying for her old ass. Next to her were two whores I'd never seen before. All of them were holding glasses. Sam handed us each a glass and started pouring.

"What's going on, Sam? Looks like you havin' a little party back here." Lou grinned, eyeing the two new whores like a dog drooling over a steak as we took our seats. Shit, he might as well have just grabbed them by the hand and took 'em upstairs, because he obviously wasn't going to be able to concentrate on business until he did.

"The party's for you and your beautifully sadistic brother." Sam laughed, placing his hand on my shoulder and squeezing this blissful look on his face that even those whores on his lap couldn't have given him.

Sam walked around to his chair and took a seat. "I just wanted you cats to understand how important you are to me and what I do."

"We appreciate that, Sam," Lou replied sincerely.

"Good, because there's another piece of business I'd like to discuss with you two."

Lou puffed his cigar. "Well, you know we're always open to talk business, Sam."

"Good, because we've been doing business for a long time—you two servicing one part of the community, and little old me servicing another. I think it's time we come together, like me and Wilma. Together we can take over all of South Georgia, possibly even the whole damn state. Big Sam and the Duncan brothers. What do you think? We can do it just like those Italian cats do. I'll be the godfather; Lou, you'll be the under boss, and Larry, you be the consigliere. We'd scare the shit out of a whole lot of people and get rich doing it."

Lou puffed on his cigar a few more times as he thought about it. After a minute, he said, "Sam, Larry and I have a lot of respect for you, so I'm going to give it to you straight." I knew Lou was about to go into one of his speeches, so I settled back in my chair. "What we do, our little business, was started by our pops, so it's a little sentimental to us. He used to loan money to share croppers during the winter when times were bad, and in the spring when they needed seed. Some say he was a pariah, leeching off of black people's misery; others said he was a godsend, helping folks when no one else would. I'm not sure which one it is, but I just know we're not letting it go cheap—if we let it go at all."

"Look, fellas, I'm not trying to screw up no family legacy or anything. I'm just trying to get paid, and expansion is the answer to that. What we build together could be way bigger than anything your pops even thought of. Why don't you take a little time to think about it and come up with a price for me to buy in?" Sam suggested. "I'm going out of town for a few days, so we'll talk when I get back, okay?"

Lou and I looked at each other, and seeing no concern in my expression, he nodded to Sam..

"Just keep an open mind."

"Sure, Sam. We'll talk to LC and get back to you," Lou said, grabbing a breast of each of the girls. "Hell, there could be a lot of benefit in going into business with you."

Lou

17

"You sure you want him coming with us?" Larry glanced back at Levi, who damn near took up my entire back seat. Larry had my back. He was trying to make sure that I didn't do anything stupid, but it had been a long time since I'd lived my life looking backward. I'd already made up my mind how this was going to go down, so anything else was going to be a huge disappointment.

"Yeah, I got a feeling he's going to come in handy," I replied, checking out my 'fro in the rearview mirror before I opened my car door to head inside and deal with this bullshit. "Come on, Levi. Let's go say hello to our old friend."

Levi and Larry stepped out of the car as I looked around. There wasn't a customer in sight at this hour of the day, which made me wonder how the hell this place stayed in business at all. If I didn't know better, I'd have thought it was a front for something else. That's just how my mind worked.

Larry liked to get the most for his money, and since he didn't believe in paying for most things, his next thought didn't surprise me at all. "Want me to fill up the tank first?" he joked, pointing to the two gas pumps we passed as he followed me inside.

There was nobody behind the counter, so I let Levi ring the bell. He seemed to get a real kick out of it.

Old Man Byrd looked about ready to shit himself when he spotted not one, not two, but three Duncan brothers waiting on him when he walked in from the garage, especially since the nicest Duncan brother was the only absent one. He threw up his hands like we'd entered with guns blazing. I guess our reputation preceded us.

"Now look, fellas. I don't want no trouble." His voice came out all shaky and scared. I was afraid his old ass was going to have a heart attack before I got a word out of my mouth.

"Trouble?" I turned to Larry as if Byrd's words were unwarranted and downright offensive. "Why would you think we're looking for trouble, Mr. Byrd? We just came for a little visit. Isn't that right, Levi?"

Levi nodded, and poor Mr. Byrd's bald head broke out in beads of sweat. That old man was scared to death—but you know what they say about cornered rats.

"Well, your brother ain't here," he snapped, pulling out a shotgun from under the counter like that would be enough to send us on our merry ole way. Unfortunately for him, he barely had time to point the damn thing before Larry had a .45 pointed at his head.

"That's 'cause you fired him, ain't it?" Larry shouted, pulling back the hammer. "Now put down the damn shotgun, old man."

Byrd placed it on the counter.

"You wanna tell us why you got a problem with our brother?" I asked, all nice and polite, leaning my arms on the counter to get a little closer to him.

"Look, fellas, I . . . I really don't want no trouble." Mr. Byrd comically shook his head and waved his hands like that would reinforce his stance and get us moving along. "LC is a good kid, but he's become less reliable lately. I'm trying to run a business here. I'm just one person, and if I hire someone, I really need them to show up on time. I can't be around like I used to."

"You see, now you're speaking my language. I get that you're running a business. Hell, I run a business too, and I depend on my employees to be reliable."

"Uh-huh!" Larry chimed in, lowering the gun.

I kept my eye focused on Mr. Byrd as I continued. Hell, I'd be lying if I didn't admit that a part of me—no, all of me—was enjoying this game. "Mr. Byrd, how old are you?"

The look on his face almost made me burst out laughing. He didn't know where the hell that question came from or where I planned on going with it, and he looked like he was about to die from fright.

"I'ma be sixty-seven my next birthday come June." Of course he left out the second half of his sentence—"if I have a next birthday"—but we could all feel his concern about his lifespan hovering in the air.

"You been around a long time. How long you been running this place?"

"Damn near forty years. I bought it when I was twenty-seven. Back then they ain't let us barely own anything, but they didn't want us coming into their gas stations neither." He said it in that way that let me know he was doing the dance for his life. "After all these years, I done made my peace with the reality that I'ma work in this place till I'm in the grave." As he finished, Byrd's eyes grew wide at the realization that he'd been the one to utter the first mention of death.

"Well, you've done your part," I answered seriously. I even smiled at him real friendly, anxious to throw off the scent of eagerness. "I'm sure you and your wife want to retire."

"Heck yeah, but who in their right mind is gonna want to buy a broken down gas station on this side of town?"

"I don't know. My brother seems to think this place would be a good investment. How much you wanna sell it for?" I was finished with all the foolishness and ready to get down to brass tacks. The bug-eyed look he gave told me I'd surprised the hell out of him with my question. He had seemed a whole lot more comfortable with the idea of me coming to kill him, but then he took a few steps closer.

"You serious?" The old man raised an eyebrow.

"As a heart attack," I responded, knowing good and well that I had damn near given him one.

"Ten thousand dollars," he said weakly.

"Ten thousand?" I repeated.

Larry and I turned to each other, but neither of us said a word. Instead, I tossed him the keys to my car. Larry went out the door, while I did a little show of checking out the place, looking under the hood, so to speak.

"Here's your money," Larry announced, handing him the ten thousand dollars he'd gotten from the trunk of my car.

The thing that old man would never know was that I would have paid twice what he asked to get what I wanted. In my business, an initial offering is just that: the first step to open up the negotiations. I'd learned that from my trips up north, where everyone seemed to be up for bargaining and no first offer was ever considered. Lucky for me, the South was still running behind the times.

Old Man Byrd gingerly counted out the cash and then recounted it. Didn't take a genius to realize that he'd never seen that much money in his life. After he finished, he held out his hand and we shook on it.

"Now I'm gonna need a bill of sale for that. You know, to make it legal and all."

"Course." He went scurrying around the counter to write one up before I changed my mind. If he wasn't so damn old, I was sure he would have clicked his heels.

"And I'm also going to need you to do me a favor." My voice dropped and got real respectful, like it did when I was feeling generous, which I was at the moment. Nothing pleased me more than not having to resort to violence to get what I wanted, and since this shit had gone even smoother than I had hoped, I was feeling magnanimous.

"Sure, sure. Anything you like." Geriatric or not, he would have damn near dropped down on all fours after unloading this spot for that much cash.

Twenty minutes later, when I'd returned from the old man showing us around our new place of business, I heard a car pull up. Byrd was already packing his shit, getting ready to get on with his new life. Through the window, I could see LC and Donna in her fancy-ass debutante mobile, with him behind the wheel. It made me wonder if the whole reason he dated her stuck-up ass was to get himself an automobile upgrade.

"What the hell are y'all doing here?" LC shouted the moment he hit the door, looking straight at me. He shut it just as quick, glancing around nervously. "And where's Mr. Byrd?"

Deciding to have a little fun with him, I winked at Larry and said, "I told you I'd straighten things out with Old Man Byrd if he fired you, didn't I?"

LC walked over to the counter and picked up the shotgun as he confronted me angrily. "Oh my God, what did you do? Where's Mr. Byrd?"

"This wasn't just on Lou, little bro, Old Man Byrd had to go. You're just going to have to get use to that, LC," Larry said simply.

LC's hands went up to his face with horror etched all over it. He crumpled to the floor in some kind of agony, like he'd just lost his father or something.

"You fucking murderer! I'm calling the police!" Donna screamed out at me, but LC wisely grabbed her arm and shook his head.

"Murderers?" I echoed. "You know what, Donna? If I were you, I'd stick to sucking dick and not Duncan business, 'cause you don't know what the hell you're talking 'bout."

"Everything all right in here?" The back door swung open and Byrd walked in from the back of the shop. Donna damn near fainted. Seeing his old boss, LC let out a sigh of relief then turned angrily toward a laughing Larry and me. "Why's everyone look like they just saw a ghost?" Byrd asked.

"We were just playing a little joke on LC before we told him the good news."

"You bastard," Donna sassed, hand on hip, as she glared at me. When LC turned his back, I stuck out my tongue then slowly ran it across my lips suggestively. She jumped like I'd actually been playing with her clit.

"What do you mean, good news? You giving me my job back, Mr. Byrd?" LC was all smiles, but not for long.

"No, son. I can't do th—" Byrd said before I cut him off.

"But I can." I handed LC a piece of paper, which Donna quickly snatched out of his hand.

"Oh my God, this bill of sale is in your name, LC."

LC removed it from her hands. "What are you taking about?" He began to read the paper, and his eyes grew big. "Get the fuck outta here! We own this place? You bought this place, Lou?" LC was damn near jumping up and down by this time. How quickly shit turns around.

"No, little brother, you own the place. Larry and I are going to use that building in the back with tires in it for our offices, maybe open a title loan shop like the white boys across town. But the gas and service station belong to you. Now you can work for yourself, put that college education to use like Ma wanted." I could see LC's wheels already turning. I don't think I've ever seen the kid happier.

"Are the tow trucks included?" he asked. He was walking around touching things like it was all a dream.

"Everything's included," I replied

"Well, I'm going to leave you fellas. Good luck." The old guy looked ready to cry.

"Don't worry, Mr. Byrd. I'll take good care of her and make you proud," LC declared.

"I'm sure you will. Now's the chance for you to make all those changes you been talking about." Mr. Byrd shook everybody's hands then headed out the door.

"So what are we going to call it?" LC asked.

"I think we should call it Duncan Brothers." Larry smiled in approval of his own suggestion. "It makes all the sense in the world, especially since LC's gonna be fixing the cars up front, and we're going to be running the other businesses out back."

"I hate to burst everyone's bubble, but this just isn't happening. LC is going to school to be a respectable businessman. He's not running a gas station. It's beneath him. Ain't that right, baby?" Donna looked over at LC, expecting him to agree. She was too dumb to realize her words were falling on deaf ears. Guess that pussy wasn't as good as either of us thought it was.

"Donna, go sit in the car and let me talk to my brothers."

"LC, I don't plan on marrying a goddam grease monkey!" she shouted as she slammed out the door and jumped in her car. "Wait till Daddy hears about this."

"You sure about this? She might take off in the car." Larry glanced at LC, who was sliding his hand down the side of the wall, feeling this new opportunity.

"I ain't worried about her. She ain't going nowhere." LC showed us the car keys as he went behind the counter and pulled out a bottle of Johnny Walker Black and some paper cups. He filled each cup halfway then handed them to us, raising his in the air and making eye contact with each of us, including Levi. "To my brothers, the Duncan brothers: I know I never say it, but I love you more than life itself, and no one will ever come between us."

I couldn't help but get a little emotional. Maybe, just maybe, that boy was starting to learn just what it meant to be a Duncan.

Chippy

18

"Lovin' you is easy 'cause you're beautiful, and making love with you is all I want to do." I sang Minnie Riperton's big hit at the top of my lungs, feeling every minute of it, and I didn't give two shits which one of these girls banged on my door to get me to stop. It had been almost a week, but my man was coming home, and far as I was concerned that was reason enough to sing.

"La la la la la . . . la la la la la . . ." I kept going, and even though I couldn't hit the high notes, I tried 'cause I felt that way about Sam. Hell, I'd been working from sun up to sun down to make enough money so we could fly away from this spot and do some of the things we'd been talking about. I was certain that I'd made double or triple what those other girls brought in. Sam was gonna be real proud of his girl Chippy, I thought as I slathered Palmer's cocoa butter cream all over my body, down my long legs, flat stomach, and nice round breasts. Boy, I couldn't wait till it was his hands rubbing all over me.

I went over to the mirror and fixed my hair so that it looked exactly how Big Sam liked it. Since we'd met, nothing gave me more pleasure than seeing him pleased with me. There was so much I had to do to get ready so that we could celebrate our future together. Hopefully this would be the night when we could finally leave this place. I dabbed some perfume behind my ears and in between my breasts so that when he stuck his face there he'd get a nice big whiff that would drive him wild. I caught my expression in the mirror, and even I could see how beautiful I looked, like a woman in love. That's when I heard the unmistakable sound of Sam's car pulling up to the building.

"Sam's home! Sam's home!" I shouted as I raced down the stairs.

The click-clack of my heels must have sounded like a herd of wild elephants and not at all ladylike, but I didn't care. My man was home, and I couldn't wait one more minute to set my eyes on him. As I came in the main room I damn near had to push through the bodies to get to him.

"There's my Chippy," Big Sam called out. Yeah, he was certainly something. Damn if that man wasn't looking better than ever and more fuckable with every moment. The way he stared at me as he caught my eye made me go weak in the knees. Sure, I'd been mad at him for the last three days for leaving and not taking me along on this trip, but the moment I set eyes on him, I couldn't be mad anymore, and he knew it. That man had me wrapped around his finger, but as long as he kept loving me the way he did, I preferred it that way.

"Sam!" I squealed, almost jumping in his arms.

He hugged me and gave me a quick peck on the cheek before letting me go, which seemed weird. It was the first time he'd ever done that. Guess he was trying to keep the drama down since the other girls could be so petty and jealous.

"Honey, I went way over my quota 'cause I wanted you to be real proud of me," I announced, expecting him to show me just how much he appreciated my hard work in front of all the others like he always did.

"I'm always proud of you, Chippy," he mumbled. When I went to grab his hand, he actually shook me off. That's when I noticed him taking the hand of a girl a little younger than me who was standing behind him. She was a pretty, caramel color, with an Afro, big tits, a small waist, and short but shapely legs. She was giving him googly eyes and holding onto him like he was all hers.

"Ladies, I want everybody to meet my new special someone. Her name is Crystal, and she's going to staying with us a while."

"Hi, y'all," Crystal answered shyly, clinging to Big Sam as she glanced around and took in her surroundings. "This certainly is a pretty place."

"Now, I want each and every one of you to treat her real nice, 'cause she means the world to me," Sam announced flamboyantly as he wrapped his arms around the little heifer like she was me.

Big Shirley turned with a big smirk to gauge my reaction. "Well, well, well, looks like there's a new sheriff in town."

"What the fuck? That's exactly what you said about me!" I shrieked more out of shock and hurt than anything else.

He leaned over and gave her a kiss like I wasn't even standing there in front of his face dying.

"Crystal, let me show you to your room," he said, taking her hand and leading her toward the stairs—but not before glaring at me with pure hatred.

None of this was making sense. To add insult to injury, that bitch had the nerve to be carrying all these shopping bags, showing off that he had taken her out on a spree the same way he did me—except this time he was using the money I'd been earning for our future. I swear seeing that made something in me snap. Before I could stop myself, I dove on top of that girl and commenced to beating her ass. I grabbed handfuls of her hair in my fists and tried my damndest to rip the pretty straight out of her. If she thought she was going to come into my world and take my man, she had another thing coming.

Sam snatched me up like a sack of potatoes; then he reached back and smacked me so hard I saw stars as I tumbled to the floor. "Bitch, have you lost your damn mind?" he shouted at me.

"If I have, you caused it! And who the hell is this bitch?" I got up from the floor and got in his face. The fact that he had smacked the shit out of me less than a minute ago was totally gone from my mind.

"You better get the hell out my face!" The look of pure rage he shot me set my stomach fluttering with fear. I didn't understand. He berated me, "Your problem is you think you're so goddamn superior to everyone because you read a few books and shit. Well, let me tell you something, bitch: There ain't no difference between you and the rest of these whores. You're a prostitute, Chippy, the lowest form of woman there can be, and I'm your pimp, lord, and master. You better remember that." He slapped me again and I went reeling.

Then he turned to Crystal, sounding all sweet and loving, "You all right, darling?"

"Yes," she answered sweetly, like she hadn't just witnessed him beating another woman, "but, baby, why did she do that?" Poor little Crystal squeaked, clutching onto Sam like they were in the ocean and he was her life preserver. Instead of telling her the truth, that I was his woman and she had to go, he actually held her tighter as she cried.

"There there, baby girl. We're gonna go upstairs and daddy is going to make everything better," he promised as they headed up the staircase, leaving me lying in a heap.

I looked up and saw all the girls trying not to stare at me, and I knew they were feeling sorry for me. Damn him.

"C'mon, Chippy." Little Momma helped me to my feet, but I snatched my arm away from her and raced up the back stairs to my room. It took me all of two minutes to throw my stuff in a suitcase and head out the door. If he thought I would ever put up with being replaced, he had another thing coming.

"It's all right, Chippy. I promise you'll get used to it." Little Momma entered my room and tried to console me, but I knew that she could never understand how I felt. None of them had the relationship that I did with Sam.

"I'm not getting used to shit."

He was standing in Crystal's doorway when I exited my room for the last time. Fuck him.

He snarled at me as I passed him. "Where the hell you going, bitch?"

"As far away from you as I can!" My voice came out much stronger than I felt, and for that I was proud, although the rest of me felt shaky and scared. Big Sam burst out laughing, like I'd said the funniest thing he'd ever heard, slapping his hand against his leg. I kept moving toward the door.

"You wanna leave?" His tone stopped me in my tracks. "Well, you about to learn the rules of the game. You can go, but you leave with exactly what you came with." He ripped the suitcase out of my hand, and when I resisted, he punched me in the face like I was a man. Then, in a much softer but equally threatening tone, he said, "I'ma put this back in your room, 'cause you'll be needing it when you come back."

It was Sam's sinister laughter that I heard all the way to the curb and into the rain, but I just kept moving.

LC

19

It was raining so hard I could barely see three feet in front of my face, so I sent my cousin Harold, who'd been working at the station pumping gas, home an hour early. It didn't make much sense to be paying him with the rain coming down like that. Only a crazy person would venture out for gas on this night. I'd actually planned on spending the night on the cot in the back so I could finish up painting the new convenience store we were putting in. Larry and NeeNee had already spent most of the day putting up drywall and spackling, so I was hoping to do my part and get it painted before the trucks came in the morning.

I checked my watch as I reached for my poncho. "Okay, time to turn off the pumps."

I guess I'd spoken too soon about someone venturing out in this weather, because the door chimed, letting me know someone was coming in. A soaking wet woman entered, holding a newspaper to cover her face and head from the rain. As she got closer, I saw the water clinging to her jeans and T-shirt. I couldn't believe anyone would be walking in this storm without so much as an umbrella, not to mention a coat or sensible shoes.

It had been raining so hard I couldn't even see the pumps, so I anticipated a good cussing out because she'd had to get out of her car in this shit to tell me to pump her gas.

"Ma'am, I'm so sorry. I didn't see you pull up," I said as I pulled the poncho over my head.

"LC." The voice sounded familiar, but I was still astonished when she lowered the newspaper and I recognized her face.

"Chippy?" That's when I noticed her swollen black eye. "Jesus Christ, what the hell happened to you?" I felt myself getting angry at the sight of her battered and bruised face. "Who did this to you?"

She looked up at me, mascara running down her cheeks from either the rain or her tears. "Sam did it to me. He hit me so hard I saw stars." Her tears started anew.

Her answer didn't surprise me, but it sure did make me want to put a hurting on him. "I never liked that guy. You got to get away from him." Normally I didn't hand out relationship advice because it really wasn't any of my business, but I couldn't help it. Any man who puts his hands on a woman is scum and deserves all the shit he gets.

Something about the lighting and the simplicity of the jeans and T-shirt made me realize she was younger than the twenty-five years I'd given her credit for. I'd only seen her with a face full of makeup, fake eyelashes, hot pants, cork heels, and halter top, all of which made her look a lot older than I now saw that she was.

I took the wet newspaper from her and helped her into a chair. "You know, I wouldn't have recognized you without the lashes and makeup," I said.

She looked embarrassed as she started to pat her damp, matted hair and wipe at the runny makeup. "I look a mess."

"No, you're pretty," I said. "It's good to see the real you." I leaned close and touched her eye tenderly. "Let me get you something to put on that." I went over to the freezer and pulled out a bright red ice pop. "Here. Put this on your eye. It should help, and when you're done you can eat it," I joked.

"Thank you," she answered softly.

We sat together quietly while she held the soothing ice to her eye. After a while, I spoke up. "You know you can't go back there. You're better than that."

She nodded and agreed, "I'm not going back there, but I got to find a job, and I've got to find some place to live."

I glanced over her shoulder at the rain still coming down in sheets. That wasn't going to happen today.

"You hungry? I was about to close up shop, and I know someplace where you can get a dry set of clothes and a good meal."

Her face spread into the first smile I'd seen since she came inside. "That would be real nice."

I shut down the shop and handed her my poncho to put on, because there was no reason for her to get wetter. She looked ready to refuse, but I wasn't having that.

"Take it. You don't want to catch pneumonia."

We stepped outside, and I ran for the truck. I turned the heat all the way up so she would be a little less uncomfortable until I could get her a change of clothes.

Neither of us spoke as I drove the few miles to my house. One thing I knew was that NeeNee would be cooking. She always seemed ready for company, whether it was two people or twenty-two, because Lou and Larry had a habit of bringing home strays and large groups back to the house. It was their way of never letting a party end, but NeeNee, she never seemed to mind. Actually, she always said the more the merrier.

"Where are we?" Chippy asked. I drove down the long country driveway, stopping the truck in the driveway of my simple one-story house.

"Welcome to the Duncan farm." I held out my hand like I was some waiter at a fancy restaurant.

"Is your brother Lou here?"

"Nah, his car's gone, which means he's gone." I was sure she was thinking about the friendship between Lou and Sam. "Don't worry about him. I'll take care of my brother. Now come on in. I want you to meet NeeNee." I led her into the house, out of the rain.

NeeNee did a double take when she spotted Chippy coming through the door behind me. Then she gave me a look like this would be some big secret between us. She'd always been super nice to Donna, but I knew she didn't really care much for my girlfriend. Well, I'd have to get busy setting her straight.

"And who do we have here?" NeeNee hurried over like a big sister being all nosy.

"This is my friend Chippy and—"

"Charlotte, ma'am. My name's Charlotte. Chippy's just a nickname." She stuck out her hand to NeeNee, who ignored it and moved in for a hug.

"Yes, Charlotte," I repeated, feeling like an idiot.

NeeNee took one look at her and removed my poncho off her shoulders. "Girl, you are soaked. Let me get you out of those clothes. Give you a hot shower and wash off some of that cold. Come on." She led Chippy through the back of the house.

After a few minutes, I heard the shower going, and then NeeNee came back in the kitchen, staring at me like she had never seen me before.

I tossed up my hands. "What?" I said defensively. "She's just a friend in trouble. I'm trying to help her, that's all."

"Let's say that's true. What about Donna?" She pressed on, still giving me that look as if to say, "You sly devil, you."

"This isn't about Donna. I'm allowed to have friends," I insisted, ready for this conversation to be over. "But for the record, Donna's gone for the weekend."

NeeNee's eyes began to darken with worry. "LC, you know that poor girl's been abused."

"I know. Big Sam gave her that black eye. That's the reason I want to help her get away from him. That's all this is. Now do you get it?"

"No, I think you're the one who doesn't get it." NeeNee sat down on the chair next to me like she'd suddenly grown tired. "Sam mighta beat her up, but what he did was tame compared what someone else did."

"What are you talking about?"

"When that girl took off her clothes, I could see all these scars on her body. It looked like somebody was using her back as their own personal ashtray. It's not right that somebody would put a young girl through all that. She can't be more than nineteen years old. It's just not right." NeeNee shook her head. I knew she wanted to have kids with Larry, and with a heart that big she'd make a great mother. Hell, she already took better care of us than any mother could.

"Shit. What am I gonna do?"

"Well, for right now let me get you kids some food. A full belly is always a good place to start." NeeNee rose up and went over to a cabinet and pulled out a bottle. She poured some in a glass and then popped open a can of Seven-Up, pouring that in it too before she handed it to me. "Give this to her. Tell her I said to drink it." NeeNee then started messing around with the pots.

When I knocked on the door, Chippy got shy, opening it only slightly when she saw it was me, but I was struck by something and couldn't stop myself from staring. NeeNee had loaned her a dress to wear while her clothes were drying, and even though it hung on her slight frame, there was something really sweet about it. Without the runny mascara and makeup, her hair pulled back in a ponytail, she looked so innocent. So beautiful.

"NeeNee said to drink this." I handed her the glass. "Come on out to the kitchen when you're ready. She's making us something to eat. You haven't tasted good food till you've had some of NeeNee's cooking."

"Okay." Her eyes were downcast, nothing like the sassy smart girl I'd grown used to. I gave her a wink, hoping it would help her to relax. I wanted her to understand that we were her friends, probably the only ones she had in this town.

"Hey, I just wanted you to know you're safe here."

Chippy

20

I stretched my arms out, trying to get my bearings as I looked around the room and saw a poster of Doctor J looking down at me. For a split second I'd forgotten where I was and how I'd gotten there. I saw my clothes pressed and neatly folded over a chair, along with a washrag, towel, and toothbrush. This had to be LC's room, I thought when I spotted the three bookcases that lined the far wall of the room.

I got out of bed and happily thumbed through the books. There had to be a thousand books on those shelves, maybe more. I wondered if LC had read them all. I heard some music coming from the other side of the door, telling me that someone else was up, so I chose a book to read, scooped up my clothes and toiletries, and headed for the bathroom.

Fifteen minutes later, I went into the kitchen, where I found Miss NeeNee standing over the stove, frying some chicken. She had to be one of the nicest women I'd ever met. And boy, could she hold her liquor.

"Thought you was going to sleep all day," NeeNee said with a laugh.

"I'm not used to getting up early. What time is it?"

"About quarter to ten," NeeNee said, taking some chicken out of the frying pan. "And here I am thinking you didn't get up because that gin knocked you out. You kept up pretty good last night. You not hung over?"

"No, I been drinking since I was twelve. It makes the pain go away, at least for a little while anyway." I sniffed the air. "That smells so good."

"I'ma sell chicken and biscuits down at the gas station today. Now that LC's got everything fixed up, they been getting a lot of people down there. That station's going to be good for everyone." She leaned over and passed me a plate. I picked up a piece of chicken and bit into it.

"Well, you better make a whole lot of it, 'cause those people are going to lose their minds as good as this bird tastes. Colonel Sanders ain't got shit on you. Damn, what you put in it?"

"I ain't got time to show you right now, but if you wanna learn, I'll teach you."

"I'd like that. I can't cook shit." I devoured the chicken leg and picked up another.

"Well, you stick with NeeNee and I'll teach you."

"So, where's LC? I don't see his tow truck outside," I said. "Then again, it's Saturday. I guess he must be with his girlfriend."

NeeNee turned around to face me, sucking her teeth and rolling her eyes. "Girl, please. That boy been at that gas station painting since the crack of dawn. And as far as his pain-in-the-ass girlfriend's concerned, she's out of town for the weekend."

"Really?" I let my excitement slip.

"Really," NeeNee repeated with a laugh, which made me like her even more. "Soon as I finish, we gonna take this food over there for him to sell. I just got to figure out how to pack it all up."

I glanced over at the chicken and biscuits piled all over the counter like she was expecting a real crowd. The idea came to me quickly. "How about if you cut the biscuits and put the chicken in between, and then wrap them in some paper like a sandwich? You can even use old newspaper and tie them with some kind of twine if you have it."

Her face lit up. "Charlotte, you're a genius. I swear you need to do something big in this lifetime, 'cause you got good ideas. And that came so easy for you," she told me, reaching for some newspaper and putting the first one together.

"Thanks. And you can just call me Chippy. I'm kind of used to the nickname now," I said, enjoying the easy camaraderie between me and NeeNee. "Let me help you." I jumped in to lend a hand making sandwiches.

It took us no time, and when we were done, she had forty-six of the best fried sandwiches in Georgia, ready to sell for one dollar a piece.

"Hey, hey, hey. Morning, Nee." Lou came in, looking Ron O'Neal kinda fly in a powder blue bell bottom suit, white shirt with big lapels, and a pair of groovy platforms, but it was the perfectly coiffed afro and gold chain hanging around his neck that really stood out. He looked over and saw me sitting at the table and tried to be nonchalant. "What's happening, Red?"

"Morning." I returned the greeting even though I wished he hadn't noticed me. Lou was too close to Sam, and that made me nervous.

He reached over and grabbed one of the sandwiches before we could wrap it. Taking a bite, he raved, "Damn, girl, you put your foot in this. LC might be right. We just might have to add a restaurant to that gas station."

"You always said he's the smartest one of us all," NeeNee replied.

"He is. Ain't no doubt about that." I was surprised to hear Lou, with all his ego, acknowledge something like that. These Duncans sure were a strange brood. "Where's Larry? He's supposed to drive me to the bus."

"He's going to meet us at the gas station. He had something to do with Quincy." NeeNee smirked as she packed up the last of the sandwiches and headed for the door, followed by Lou. "Come on, Miss Chippy, you don't want to be left here by yourself until you're properly introduced to Levi and his pets."

I'd seen Levi's huge ass before, but what the hell did she mean by his pets?

When we got to the shop, there were three big trucks being unloaded out back. I could see LC through the picture window up front, in his coveralls, talking to two white men who looked like salesmen. They were hanging on to his every word. I'm not going to lie; there was a certain sexiness about him that turned me on.

"LC really fixed this place up," NeeNee gushed, clearly impressed with the level of work he'd done. Guess I didn't notice because I'd never been there before, but once she said something, I could see all the new touches.

When we got out of NeeNee's car, Larry came out wearing a bandanna wrapped around his head and a wife beater, smiling from ear to ear.

"That boy's in there schooling those white boys like he's one of them. They done gave him enough refrigerators, freezers, and shelving to furnish the whole damn store for free, just so he'll sell their shit. He even talked the cat from Pepsi into paying for a big-ass Duncan Brothers sign to hang out front as long as it has their logo," Larry said, sounding excited.

"Yeah, well, the resident genius is not going to like it, but he's going to have get his hands dirty while you drive me to the bus station," Lou said.

Lou and Larry went inside to talk, while NeeNee and I set up a table out front and started getting the chicken and Pepsi ready for sale. A few minutes later, LC stepped out the front door alone. He smiled at me before he turned to NeeNee, and I felt myself blushing.

"Hey Nee, you think you and Harold can handle the shop while I take a ride out to the country? I gotta take care of something for Lou."

"I got this, LC. You go on and handle your business."

"What about you, Ms. Charlotte? You wanna take a ride?" He gestured toward the tow truck.

"Look, I appreciate everything you did last night, but maybe I should just go back to Sam's. I'm not trying to get in the way of your business or anything." As much as I liked LC, I did not want to be a bother. It was one thing to bring me out of the rain, and another to have to put up with me the next day.

"We're friends, right?" he said.

"Yeah, of course we're friends. I just don't want to be a burden."

"Then stop all this foolishness and take a ride with me. Ain't nobody around here letting you go back to Big Sam's. Tell her, Nee."

NeeNee didn't say a word. She just pointed to the truck, and I started to walk.

Larry

21

Lou and I stood in the convenience store part of the gas station, staring out the window at LC and that whore Chippy as they got into the tow truck. I sure hoped LC knew what he was doing, because having that wench around could be more trouble than it was worth.

"What's the deal with them?" Lou asked.

I watched them pull away then shrugged. "I don't know. From what I hear Sam beat her ass pretty damn good last night and LC turned into Captain Save-a-Ho, rescuing her like she was some damsel in distress. Bitch spent the night in his room last night. Nee seems to think she's sweet on him."

"She can't be too sweet on him, 'cause when I got home LC was 'sleep on the sofa while old girl slept in his bed. Shit, if that was me, I woulda been in there tearing her fine ass up." Lou looked like he was about to slobber all over himself. When it came to pussy, he was worse than Levi. That shit just fucked his head right up, 'cause he had no self-control whatsoever.

"Thank God not everyone thinks like you, Lou. What I'm more worried about is if this whore's gonna cause us any blowback from Sam. You know we still gotta sit down with him this week."

Lou swiveled his neck in my direction, shaking his head. "Now you're worried about Sam. A few weeks ago you were ready to go to war with the man."

"That was different."

"Excuse me, Mr. Duncan?" We turned to see one of the white men who had been talking to LC. He approached us.

"Yes, how can we help you?" Lou put on his best white-boy voice.

"Your brother said I was to give this to you if he wasn't here." He handed Lou a check.

"What's this?"

He patted Lou on the back. "It's an incentive check for carrying Pepsi products in your store, and at your event on the fourth."

"Event?" Lou looked kind of confused until I elbowed him in ribs.

"Yeah, you know, First Friday, LC's grand opening."

"Oh yeah." Lou shook the man's hand. I shook his hand also, and we headed for the door.

The second we stepped outside, Lou handed me the check and said, "How much did we pay for this joint?"

"Ten grand. Why?" I looked down at the check and did a double take when I saw the amount was $5000.

"Because our little brother figured out a way to pay half the place off, and he didn't have to bust one head."

"You know, Lou, Ma always said this family would rise and fall on LC's shoulders. I know you're the oldest, but I think maybe we should start listening to him a little more." I opened the door to the little sports car I was driving.

"Larry, that's exactly why I'm going outta town, remember?" Lou replied, opening the passenger door then giving the car a once over. "Whose car is this?"

"Oh, this? This used to be Quincy's car, but it's ours now." I laughed. "Corvette Roadster Convertible. The body's a little rough and the transmission's just about shot, but I'm sure we can get three grand out of her, maybe a little more. You should have seen LC when he saw it. I thought the little bastard was going to bust a nut he got so excited." We both got a kick out of that as we got into the car.

Lou said, "Let LC work on it, and when she's purring like a kitten, bring her over to Ralph's and let him paint it. I saw one of these in New York, and the cat said he paid over ten grand for it."

"Damn, it's a good thing I showed Quincy what was in those two barrels or he wouldn't have given up shit."

Lou's head snapped in my direction and his face became hard. "What two barrels?"

"You know the barrels with those two hillbillies from Valdosta. The ones we got soaking in vinegar."

Lou's eyes flashed with anger. "You idiot! What the fuck is wrong with you? You trying to get us all locked up? I thought I told you to give those barrels to Levi so he could get rid of them."

"I'm going to, but you also said you didn't want me to kill Quincy, so I needed something to make him think I would, which he does now. Why else do you think we have the title to his car? Shit, I shot half his foot off and the bastard still wouldn't give up our money."

He took a deep breath to calm himself down. Placing a hand on my shoulder, he said, "Larry, man, that's just not smart and you know it. You can't be putting the whole family at risk like that, 'cause all we got is us. What would Momma say?"

I sighed, giving in, "Yeah, you're right. It was fucking stupid. Look, I'm sorry. And don't worry; I'm gonna take care of it as soon as I drop you off. You got my word."

Lou stuck his hand out and I slapped it. "Little brother, that's good enough for me."

Chippy

22

"So, did you get a good night's rest?" LC asked when the song we were listening to ended and a commercial for a personal injury lawyer started playing. We'd been driving for about ten minutes before he even spoke, but it wasn't one of those awkwardly silent rides. It almost felt like we were on a date, the way he had his arm over my side of the seat as we rocked to the music on the radio.

"Best I had in a long time. That was your room I slept in, wasn't it?"

"Yeah, that was my room," he said. "What gave it away?"

"The books. All those wonderful books. There had to be a thousand of them."

"Eight hundred fifty-six, to be exact." He looked at me and chuckled. "Only you would bypass all the football, basketball, and baseball trophies and see my books."

"What can I say? I love books. Have you read all of them?"

"Most of them. When I was coming up, my pops used to make us work on the farm, but he'd pay us every Friday, and instead of buying candy, I'd go down to the store and buy me a book." We had more in common than I thought.

"What about this one? Have you read *Pimp*?" I pulled the book I'd taken from his room out of my bag.

"Matter of fact, I have. Several times. Iceberg Slim is one of my favorite authors."

"I took it out of your room," I admitted. "You think I'll get anything out of it?"

"That depends on if you're really planning to go back to Sam."

I didn't answer, and he stared at me like a disappointed father. "You can't be serious. After what he did to your face?"

"I don't have anywhere else to go." I could feel tears well up as I touched my eye subconsciously. I'd completely forgotten about my bruised eye and face.

"Yeah, you do. You can stay with us."

"Let's see what your brothers have to say about that," I replied, thankful that the commercials were gone and the DJ was playing music again.

We drove a ways out to an area he called Okefenokee Swamp, where he turned up a dirt road and followed it to the sorriest looking shack I'd ever seen. The old house, if you could call it that, didn't look like there was even any running water inside. A gaggle of messy kids all under the age of ten were running around playing without shoes. An old, rusted car sat on some bricks in the driveway. When they saw us, the kids started jumping up and down.

"LC, LC, what did you bring us?" A cute little girl, about six years old, who looked like she'd been playing in the dirt, ran up to us when we got out of the car.

"What do you mean?" he said, looking comically stern.

"Please, please!" she begged as the others joined her, all screaming his name.

He reached into his overalls and pulled out five suckers and handed one to each kid. You would have thought he gave them gold as they excitedly ripped off the wrappers and shoved them in their mouths.

"You spoiling them kids." A heavyset woman who I could tell appeared older than her age called out from the porch as we approached her.

"Ms. Ruby, you know I didn't do no such thing," he answered in a friendly tone.

"I'ma send them to live with you when their teeth rot out of their heads." She laughed, throwing her arms around him. "Boy, it's good to see you. I heard you was down the road visiting with Ms. Emma a few weeks ago."

He released the embrace and turned to me. "Ms Ruby, this is my friend Charlotte."

"Well, well, well, she's real pretty, LC." She pulled me in for a hug. Between her and NeeNee, it was fair to say that LC knew a lot of huggers.

"Thank you, ma'am," I answered feeling slightly embarrassed by the attention.

"And she ain't got her panties in a bunch like that other heifer you brought around here. You need to marry this one."

I shook my head, anxious to fix her presumption. "We're just friends."

"Friends are good. My husband and I started as friends. That's a smart way to go. Too many people base their relationships on sex nowadays."

"Ms. Ruby!" LC admonished her, clearly embarrassed by the conversation.

She had a sparkle in her eyes as she continued. "Well, I'm telling the truth. This whole free love thing they got going in San Francisco is making these young people crazy. Martin and I been friends and gonna stay friends, and that makes our marriage better." I blushed when I felt her eyes on me like she was giving me some private information.

"You all right? Lou wanted me to bring you this." LC reached into his back pocket and handed her an envelope. It brought a big smile to her face.

"You boys are saints." She threw her arms around him again then opened the envelope, which I could see contained cash. "Martin told me to say thank you for all your help. And he'll pay you back on time."

"Martin's a good guy. We just want to make sure you're okay till he gets home. It was nice to see you, Ms. Ruby. I got to get back to the station," he told her as he took out his keys.

"Nice to meet you, ma'am," I said as we made our way back to the truck.

"Charlotte, you're welcome anytime," she yelled after me. The kids all gathered near their mom, sucking their lollipops and waving as we pulled away.

"What was that?" I asked, not able to keep the bitterness out of my voice. I had an idea, but I wanted to hear it from him. If it was what I thought, I knew I wouldn't be able to hold my tongue. Last thing I wanted to hear was that he took advantage of people like Ms. Ruby, with all those kids she had to take care of.

"The Duncans have a business where we lend money to people who can't seem to make it through the month," he informed me.

"You mean like a loan sharking business?" I snapped. It wasn't like I was dumb or nothing.

"Yes, and we loan money to gamblers and certain people for interest, but not Ms. Ruby—at least not more than she can afford. Lou wouldn't take a dime from the mothers whose husbands are off at war, or even in jail, for that matter. That would be the lowest of the low."

LC's explanation made me feel guilty for thinking the worst, but I guess after what had happened with Sam, I had lost faith that people could actually be good.

"That's nice. Real nice. You're good with kids," I said, thinking about how those kids' faces lit up at the sight of him before he even gave them anything.

He turned to me with a big smile on his face. "Yeah, I really like kids. I want a whole house full one day."

I nodded silently, and for the first time since I left Sam, I was beginning to feel sad for another reason: I would not be the one to give him those kids.

Big Shirley

23

I had to stop and catch my breath because I'd been walking for almost thirty minutes in the hot Georgia sun. However, it was all worth it when I saw that Deuce and a Quarter about a hundred yards down the driveway outside the tin-roof farmhouse. It meant Lou was home. I hadn't seen him in a few days, but he'd always said if I was in trouble or needed his help, he'd always be there. I guess now was when I found out if he was a man of his word or as full of shit as his friend Big Sam.

I took a deep breath and headed toward the house. As I got closer, dogs started to appear out of nowhere, barking like some type of country alarm system. By the time I got to the house, there had to be about twenty of them, and most of them were growling and baring teeth as they closed in on me.

"Hello! Anybody home?" I shouted, praying someone would call them off and come to my rescue. They were about two feet away from my ass now, and I was scared to death. I was tempted to run, but all my life people had been telling me not to run from dogs. I bet their asses had never been surrounded by a pack like this. "Help! Anybody, please, help! Help me!"

"Shirley, what are you doing here?" A voice yelled from my left, scaring the shit out of me even more than the growling mutts. I turned and saw Lou's brother Larry sitting at a redwood picnic table with about five or six guns in front of him. His other brother, Levi the simpleton, was walking toward a barn, carrying two big-ass barrels like they were soda cans. "You trying to get yourself killed or something?"

While that fool was rambling, those dogs were steadily getting closer to me. "Um, Larry, you think you can call off the dogs?"

"Levi!" Larry screamed. "Call these damn dogs."

Levi whistled one time, and the dogs seemed to disperse and disappear.

It took me a moment to get myself together. I walked over to the picnic table, making sure my good side was facing him. "Hey, Larry, I came to see your brother Lou. Is he around?"

He shook his head. "Lou ain't here. He's outta town."

Larry's words were like a punch in the stomach and would probably end up being the reason I got my ass kicked that night. I'd dragged my sorry ass all the way out there for nothing, because ever since Chippy left Big Sam, he'd been on the rampage about his damn quotas. I had to give it to her; she really must have made him a lot of money, 'cause he was pissed to be missing those dollars. And with this fucked-up face, I just couldn't get these niggas to fuck me like they used to.

All of a sudden, the dogs sounded like they were attacking something around the back of the barn. The first thing that came to mind was that they must be attacking Levi. "What the hell's going on? Is your brother all right?"

Larry smirked. "Oh, nothing. Levi's just feeding the dogs their favorite food. You know, it's amazing how much they like pickled meat." He started cackling like he'd just said something really funny.

"So, you know when your brother's going to be back?" I asked.

"Ain't no tellin'. You know Lou. He's always gotta be the last one to leave the party. Last time he went outta town he stayed a month."

"Fuck!" I said out loud. Of all the times for him to go outta town. "Hey, Larry, you think I could borrow a few dollars until Lou gets back?" I could tell by his smirk that the answer was no, so I made a desperate move. "I'll suck your dick."

I knew Larry hadn't bought any pussy since he'd come back from Vietnam, but it was worth a try. Shit, when Sam and I first came to town, I used to fuck him and Lou all the time.

"What the fuck is wrong with you, Shirley? You know damn well I don't buy pussy. You lucky Nee's not around, or you'd be eating one of these guns."

I threw my hands up defensively. "I'm sorry, Larry. I just need to make some money."

"Well, you ain't gonna make it from me," he replied as his mountain of a brother Levi walked up from behind the barn.

"D–d–done, L–l–l–Larry. The d–d–dogs are fed." He stared at his brother, waiting for approval.

"Good job, Levi. You might as well take the afternoon off and work with your birds."

Levi turned, finally noticing me, and his whole demeanor changed. "I know y–you. Y–y–you're pu–pu–pussy!" He was grinning at me like I was the most beautiful creature he'd ever seen. I had to admit it actually felt good. "I–I l–l–l–like pu–pu–pussy."

I turned to Larry. "Why y'all teach him that? That boy thinks all women are pussy."

Larry looked at me, unapologetic. "Aaaaaaannnnnd, what you tryin' to say?"

I shook my head, turning back to Levi. "I got a pussy, but that don't make me one. And just so you know, all pussy might be good pussy, but this is not good pussy. This is great pussy." I ran my hand down my body, hugging every curve. "This is aged to perfection, grade-A pu–pu. If Lou was here with some money, I'd show you."

Once he could stop laughing, Larry said, "He's got his own money. If he really wanted some pussy, he could buy it. Lou just takes care of that shit so you bitches don't take advantage of him."

I couldn't tell if he was lying. "Where'd he get money from?"

"He works hard for it, just like the rest of us Duncans. Levi's probably the best cock trainer in Georgia," Larry bragged. "Not to mention the fact that he gets a check from the state and the feds every month for being slow."

Well, that just changed the whole situation. "So, Levi, you want a blow job?"

"N–n–no, I w–w–want some pu–pu–pussy." Well, the boy sure knew what he wanted.

"I'll be damned. That boy's never had a blow job, has he?" I turned to Larry for conformation, but he just shrugged. "Okay, Levi, Big Shirley's going to give you some pussy, but she's also going to give you a lot more. Would you like that?"

Levi nodded his head like an eager kid. He looked kinda cute. I took his hand.

"Shirley, don't you take a dime from him until you're finished, and you settle up with me then. You hear?" Larry said sternly.

"Yes, loud and clear," I said, happily leading Levi toward the house. "You know, Levi, this might be both our lucky days."

24

After two shots I had a buzz, so I left NeeNee, Larry, and Chippy to finish off the bottle they'd opened. I gotten up early, so I figured I'd get a catnap in my room, then when Chippy was ready for bed, I'd head back out there to the sofa. However it was damn near dawn when Chippy found her way to my bedroom, and she wasn't in the mood for sleeping at all when she climbed in the bed and on top of me. She moved her hands against my stomach and slowly down my body.

Chippy kissed me, and I kissed her back, ignoring the alcohol on her breath and concentrating on how soft her lips were. I loved the way she kissed, gently sucking on my tongue as it slid inside her mouth. I hated to admit it, but she brought out things in me I didn't know existed. I'd never had a woman kiss me so passionately. She sent shivers down my spine at the thought of what else she could do with her lips.

She straddled me, taking off her shirt and then her bra. I lifted my hands and cupped her perfectly round breasts then slipped my finger into her mouth, and boy, did she know how to suck. Of course, I imagined it being something else in her mouth, and just that thought started to make me crazy. Every hair on my body felt electrified by the sensuality of being touched, almost as if our bodies were not strangers but had been in this position too many times to count.

She leaned in and kissed me again, and I grabbed her around the waist and pulled her closer to me, our bodies so on fire with lust for each other that I could feel the heat. I rolled her over so that she was on her back. I kissed her lips, then her neck, then I kissed and sucked her nipples like they were the sweetest fruit I'd ever had. I listened to her moan, loving the way she reacted to my touch. She made me feel like I was the only man she had ever truly given herself to. I continued to kiss my way down her belly until I found her neatly trimmed, heart-shaped pubic hair.

I made up my mind I was going to do something I'd never done before. I'd attempted to do it to Donna once but I was shunned. I kissed my way down Chippy's pubic hair until I found the little bump, or clit as Larry put it. Lou had always made sex about him and that horse dick of his, but Larry, despite his rough exterior, always preached that you had to know a woman's body. From all the shit NeeNee talked to her girls, he must have known what he was talking about.

I stuck my tongue out, licking her clit until Chippy started to squirm and moan, which just motivated me to lick her more. I knew I was doing something right when she raised her legs and used two fingers to pull back the hood of her clit to give me greater access. It seemed like the more effort I put in, the more reaction I got, so I just went for broke, sucking her entire clit into my mouth and running my tongue over it repeatedly in the process.

"Oh God daaaaaaaamn," she hollered, placing her hands on my head. "That feels so good, baby. So good. Don't stop. Please, don't stop."

Her encouragement just made me work harder, and I began to lick not only her clit, but her whole damn kitty-kat. At this point, she was starting to sweat and so was I, but I didn't let that stop me, because pleasing her was so much fun.

"Oooooohh, shhhhiiiit! Oooooohh, shhhhiiiit!" she moaned, sounding almost as if she was in pain, but I could tell by the way she kept holding my head in place as her body squirmed that it hurt so good. "Oooooohh, shhhhiiiit!" She let go of my head, and her entire body just went spastic as she pushed me away.

"You okay?" I asked.

"Yeah, I think so," she panted, covering her kitty with her hand, trying to catch her breath. The way she was looking at me made me feel like a king, like I'd really accomplished something. "Shit, that was my first time."

"Your first time?" I gave her a look. Did she really expect me to believe she'd worked at Sam's and never done this before?

She must have read my thoughts, because she explained, "Yes, my first time cumming, silly. I always wondered what all the hype was about, and now I know. Damn, I felt like I was having an out of body experience."

"For real?" I probed, deciding at that moment that I liked eating pussy.

She nodded her head, smiling. "Come here." She reached for me, pulling me up until my face was close to hers.

"I want you," she whispered as a warm hand slid into my boxers and clasped over my dick, sliding expertly up and down the shaft. Here we were, two half-naked people in a bed, lusting for each other, and as much as I wanted to explode inside of her, I couldn't. Not this way.

"I want you, too, but I can't," I said, almost to remind myself more than her that I had a girlfriend who I didn't want to hurt. Unfortunately, I could see that someone was going to get hurt. In fact, from the look that Chippy gave me, I knew someone had already been hurt.

"What do you mean, you can't? You want this just as much as I do." She tried to force me down on her, but I stopped her.

"I do, but I can't. I'm not a cheater, Chippy. I'm a lot of things, but a cheater's not one of them. I can't believe I let it go this far."

"LC!" Larry screamed out from the other room. Talk about bad timing. I needed to stay put and make sure that she was all right, that she understood, but life would not conform to my needs at this moment. "Man, your old lady just pulled up outside!"

"Shit! She never comes here." Chippy and I exchanged a look. "Don't be mad."

"LC! You need to get out here." Now it was NeeNee's voice sounding an alarm as she called my name. I pushed Chippy aside, pulling up my boxers and scrambling for my pants. Grabbing my shirt, I raced out of the room, slamming the door and leaving her alone in my bed.

"Where is she?" I snapped as I hurried into the room.

Larry burst out laughing so hard he could barely get the words out of his mouth. "She's surrounded by the dogs."

"Dammit." I gulped, running for the door.

Chippy

25

I walked in the kitchen and glanced at Larry and NeeNee, who were sitting at the table sharing a cigarette like two cats that ate the canary. To be such a strong man, Larry looked so weak. I picked up the pack of cigarettes off the table, sliding one out, then bent over so Larry could light it. I took a long drag, sharing eye contact with NeeNee, who looked like she wanted to say something but didn't. I strolled over to the kitchen window, sighing when I saw Donna standing next to her car, talking to LC. I couldn't hear what they were saying, but Donna was smiling and giggling like a school girl who'd just been asked to the prom. I knew I didn't have a right to be, but I was hurt.

I was having the time of my life, hanging out with LC and his family. In fact, I was starting to feel so comfortable around LC that after a few drinks, I'd crawled into bed with him and got something started between us. It felt so different than all the men I'd been with at Sam's; it even felt different than it was with Sam—and then, just like that, she'd shown up and ruined it. She had everything I wanted: a good man, money, and most importantly, a fucking life with a future.

I sighed, turning back to NeeNee and Larry. "She's real pretty, isn't she, Nee? I like her hair. It makes her look like Jane Kennedy."

"Jane Kennedy my ass." Larry laughed, getting up and walking out of the room.

NeeNee sighed, walking over and placing a comforting hand on the small of my back. "I guess. I don't much like the uppity bitch myself."

"That doesn't change the fact that she's pretty, NeeNee."

We both took a moment, staring out the door. "Yeah, she's cute, but being cute don't make you pretty. You're much prettier than her."

I touched my bruised face. "Not with my face looking like this I'm not."

"Your face will heal. It's starting to get better already." She smiled, touching my black eye then my hair. "Oh, and for the record, that bitch is wearing a wig. It's an expensive wig and might look real, but that shit's a wig. I knew her nappy ass in grade school." We both laughed.

"You know she don't even appreciate him, Nee. If she supported him the way she should, he could do anything in the world. He's really smart, and not just book smart." I turned back to them. I couldn't stop staring at her.

NeeNee turned to me slowly, speaking very candidly. "You really like him, don't you?"

"Yeah, he's my friend. The first real male friend I think I've ever had."

"Girl, you must think I popped out of my momma's pussy this morning. You don't look at LC like he's your friend, so you can take that shit somewhere else." NeeNee gave me this look that said I shouldn't waste her time with storytelling.

I hesitated, not sure if I even wanted to admit to myself how I was starting to feel. "So what? What if I do like him? That's not going to change anything. He's made his choice. He's planning on marrying that girl, with all her fancy ways and expensive things." I huffed, growing more jealous by the minute.

"And you're just going to let her have him? Chippy, that girl's on the ropes and she knows it. Her woman's intuition is kicking in like a motherfucker. She can sense something's wrong with her relationship, and that something is you."

"You don't know that, NeeNee," I said, although a big part of me hoped she might be right.

"The hell I don't. She don't ever come over here. She thinks she's too good for us country folks," NeeNee huffed. "Shit, she done got everything she ever wanted with her expensive clothes, flashy jewelry, and fancy car. Why you fittin' to let her have LC too?" She shook her head.

"Because he's not mine! He's hers; trust me." She had no idea of the rejection I'd just faced trying to make him mine. I'd never had a guy say no to me, and as far as I was concerned, it was humiliating.

"Well, Charlotte, then I must be wrong about you. I thought you were scrappy, the kind of girl who grew up fighting for what she wanted and always got it. The woman they called Chippy and she claimed it."

"NeeNee, you're right. I have spent a lot of time fighting and proving myself and having to work for every little crumb of kindness this world's shown me, and maybe that's why I'm not going to do it anymore." As soon as the words were out of my mouth, I knew they were true. I was tired.

She gazed over at me. "Are you sure?"

"There's a spark, but I'm not sure if the candle's lit. I'm not going to fight some woman over a man who may or may not want me. I don't even really know him, and he damn sure doesn't know the real me," I protested, starting to feel genuinely terrified for some reason.

"You think you have to know a man for a long time before you know him? Do you know how long I chased Larry's sorry ass before he realized I was in the room? Sometimes men don't know what they like. It's up to us women to show them." NeeNee smiled. "He's quite a good catch, Charlotte. If you really like him, you need to fight for him."

I turned to NeeNee. "No, I'm done fighting over men. Three days ago I fought for a man I would have given the world to, and come to find out he didn't give a shit about me. Next man I give my heart to is going to fight for me just as much as I'd fight for him, and I mean that. Besides, LC's my friend. I would rather lose his heart to her than lose his friendship."

"She's not going to make him happy. Mark my words that if LC winds up with Donna, she will make him miserable."

"Well, that's not my problem. I have other things to tend to." I shrugged my shoulders, my mind already moving on to other things. "Can I use your phone?"

"Sure." She motioned to the phone on the wall.

I made my way over and dialed a number from memory. When I heard the voice on the other end of the phone, I almost hung up.

"Hello! Hello!" my mother shouted into the receiver.

I glanced over at NeeNee, taking a deep breath before I said, "Momma."

The phone fell silent for a good three seconds. I was fully expecting a barrage of insults and curses, but none ever came. "Charlotte, baby, is that you?" She called out my name in an unfamiliar tone that made me suddenly homesick for a place I couldn't get out of soon enough.

"Yeah, Momma, it's me."

"Baby, where have you been? I been looking everywhere for you. You had me worried sick." She actually sounded concerned.

"Momma, I just thought . . . You told me to get my ass out your house." There was momentary silence on the line again.

"I was drunk, and I shouldn't have said and done those things. I'm sorry, baby." My mother had never apologized about anything in her life. Who was this woman? "Charlotte, you got to come home. I need my baby back. I need you, girl."

"What about him?"

She paused again before telling me, "He's gone. He left me not long after you did. Come on home, baby. Let's be a family again."

I hesitated, taking a breath. I realized there was only one place that I wanted to be. "Okay, Momma. I'm coming home," I told her before I hung up.

When I turned around, NeeNee stood in the doorway, staring at me. "You sure about this?" I could see in her face that she was thinking about the scars she'd seen.

"Yeah, he's gone and she wants me to come home."

"What about her drinking?" NeeNee questioned me, sounding worried.

"She was sober, NeeNee. For the first time since I can remember, Momma was sober," I said, staring out the window at LC and Donna getting all touchy-feely, which only served to make me more determined to leave this place. NeeNee followed my line of vision out the window.

"Sure wish it was her about to leave and not you," she huffed, shooting Donna the stink eye through the window.

"Me too, but it ain't."

She gave me a hug. "Damn, girl, you going to miss our grand opening."

"I know." I got my purse and pulled out one of the only phone numbers I actually had. "Gonna need to use your phone one more time."

John

26

My first day on my new job wasn't as I'd imagined it.

The rickety station wagon they had me driving reeked of burnt motor oil, mold, and old people. Still, it was better that it smelled of those things than of the cargo that was concealed in the car. It was an amazing job by the cartel back in Houston that it didn't smell overwhelmingly of marijuana instead.

I'd just crossed into fucking Georgia with its goddamned peaches and racist Confederate flags, relying on the map that lay open across the seat beside me. I was already tired, almost missing my exit off I-10 back down by Tallahassee, but I didn't want to stop to rest until I got at least to Virginia. The sooner I could get to New York and make the exchange, the sooner my mother and sisters would be safe and benefitting from the money I'd made. I wished I could have gotten them to safety sooner. If I had somebody back home I could trust, I would have gotten my family to safety and maybe disappeared with whatever packages were hidden all throughout this piece of shit some idiot in Detroit dared to name a Country Squire. Thoughts of what my boss had threatened to do were torturing me even more than the fifty-five mile-per-hour speed limit I was forced to adhere to.

Again, I was getting sleepy and foolish. *Just do the job and everything will be fine*, I thought as I looked in the rearview mirror. A police car that I thought had been following me for miles finally exited at a Cracker Barrel, calming me just a little bit. To celebrate overcoming my latest scare, I grabbed my pack of Marlboros off the dashboard and lit one up.

That helped, but in such an unsatisfying automobile, I really needed some music to distract me. These radio stations around here were awful, though, with their endless country twang, and I'd been punching the eject button since I was back in Louisiana, trying to get whatever tape was stuck inside to pop free.

From Houston, I'd brought a few eight-track tapes, The Steve Miller Band and The Jackson 5, but I couldn't even play them until this one was unstuck. "Dammit!" I cursed, angrier than I should have been over such a thing. I guess I was tired of feeling so helpless.

I figured I'd try one last time before screaming. I jammed the eject button, but this time did it at an angle, hoping the button would finally catch on something. When I felt it resist against my thumb, I held back on my excitement. When the tape popped free and landed on the floor, I let it all go.

"Yes!" I triumphantly crowed, free to have some sanity and get my boogie on the rest of my trip. *Who in the fuck listens to Perry Como?* I thought as I read the faded label with the smiling gray-haired man who mocked me. Nevertheless, I swiftly cranked down the window as I prepared to ditch the old people's music once and for all. When I reached down to grab the eight track tape off the floorboard, it slid away from my grasp.

I ever so briefly slid out from under the steering wheel and extended my fingertips as far as they could go. It was so close, and with a final stretch, I got my mitts on the tape. Preparing to toss it out the window, I slid across the bench seat and put my eyes back on the road—just in time to see the brake lights on a bright green pickup truck as it stopped to make a left turn.

"Oh, shit!" I yelled as I yanked hard on the steering wheel to avoid running up under the truck. As I left the road, I felt the bulky wagon leave the ground just before it careened down a hill and crashed head-on into an oak tree. Believe it or not, I felt fortunate to have hit the tree, because the thick trunk had kept the Country Squire from a worse drop.

"Boy, ya done fucked this one up bad," the stupid country sheriff with a badge offered from below a little while later. He had climbed down into the ditch where the car was releasing steam into the air from a busted radiator. I had climbed back up to the roadside, and I wasn't standing there too long before the sheriff, who just happened to be driving by, pulled over to see if he could help. Now he was examining the outside of the car. The odor of antifreeze traveled up to my nose from the radiator steam. While unpleasant, I was just glad it wasn't the smell of the cartel's crop burning inside. If the car had caught fire, I would be running for my life, though there would be nowhere to hide.

Even if the marijuana was still intact, I was in a bad situation and in need of a solution. The cartel higher ups didn't want idiots; they demanded those who could think on their feet.

"Hell, I'm just glad you came along," I lied, nervous about how well my gringo accent was playing now that I had to put it to the test.

The sheriff moved on from the outside and was combing through the station wagon's interior, nudging at things with the butt of his flashlight. The closer he came to one of the loose panels where the marijuana was stowed, the more my anxiety rose. I nervously maintained my smile, keeping my hand near the revolver beneath my Hawaiian shirt. This road didn't have that much traffic about now, so there would be no witnesses if I acted fast and timed it just right.

"Hey, son?" he called out as something caught his attention.

"Yes, sir?" I replied as I leaned over, bracing my foot as I prepared to pull my gun from my waistband.

"Mind if I ask ya somethin'?" he questioned as he got near the panel by the backseat I was worried about.

"No. Not at all, officer," I said, flashing a smile as I tried to position myself where I could get the upper hand before he could return fire. There was no way I was a better shot than him, so surprise would be my only chance.

"Are you really from New Jersey?" he asked, looking back at me suddenly, like I'd come down in a UFO.

"Yeah. Name's John, by the way," I said, struggling to conceal my nerves and my accent. Figuring it would impress this Southern hick, maybe distract him from his impromptu search of the car, I added, "I've been on the road selling Bibles, sir."

"Well . . . where they at?" he said as he eyed me curiously.

"What can I say? I'm a successful salesman," I replied with a cocky wink and my best Jersey accent. "And when it's the Word of the Lord, people can always use that." I made the sign of the cross. My grandmother would've been so proud of me.

"Hmm. Well, I'm sorry to say that your trip back up North is gonna be delayed," he said, and I felt my heart start racing. "This here wagon is definitely gonna need some repair work."

"Oh, noooo!" I was genuinely worried about my trip and my family. Any delays would not be good for my mother and my sisters.

"Don't worry though, John," he said as he stood up straight and adjusted his belt around his large waist. As he hiked back up the hill, I offered my hand to assist him. He had no idea how close he had been to making the major bust that could have cemented his career—but would've cost him his life. "I can have you towed up the road yonder to the next town. Somebody there should be able to fix it and get you back on your way."

"Oh," I said, hopeful that I could be back on the road before sundown. "What's the name of the town?" I asked.

"Waycross," he replied as he pointed due east.

Lou

27

After riding three busses for almost twenty hours in a cramped seat, I'd finally arrived in Atlantic City, New Jersey, where I'd immediately found a diner so I could have something decent to eat. My next plan of attack, since I couldn't handle my business until the morning, was to find me a cathouse and release the black snake on the local population. That's when I met Loretta, the black-as-night diner waitress. She had to be ten years my senior, and she wasn't much to look at in the face, but her juicy ass and firm, oversized tits sure were a welcome sight to an old pussy hound like me. What most brothers didn't know was that them ugly gals had some of the best pussy in the world. They usually weren't much when it came to sucking your dick, but they'd fuck the black off you every time if you let 'em.

Loretta and I had made small talk to start with, but once I found out she was single with her own place, I slapped down a five spot as a tip to open her nose then nursed a cup of coffee until the end of her shift. Twenty minutes later I was in her place, fucking the shit outta her while saving myself the cost of a whore, a hotel room, and breakfast.

After a breakfast of eggs, grits, country sausage, and hash browns I had thanked Loretta with a good fuck before I got showered and dressed. On my way out the door, she kissed me then pleaded with me to come by the diner after I handled my business. I didn't make any promises but said I'd see what I could do, because you never know when a better opportunity would present itself.

"Lou Duncan! It's really good of you to meet me today, especially since I know it was out of your way," Tony Dash, the suave Italian capo of the Russo family, greeted me as I entered the large, fancy restaurant deep in the bowels of A.C.

"Hey, Tony, after the good time you showed me in New York, how could I not show up with a smile on my face and fuckin' ask questions later?" We hugged. Tony loved black pussy more than anyone I'd ever met, and got plenty of it—for both of us—the last time we were in New York together.

"We did have a good time, didn't we?" he said with a smile. "So, how was your trip from Georgia?"

"Long as I got here, that's all that matters. The South is fine, but there is nothing like being in A.C. The air smells better. Maybe it's the salt from the ocean." There was something about the way the adrenaline in my body changed when I arrived in the city.

"It smells like shit!" A guy who resembled Tony, only a few years younger, cut in as he approached us. "You got to go to the Poconos if you want to experience real fresh air," he said as he plopped down next to his brother. "Hey! Hey! What the fuck I gotta do to get some fuckin' service in here?" He snapped his fingers at the waiter, who looked terrified as he rushed over to him.

"Sal!" Tony's voice came out as a warning to his brother. I'd heard that Sal was violent and brutal if you ever got on his bad side, which I made a mental note to never do. "Have some goddamn respect. We got company."

Sal looked me up and down before deciding I wasn't worth his attention. "What? I'm hungry," he said to Tony.

"Why don't you go eat up front with the boys? Lou and I need to talk." Tony made it sound more like a demand than a suggestion.

"Fine! But they better fuckin' feed me soon." Sal got up and stomped into the other room.

"I'm sorry about that." Tony sighed, frowning as his brother disappeared out of sight, his complaints still ringing behind him. "What the fuck am I going to do? He's family. But enough about him." He leaned in close and spoke a little lower. "The reason I invited you here is that the Russo family needs a heroin trafficker, one that we can trust to handle the Southern territories."

"Are you serious?" I asked, because truthfully, I couldn't believe what I was hearing. This was an opportunity to be a major player. Sam was going to shit himself when he heard this.

"Well, I'm not exactly ready to shake hands on it, but I need to know if you think you can handle that much product."

"You're saying you want me and Sam to be the Southern arm of the business?" I checked to make sure I had heard him correctly.

He nodded. "Look, I've only dealt with you. I don't have any idea who your guy Sam is other than what you've told me. I thought you were working with your brothers," he said.

"I do work with my brothers on some things, but I'm moving the drugs for Sam. He runs a cat house in Georgia, among other things, and he has a lot of connections for all kinds of things in South Georgia."

He sat back in his chair. "Lou, one of the reasons I thought about you is because I'm a family man, and the last few times we met, you made it clear that so are you."

"Wait, wait, wait," I said, desperate to set things right before he took the offer off the table. "I am a family man. My brothers and I are thinking about approaching the biggest numbers runner in Georgia. Well, approaching his widow, since he just passed away. It would be a huge come up for us," I told him, my voice laced with the dread I felt in the pit of my stomach at this idea, even though I knew it sounded good.

"You don't sound so excited." Tony replied upon hearing the trepidation in my voice.

"Nah, it's a great opportunity, but . . ." I trailed off, not sure how to continue.

"But what?"

"You know, it would cut out Sam, and I'm not sure I can do that. The two of us are tight, and he wants to take over this numbers business as well."

"And you don't want to step on his toes? That what you trying to say?" Tony asked.

"Yes. No. Well, it's just that my brothers think I need to get out from under Sam and to be my own boss. To stop being a hired hand, even though he did just offer me the chance to be a partner."

"And what do you think?" He sat back in his chair, curious to hear my response.

"Why make an enemy of my best friend? Sam is like a brother to me," I admitted. The two of us had been hanging pretty close for the past five years.

"But he's not your brother," Tony reminded me matter-of-factly. "You have a brother. You have three brothers, so I don't see why you need another one."

"Yeah, but we work so well together," I told him, realizing just how much I didn't want to compromise my friendship.

"No," he corrected, "from what you been telling me, you work for him. He's the real boss. You're just fucking so much of that free pussy he's giving you that you can't see it."

I fought the urge to tell Tony that he was starting to sound like Larry.

"And your brother LC?" Tony continued, "I would listen to him. He sounds like a smart guy."

"Yeah, that's what people keep telling me."

"Let me tell you something. The only people I partner with are family. You can see that my brother is a real idiot. I admit it, but I know exactly who he is, and as much as he annoys me, Sal has my back in a way that a friend can never have. You want to go into business, then do it with family. That way you'll always know what you're getting. There won't be any surprises, and they'll have your back even if they're hating you. They have no choice," he told me.

"My other brother, Larry, he doesn't trust Sam at all. In fact, he can't stand the guy. Thinks he's corrupt and untrustworthy," I admitted.

Tony shook his head. "I would trust my brothers before I trusted that guy. What does your brother have to gain by lying to you? Nothing. But that Sam guy? He could stab you in the back and you wouldn't even know it until it was too late, and then you're lying there dead." His words jarred something in me that I didn't want to think about. I didn't want to be disloyal.

"But he's like my brother," I argued again, even though I was repeating myself.

"But he's not your brother. My brother and I fight, but you let anybody else try and fight me, and my brother will kill them. I bet your brothers are the same way. Would Sam do that for you?"

I shook my head. If I was being honest with myself, I knew he wouldn't.

"This man Sam has you doing his dirty work and he ain't even paying you that well."

"Tony, that's a lot for me to think about," I explained. I'd left Georgia certain about a lot of things, and in one meeting I suddenly wasn't sure about anything.

"You keep sleeping on this guy Sam and one day you're going to wake up with a bullet in your back. Remember I said it."

Chippy

28

I looked up in the sky, and the clouds overhead mirrored my mood, mostly because I'd spent the past five hours reading *Pimp,* the book that I'd taken from LC's room. It had opened my eyes to a lot of things about Sam and the way he'd manipulated me. I was trying not to let it bring me down, though, because I preferred to focus on how it felt to finally hear my mother's voice, finally sober, telling me to come home. She didn't have to ask twice before I made the decision to leave Waycross—well, that and the way LC had made me feel when he jumped out of bed and ran to Donna that day.

"You sure this is it?" Calvin asked.

Calvin was one of the few tricks whose number I had, and probably the only one I trusted enough to ask for a ride all the way to Fayetteville. Sure, I had to fuck him before we left, but I wasn't gonna do the eight-hour trip on no bus, stopping in every hick town in between on the way. He said he had to be to work, but the chance to get some pussy away from the watchful eye of Big Sam was too good to pass up. The way he was talking, the fool probably thought he was going to replace Sam as my pimp. If he did, he was in for a big surprise. Yes, I made him some promises, but he'd also given me quite a bit of cash and a ride home.

"Yeah, this is it."

"So, exactly who lives here anyway?" he asked at the end of our journey.

"A friend," I replied, lying as I stared up at the gables and rose bushes that surrounded the stately front porch. Nothing had changed about them, and probably the same for the people inside. "Now, are you gonna pull around the corner and let me suck your dick, or keep asking me questions?"

He didn't take long to make his decision, quickly parking the car and unzipping his pants. I knew just how to get him off, so it didn't take long for Calvin to finish and fall back in his seat.

"Damn, Chippy," Calvin gasped, his limp dick still outside his pants as he stared adoringly at me. I ignored him, checking my hair in the rearview mirror. "I ain't never had anyone make me do the Spiderman like that. Say, when you coming back to Waycross? I'll pick you up."

"I ain't comin' back, Calvin," I said with a grin as I left his company. Closing the door to his pale blue Buick muffled his protests. To leave a customer, and not the other way around, gave me some pleasure.

I walked around the corner then ducked behind some bushes until Calvin was gone. That determined bastard circled the block three times before he gave up and drove away.

I finally made my way to the house, but something kept me standing there outside of the house where I grew up, feeling like a ghost from my own past. As I reached out to push the doorbell, the voice in my head screamed for me to stop this nonsense and run away again, but I was hardheaded to a fault, even with myself. As much as I wanted to run, I also wanted to finally meet the mother I'd always wished I had, the woman on the phone who sounded and treated me so different from the one who raised me. It had been a long time since I'd felt truly welcome or at home in this house, and now, with her begging me to come back, I couldn't help imagine how different it could be.

With just the two of us, life really could be so much better. I could even go back and finish school, and maybe go to college like LC. The whole ride home, I'd thought about the life I never had that suddenly seemed within my grasp. It was a normal life that didn't look one way from the outside and another once you entered the door.

"Oh my God, Charlotte." The softness of my mother's voice caught me off guard, and it only accelerated my discomfort when she grabbed me in a bear hug and squeezed me so tight I thought I would burst. "Girl, I missed you so much."

"I missed you too, Momma."

She relaxed her hold on me, staring at me closely. I felt myself shrink under her intense gaze, because I expected the criticism and demeaning comments to follow. My mother had never taken the opportunity to build me up when she could tear me down. "You look so grown up. You're beautiful." She touched my face, and I was glad that the black eye had faded.

"Thank you, it's the makeup and the hair," I replied, my voice shaky with emotion at this kinder, gentler version of the woman who had birthed me. Although it had only been a few months since I'd left, I knew that I couldn't possibly look like the same person. I'd done things that I couldn't imagine when I walked out the door.

She hugged me again. "Baby, I'm so happy you're home. Now get on in this house so I can put some meat on those bones of yours. Looks like nobody's been feeding you." She hustled me inside and we went straight to the kitchen.

My mother got out her favorite cast iron skillet, along with some other pots, and started to cook. In spite of everything that had happened, it felt good to be home.

"So how are you doing, Momma?" I asked as she hurried around the room, preparing food.

"I'm good. A lot better now that you're here. Where were you anyway?" She started chopping a potato as she waited for my response.

"Well, first I went down to Savannah; then I went Jacksonville and spent the night at a fancy resort with a friend, and then, after that, I went to Orlando and Disney World. Momma, it was so beautiful down there. It was almost like a dream."

She stopped cooking for a second and turned to me. "That all sounds good, but Disney World ain't cheap. Where'd you get the money to do all of this jetsetting? You're not in any trouble with the law, are you?"

"What? No!" I shook my head. "My friend paid for it." I didn't want to lie, but I also didn't want to tell the truth.

"Your friend paid for it, huh?" she asked curtly. For the first time since I'd arrived, my mother was starting to judge me. "I hope you didn't let your friend get up under your skirt. You know that's all they want."

Well, that was a punch to the gut. "No, Momma, my friend's a girl. Her . . . her name's Donna, and her daddy's a doctor down in Waycross, Georgia. That's where I've been staying. I even had a job."

"A job doing what?"

"Working at a convenience store at a gas station. I worked for a real nice man named LC Duncan and his family."

She looked at me skeptically but didn't say anything as she kept on cooking.

"So, if things were so great, then why'd you come home?"

"Because I missed you, Momma." I jumped up, hugging her with tears running down my face. "I missed you."

"I missed you too, baby." She smiled and set the plate of eggs, bacon, hash browns, fried green tomatoes, and biscuits in front of me, hovering nervously. I could tell how much she wanted my approval.

I knew things were different from the way she was making such a fuss over me. My mother had never cared one bit what I thought, but this was a different person. She waited for me to take that first bite, and since it looked like she wouldn't budge until I did, I obliged, shoveling a huge forkful of eggs into my mouth.

"This is so good, Momma," I murmured absently, trying to calm my anxiety.

"All I want is for you to be happy. This time you're going to be happy, I swear. Just promise me you'll give this a real chance?" She asked it in a way that made it seem like she was begging me for something, and I just didn't know what. "I'ma make you those baked turkey wings you like for dinner," she told me as she got up and began to prepare the next meal.

By the time night fell, we were both exhausted as we sat down on the couch together to watch television. When Archie Bunker ended, *Good Times* came on. My mother and I howled with laughter every time J.J. said "Dy-no-mite!"

As soon as the show ended, I started yawning. She got up and turned off the television. "You must be tired," she said.

"Yeah, I am," I said, getting up and heading into my bedroom. My mother followed close behind me, talking a mile a minute.

It was strange being back in that room. I opened the set of drawers and pulled out a nightgown. I was actually surprised she hadn't thrown away my stuff. I got dressed and was about to slip into bed when my mom threw her arms around me.

"Charlotte, I'm just so glad you're finally home. I had almost given up on ever being happy again."

29

I should have been walking out of the Holiday Inn beating my chest because I'd just gotten laid, but instead I wanted to plug my ears because of Donna's nagging.

"I don't see why we can't spend the day together. We can go back inside and tell them we want to keep the room until checkout then head down to my parents' summer place." Donna took hold of my arm, trying to turn me back toward the hotel. Part of me wished I could, but I had responsibilities.

"Look, I can't, all right? I told you last night I had to open the shop this morning," I reminded her as we approached her car. The tow truck was parked on the other side of the parking lot just in case anyone got suspicious, because good girls like Donna didn't get caught in hotels with guys who were not their husbands, even though we were engaged.

"Please, I'll give you a blow job." She licked her lips coyly. At the same time, she looked around to make sure no one had heard her.

"You have no idea how much I wish I could."

She stuck out her lip and pouted. I slipped my hand around her waist and pulled her close, trying to make amends. It seemed like all the things I'd been wanting Donna to do, like spend the night and give a brother a blow job, she suddenly wanted to do. I should have been ecstatic, except for some reason, it didn't feel quite right. It almost felt contrived.

"Even if I leave now I'm going to be late. Donna, I have responsibilities."

"What about your responsibility to me?"

I gave her a peck on the lips, stepping back only to be met with the saltiest expression. Normally, she was the one too busy to spend time with me, leading me to chase behind her, but over the past few weeks, it was like everything had flip-flopped. Now she was the one acting all needy, wanting to be with me every waking minute. Who knows? Maybe the idea of me owning the shop was becoming attractive to her.

"LC, what kind of kiss was that?" she complained. "I ain't your old aunt Ethel. I'm your fiancée, who just spent the last twelve hours showing you how much I love you." She chastised me until I leaned in and planted a deep, long French kiss on her, even knowing that my mind wasn't present.

"How was that?" I laughed, wanting to make sure everything was all right before she got back on the road. Last thing I needed was for her to be upset and get into an accident.

"That should keep my mind busy on the drive back to Jekyll Island." She made a face like she was being sent to a prison instead of the luxury summer home her parents kept on a private island with a beach, where all she had to do all day was relax and have fun.

"If it's any consolation," I said, "I love you."

"I love you too, and you better call me at least five times before tomorrow," she whined.

Boy, I certainly wasn't used to this version of Donna, and I was seriously ready for her to go back to her old self. I'd never been attracted to needy women, especially not whiny, spoiled ones.

"Okay, but I want you to call me at the shop and let me know that you arrived safely."

"So you gonna come down this Saturday right? My parents are having a big seafood party, and afterwards we can make love on the beach."

I nodded. "Yeah, I'm planning on it, but we still haven't got everything together for the shop's grand opening, so don't hold me to it, okay?"

"The shop. The shop. Everything is all about the shop," she snarled, yanking open the door to her car and getting in. Okay, so maybe it wasn't the shop that was bringing out the seductress in her. "There are a lot of people on St. Simon's and Jekyll Island that would love to spend time with me, so if I were you, I'd make me a priority," she snapped before she turned on the engine and drove away. Now that was the Donna I had grown used to!

She'd driven two hours yesterday and lied to her parents so we could spend the whole night together in a hotel, and as much as I enjoyed it, I had to admit my mind was elsewhere for much of our time together. It was weird; I had been so into the chase, but when Donna finally gave in to all the things I'd been begging for, I could barely stay focused on her. Other than the issue with going to her parents' house, though, I think I'd managed to hide my preoccupation from her. At least she hadn't commented on it.

I got in the tow truck and headed to the station. Instead of taking the direct route, I found myself traveling through town and down Oak Street past Big Sam's, probably because it made me think of Chippy. I guess I couldn't blame her for leaving, but I sure wished I'd had a chance to explain myself and say good-bye. I couldn't deny my disappointment as I drove by.

Less than five minutes later, I pulled into the shop, slamming on my brakes. "What the hell is he doing here?" I murmured to myself, gazing at the 300D Mercedes-Benz that belonged to Dr. Washington. Donna's father was leaning against the car, looking out of place in his suit and tie.

"LC." He nodded to me.

I got out of the truck and approached him, my heart pounding in my chest. "Dr. Washington." I held out my hand to him, but he ignored the gesture. "I thought you were down in Jekyll Island," I asked, even though the possible reason for not being there worried me.

"There was an emergency with a patient, so I had to come up last night. I heard you opened up this shop, so I thought I'd stop by and have a heart to heart talk with you." He took a few steps back, looking up at the sign. "Duncan Brothers Service Station," he read aloud.

"Yeah, my brothers and I own the place," I replied, suddenly feeling less than confidant about what had been a real source of pride lately. Something about this man made me feel like I was still some scruffy little kid begging for scraps, and I didn't like it.

"I thought you told me that you were going to get a degree in business." He stared at me like he felt I'd been lying to him.

"I am getting my degree," I answered, feeling sweat forming on my brow.

"So why are you wasting your time in this place?" His face scrunched up like he had swallowed something nasty. "Shouldn't you be up there in Atlanta or Charlotte doing an internship?"

I took a deep breath to calm myself before answering. "Dr. Washington, I'm trying to set something up to secure my future, so that I will always have a fall back plan when I'm married to your daughter."

He laughed. "Speaking of my daughter, would you happen to know her whereabouts?"

"She's on her way back to Jekkyl Island, sir."

"Is that right? And where did she stay last night?"

Shit. Was he really going there? From the way he was looking at me, I was sure he already knew the answer. "Maybe you should ask her that."

"I'm asking you." He folded his arms, looking me dead in the face. I felt like I was shrinking before him.

"Dr. Washington, Donna and I are engaged, and I really don't feel comfortable answering that question."

He raised his hands and waved them in my face like he had no interest in hearing about that. "Your engagement still remains up for discussion as far as I'm concerned. Where I come from, when a young man wants to marry a young woman, he goes directly to her father and asks for his permission, and only after he receives that approval does he go and buy her an acceptable engagement ring—not a piece of fool's gold." His words landed sharply, as they were meant to wound.

"That ring belonged to my mother. It's a family heirloom," I shot back, feeling a sudden urge to punch him in his smug face.

He audibly groaned at my response. "Not all things are meant to be passed down, son. That thing barely had a diamond. It was more like the chip off a real diamond."

"When you love someone, you're not concerned with the size of a ring," I replied in defense.

"My daughter thinks that she loves you, but that is because she doesn't know who you really are. Nor, for that matter, does she know anything about love."

"Excuse me?" I asked, reminding myself that this was Donna's father and I needed to keep my cool for her sake.

"You don't think I know about your family? I remember your father. He was an awful, lawless, godless human being. You're all con men and criminals, and there is no way I want my darling daughter to ever be called a Duncan. Do you understand?"

Before I could give him a piece of my mind, a sheriff's car pulled up, and a dark-haired, olive-skinned man got out with a desperate look on his face. "Excuse me," he said. "Do you have a tow truck available? I need my car towed out of a ditch."

I glanced over at Dr. Washington and said, "We'll have to pick this conversation up another time. I have work to do."

He shook his head and brushed off his suit as if to remove the indignity of even setting foot on the property of my service station. "You and this clan of thieves are not good enough for my daughter. The sooner you realize that, the sooner you can get back to . . . pumping gas." He laughed derisively as he got into his car and left.

The man looked from me to the moving car. "Please, sir, I really need a tow."

"I'm sorry, but I can't right now," I told him. "I need to open up the shop. But I'll have someone here in about an hour and we'll get you all straightened out."

"How much?" he asked.

"How much what?" I snapped, still reeling from the encounter with Donna's father and the nasty way he treated me. The man rubbed his index finger and thumb together in the universal sign for money.

"It's normally twenty-five dollars, but like I told you, I can't do it right now," I told him, my tone absolute.

"What if I give you a hundred dollars?" he said, raising it to a number that I couldn't afford to pass up. No way was I pumping a hundred dollars' worth of gas in the next hour.

John

30

"So you're certain about that?"

The man who towed the car was speaking to someone on the phone back in his auto shop. He'd been nice enough to tow me right away, although he didn't hesitate to take my hundred dollars, which was four times his normal rate. His brow furrowed enough to make me nervous as I waited to hear what was wrong with the car.

"Yes, Waycross, Georgia." That was the last thing I heard before I zoned out, pacing back and forth in front of the counter separating us, my mind racing with scenarios of things happening back home. None of them were comforting.

"I got good news and bad news," he announced as he placed the phone back on the receiver, staring at me until I stopped moving and he could be certain he'd gotten my attention.

"Go on," I said as casually as I could with my heart pounding out of my chest.

"Which one you want first?" he asked, his expressionless face leading me to assume he was used to delivering bad news.

"Whichever one ends with me driving that car out of here." I leaned on the counter across from him.

"Good news is I can fix everything on the car in a day."

"Uh-huh?" I waited, certain I was about to hear the other shoe drop. And sure enough, his next bit of news was terrible. "Bad news is you need a manifold, and for this particular car it's out of stock at the factory. The only place that might have one is in Oklahoma."

"Oklahoma! How long is that going to take?" I asked, thinking it would take at least a few days. I didn't have that kind of time.

"Yeah, not exactly around the corner. It's going to take seven to ten days for it to get here. I know you need to get on the road, but I tried everybody. To tell the truth, half an hour ago I didn't think I would find it at all," he finished, offering me a look of condolence.

My hands tightened into fists. It took everything in me to keep it together. "You don't understand. You have to find that part someplace closer. I have to get on the road." My voice shook with emotion, thinking about my family and what this man who was my boss would do to them. He'd have them killed, and then he'd come after me and murder me too. I had to hold on to the counter to stop myself from sliding to the floor in a heap.

"I'm sorry," he said calmly, ignoring my obvious distress, "but these guys are the best in the state. If they say the closest one is in Oklahoma, then that's where it is. You're welcome to try another shop if you'd like."

"No, I trust you," I said. I had witnessed the guy make multiple phone calls to track down the part, so I knew he wasn't bullshitting me. "You have an honest face."

He laughed loudly. "Thanks. I've never had anyone say that before. Name's LC Duncan." He offered his hand.

I accepted his handshake. "Uh, John. John Roberts."

A car rolled into the station, so he went outside to pump gas. By the time he returned, I had managed to get myself together.

"There's a little motel out on the highway. Not too fancy. I'm sure they have rooms," he offered. If he had any idea what was worrying me at that moment, he would have known that the last thing I was thinking about was a hotel room, fancy or not. I just wanted to get the fuck out of there.

"I don't have that kind of money," I said, barely containing the anxiety I felt. Truthfully, money was not the problem, but I wasn't about to tell him that. "I didn't budget for things going wrong. Can you help me push the car outside of the shop and I can sleep inside? I won't be in your way." No way was I leaving the premises and letting that car out of my sight. Not with all those drugs in there.

He furrowed his brow like he was in deep thought for a minute, and then he said, "Well, if you don't mind staying here, there's a little room in the back with a cot. Between work and school I've spent more than a few nights sleeping there myself, so I know it's not that bad."

Man, this guy was so nice he almost didn't seem real. Maybe it was a Southern hospitality thing. Whatever it was, I was relieved that he didn't have a problem with me hanging around. *Maybe I have an honest face too,* I thought, laughing to myself.

"That's nice of you to offer," I said. "But if I'm going to be staying here, the least I can do is help you out around here. I can sweep, pump gas, anything." I kept this whole nice-guy theme going. Maybe it would get me my car faster when the part did arrive. Plus, keeping busy around this place might help the time pass faster. It would be better than sitting around worrying about my family all day.

"Yeah. Sure. We'll call you the night watchman," he joked. "I'll make sure NeeNee sends you some food every day. She loves any opportunity she can get to feed people," LC said, talking like I was one of the family or something. This was one hospitable dude.

In spite of all this friendliness, though, I still had big problems hanging over my head. "I need to make a phone call, let my people know I've been delayed," I said.

He nodded. "Pay phone's outside."

I went outside to make the call I'd been dreading. "Hello? It's Juan—I mean John," I said when a voice I recognized as Manny picked up. When he heard my bad news, he quickly handed the phone to the man who had placed me in this position.

"What do you mean you are going to miss the drop-off?" he seethed, the threat in his voice clear and uncompromising. "If you don't make that drop-off, then you will be the one who owes us the money for the drugs."

"But the part needed to fix the car will not come for a week or more," I tried to explain but he wasn't interested.

"That, my friend, is your problem, and unfortunately, it is also the problem of your mother and your sisters. I suggest you spend less time making excuses and more time figuring out how you are going to get me the money for my drugs!"

"Yes, sir," I heard myself answer, but I had no idea how the words made their way out of my mouth when I felt too scared to speak.

"Tick-tock!" he hissed into the phone before it went dead.

"You all right?" LC asked when I wandered back into the shop a few minutes later and a lot less all right.

"I will be when that part comes in." I saw a broom in the corner, so I picked it up and started sweeping.

Big Shirley

31

"You can barely see them anymore," Little Momma exclaimed as she applied makeup to cover the scars on my face. Of course she was exaggerating, but I had to admit it looked better than before.

It was just nice to finally leave the house for a night, and the fact that it was First Friday made it even better. On the first Friday of every other month, the Duncan Brothers put on a big to-do. The whole black side of town showed up, gathering 'round to watch cock fights, dog fights, and more importantly, people fights, along with music, dancing, and fireworks. It was the only time Sam shut the place down for a few hours, including Christmas and Thanksgiving. It was usually held in an abandoned lot over on G Street, but today they were holding it behind their new gas station as part of their grand opening.

"Let's go!" Big Sam hollered up the stairs, and the bunch of us girls padded down, each of us trying to outdo the others. Sam had one of the boosters come by with new outfits, and all us girls were allowed to pick one for tonight. See, this was our chance to meet and mingle with some of the men who wouldn't be caught dead up in the house—that is, until they saw firsthand what we had to offer. Sam wanted us to look good for the potential customers. We had to look better than their wives.

We showed up in a caravan of seven cars, and when we stepped out and followed Sam to our seats, heads turned.

I hadn't been by the new Duncan brothers' gas station yet, but I was impressed with the way they had things set up when I got there. They'd put up a boxing ring in the back, with plenty of chairs and bleachers, and a dog– and cock-fighting pit a little further back. Larry's girl NeeNee had a rolling barbecue trailer where she had a couple of guys working the grill while she sold plates at a real profit. And let me tell you, she could cook. Hell, there was a line all the way around the building. Then there was a stand set up where Lou's cousin Harold and some white-looking guy were selling beer and sodas at twice the regular price, and those Negroes were still buying them. Oh, and let's not forget Larry and Lou, who were working the crowd, taking bets. From the looks of things, they were all making money hand over fist.

"The twins will cart any of you and your tricks back to the house, so remember, you're not here just to look cute and to spend my money. You're here to meet new customers and to make me money. Now get to work," Sam barked at us as he took his seat. I'd learned to sit directly behind him, because you always got the good gossip first, not to mention you were out of his line of sight.

"Damn, he's fine!" Little Momma, who was sitting to my right, murmured under her breath. Following the direction of her gaze, I spotted LC about to step into the middle of the ring as master of ceremonies. I glanced at Little Momma, who seemed enthralled, until she saw me looking and then tried to play like she wasn't interested.

"Good afternoon, everybody. My name is LC Duncan. Welcome to Duncan Brothers Service Station and First Friday, Waycross. We've got some great entertainment for you tonight, folks." LC reached in his pocket, pulled out a stack of money, and waved it around. "To start with, I'd like to offer an open challenge to any man who has the heart and thinks he's tough enough to stay in the ring with Waycross heavyweight champion, Levi Duncan. Matter of fact, whoever can last three rounds will win five hundred dollars cash." All of a sudden men start pouring out of the stands and heading to the ring.

Levi, dressed in a pair of shorts and boots and a bright yellow robe with Duncan Brothers splashed on the back, stepped into the ring, looking like a professional.

"Ain't that your boy?" Little Momma asked.

"Mm-hmm, sure is. My baby covers my whole quota every Wednesday and Saturday when I come to see him," I bragged, waving at Levi.

"Shit, I need to go see him," Little Momma replied.

I cut my eyes at her. "You go near him and I'ma give you something worse than this," I growled, pointing at my scarred face.

"Fuck, I didn't know we was claiming Johns and shit," Little Momma replied, rolling her eyes sarcastically.

I wagged my finger at her. "Just stay away. Ain't none of you give a shit about him before, so stay away now."

"How much you think they're pulling in? Five, ten thousand?" I heard Sam whisper to Jefferson, his accountant, who nodded excitedly.

"At least, and that's just on the food. The real money is being made on the cock and dog fights." Jefferson pointed to the animal fighting pits. "Look how crowded they are."

"Damn," Sam said. "This place is a fucking gold mine. And we can thank the Duncans for building this all up and doing the heavy work."

"Yeah, if you can get it at the right price."

"Please. That nigga Lou might as well be calling me Daddy. I say suck my dick; he says how hard. This whole operation is my next target after I wrest control over Old Man Walker's numbers racket. I've already got it planned." The two of them laughed like they had the world in their hands.

Back in the ring, men started lining up. We watched them fight what I swear must have been the shortest matches in history. Levi was knocking most of them out with one punch. The two guys who lasted more than one round ran from him, until they were caught and knocked out.

The next thing I knew, LC had gotten back in the ring. Levi exited and was headed in my direction.

"And now, ladies and gentlemen, Waycross-born Georgia State heavyweight champion Buck Livingston will take on Blackshear's own Willis Brown," LC announced, and the crowd went wild.

Some of the girls were starting to attract customers, so I was happy when Levi came over and sat next to me. Little Momma was nice enough to give him her seat when Sam told her to tell Lou and Larry he wanted to meet.

Larry

32

"LC, I think this might have been the best First Friday we've ever had." Lou sat back in his chair, puffing on one of those big-ass Cuban cigars Sam had given him, with a two-inch thick fistful of money in each hand. While Lou relished in the moment, LC, NeeNee, and our cousin Harold happily counted what was left of the night's take. Meanwhile, me and my sawed-off shotgun sat guard, while Levi and John, the gun-toting night watchman that LC had adopted, stood guard outside the title loan offices.

"I don't think; I know," LC replied proudly.

I had to give it to the kid. My little brother had really done his thing with the gas station, convenience store, and First Friday grand opening.

There was a knock on the door that made everyone, including LC and NeeNee, reach for their firearms. I walked up to the door with my shotgun cocked and ready.

"Who is it?"

"L–L–Levi," my brother stuttered. "B–B–Big S–Sam's here to see L–L–Lou."

I checked my watch then glanced over at Lou. "What the fuck's Sam doing here at this time of night?"

"I don't know, Larry. He probably wants to talk business. You know what kind of hours Sam keeps. Let him in." Lou waved his hand for me to open the door. I reluctantly did what I was told. I didn't like the idea of anyone other than family being in that room with that much cash lying around.

The door opened, and there was Big Sam, grinning like his dick was being sucked. He had his wannabe gangster accountant, Jefferson, with him, and the ever-present twins in the background.

"It's a little crowded in here, Sam, so let's leave the twins out here with Levi and my man John," I said, leaving no question that it was a command and not a request.

He nodded and gave the twins a look. They obviously knew their place, because he didn't have to speak one word for them to understand that they were staying put while Sam came inside Lou's office.

I stepped out of the way, watching Sam enter and check out the place. He froze when his eyes landed on all the money being counted.

"Damn, fellas, y'all doing it big, ain't ya?" Sam and Jefferson took seats in front of Lou's desk. LC and I got up, flanking Lou on either side.

"Compared to you, we just squirrels try'na get a little nut." Lou gave Sam this big, shit-eating grin. I was sure his dumb ass loved the idea of Sam seeing all that money lying around. Knowing him, it probably made his dick hard. "How can we help you brothers?"

"Well, before I left town we talked about partnering, so I wanted to give you the latest."

"Sure, Sam, what's going on?" Lou replied, and for a minute I wondered if Lou was really going to consider his offer.

"I now control all of the whorehouses in South Georgia, which means I control the booze, drugs, and whores in each of those towns. Not to mention the fact that my Florida connect wants me to handle distribution in the Southeast." He paused, looking proud of his announcement, like we were supposed to get up and applaud or something.

"Always making moves, aren't you, Sam?" Lou said happily, feeding right into Sam's arrogant need for praise.

"Brother, you have no idea. And get this: I'm about to go see to Mrs. Walker. She don't know it, but she's about to sell me Old Man Walker's numbers business."

"We gonna make her an offer she can't refuse," Jefferson added, making his hands look like two guns. Lou and I shared a glance.

"Yep, I'm about to become the black Godfather of the South," Big Sam boasted. "And I want the Duncan boys to come along for the ride. With my brains and your muscle, we're going to be unstoppable."

Lou looked like he was trying to swallow something bitter. "Sam, I'm real happy that things are going well for you. I really am. But me and my brothers have decided that the only partners we need are each other. We want this to be a family thing."

The color rose in Sam's cheeks. His blood pressure must have shot up a few points, but he kept a smile frozen on his face. "Lou, you haven't even heard my offer!" He laughed, but believe me when I say it wasn't no real laugh.

LC finally cut in. "It doesn't matter what you offer, Sam. We're not looking for partners. Like you, we're expanding our business too." I was sure he'd been waiting for this moment since Sam walked through the door. What was it about those two?

Sam's smiling face became stern as he intertwined his fingers and cracked his knuckles. He purposely ignored LC, glaring directly at our older brother. "So he speaks for the Duncans now, Lou?"

"Look, Sam, nothing's changed. We're still going to do freelance jobs for you like we've done in the past, but like I just told you, we're not looking for partners."

"Especially not ones that beat up women," LC snapped.

Sam cut his eyes in LC's direction then glared at Lou again. He was probably surprised to find out that his old friend Lou was also an adversary in this discussion.

He turned his attention to me. "You sure I can't change *your* mind?"

"Sorry, Sam," I said, shaking my head.

Sam straightened out his suit jacket then gestured to Jefferson to get up. "Well then, gentlemen, I can't say I'm not disappointed, and I think you're making a big mistake, but I wish you well. I do hope you understand, though, that next time we have this conversation, my offer will be considerably less." Sam cut his eyes at LC as he passed him.

"Hey, Sam," LC called to him just as he was at the door. Damn, this was not going to be pretty; I could feel it in my bones.

Sam turned to him. "Yeah, young buck?"

"If you're headed to see Mrs. Walker anytime soon, there's no need to waste a trip." Sam looked puzzled. "We made a deal with her this morning. She's still going to be a silent partner, but we agreed to take over her husband's numbers business."

Sam exploded, heading directly for Lou. "You motherfucker!" A .38 suddenly appeared in Sam's hand, while Jefferson's punk ass went for his piece. Before he could get it out, I had the shotgun pointed at his head.

"Looks like we have a little Mexican standoff here, Sam," I said.

He pulled back the hammer on his .38. "I don't think so, Larry, 'cause I've got a gun to your brother's head, and to be honest, I don't really give a shit if Jefferson lives or dies."

"Hey, Sam," Lou said. "Relax. This is not personal. It's business. You own damn near all of the hustles in town. What my brothers and I have is a tiny piece compared to you, so there ain't no need for you to be getting upset. We all friends here, remember?"

Sam gave him a look that might as well have been a deadly bullet coming from the gun he was holding. "Fuck you, Lou." Sam flipped him the bird. "You ain't my friend. You knew I wanted that numbers business!"

"Sam, there are four mouths to feed here, and we can't get fed on your crumbs. Do you know how much work and manpower it's going to take to run that numbers business? You're going to need half your staff to run that shit right. Now how you gonna pimp half the state, build a drug empire, and run numbers? Hell, you Superman, but you still only one man."

Believe it or not, Sam looked like he was giving Lou's words some thought.

"Now, it's a compliment to you that I even learned to branch out in business. We're small potatoes compared to you, and we're not trying to be your competition, so c'mon, man. Don't let me trying to get the tiniest piece for myself end our friendship." Lou reached out his hand to shake Sam's.

"I see." Sam's head bobbed up and down as he stared at Lou. "Lou, if you were anyone else, you'd be dead right now. You know that, right?"

"I'm sure there'd be a lot of dead people in this room, Sam." Lou looked over Sam's shoulder at LC, who had a gun trained on him.

"You can have the numbers, but you have any more ideas of expansion without talking to me, and you and your brothers will be dead men," Sam promised before motioning to Jefferson to leave.

"So we still friends?" Lou, ever the optimist, checked with Sam.

"We something, but it certainly ain't friends." Sam backed out of the building with his gun still pointed at Lou. "Oh, and for the record, your free pussy card has been revoked until further notice."

From the look on Lou's face, I think that hurt him more than losing Sam's friendship.

Chippy

33

I'd been home about two weeks, and to my surprise, my mother had still been sweet and kind. I'd almost forgotten all the bad stuff that had happened to me there. It felt so good to be home in my own bed without being harassed, even if I still missed LC, his books, and the way he conducted himself. I started dreaming about him climbing on top of me and making me feel better than I ever had. In my dream, we weren't just fucking like I did with the guys at Big Sam's. No, we made love, and he was mine, and I belonged to him. I heard myself sigh at the pleasure I felt with his hand between my legs.

"Miss me?" he said, but it wasn't him, and I was no longer dreaming. I jerked myself awake to find Willie Anderson, my mother's husband, naked and on top of me.

"Get off of me!" I screamed, trying to shove him off of me. His clammy hand slapped down over my mouth, silencing me.

"I certainly missed you, Charlotte." His lecherous voice assaulted me. To make matters even worse, I could see my mother's silhouette in the doorway.

"Momma! Help me! Please help me, Momma! Please!" I screamed at her.

She moved closer to me, her voice pleading as she slurred, "Honey, when you left, so did Willie. He said that if he couldn't have you, then he didn't want me—and I can't live without him. Please, baby, just do what he wants. We need you in order to be a family."

"This is crazy!" I yelled at her through my tears. "And you're drunk!"

"Please, baby girl," she continued, unmoved by my emotional state. "As long as you're here, Willie's gonna be here.

Now do what he wants so we can all go to bed." She shut the door, leaving me with him.

"You wanna live under my roof, then you gotta pay the toll." He laughed as he shoved his fingers inside of me. I struggled to get away, but he pressed his weight against me. My fighting only turned him on.

"You horny little cock tease. You know you like it," he said, his sour breath in my face. "When you walked in this house it was because you wanted more of this. Your momma knew. That's why she called me." Willie slapped my hands away as he tried to rip off my underwear.

Thrashing around, I tried to throw him off of me, but he was too strong. He balled up a fist and banged me upside the head. This wasn't the first time Willie had hit me, but if I had any say, it would be the last. I may have come home hoping things would work out, but I also came prepared. I reached under my pillow and grabbed the straight razor that I'd taken to sleeping with at Big Sam's. Everything in me swelled into a ball of rage, ready to strike. I gripped it in my hand, flipped it open, and let my arm swing wildly, slicing him everywhere I could reach. At first he didn't know what I was doing, but as the blood oozed out of his wounds, he started to fight me. Even though he was bigger and stronger, my rage made me invincible.

The blood gushing out of him covered me, and before I knew it, we'd fallen to the floor with a loud thud. Willie was still on top of me. Even in the dark I could see the whites of his eyes bugging out in horror. He didn't move. I knew he was gone. My victim days were behind me, and I didn't feel a moment of regret. What I felt was the opposite: calm.

"Momma! Momma!" I yelled as I tried to move his heavy body off of me. He weighed more than two hundred and fifty pounds, and I couldn't get him to budge.

The door flung open and a light came on. My mother was standing there in her nightgown. Seeing her husband lying there dead on top of me, her expression darkened and she went cold. The look that she gave me made me feel as though someone had shot ice into my veins. And then she started screaming.

"What have you done?" She rushed toward me, scooping him up in her arms and trying to shake him awake. It was too late, and I for one wasn't the least bit sorry.

Relieved to be free, I scurried away from him. I watched her gently caressing his face and kissing his lips as she tried to revive him. "Willie, baby, wake up. Wake up, honey. Charlotte, what have you done?"

"I did what I should have done when I was twelve years old and that monster raped me the first time. I killed him!" I cried out. I just wanted her to stop hugging him and, for once in her life, throw her arms around me and be my mother.

"Shut up! Shut up, you whore. My husband was a good man!" she howled, still defending the worthless son of a bitch. "You're going to pay for this. You are going to jail."

"And I will let every person in this entire town know that not only did he rape me since I was twelve years old, but you knew and you never did anything to stop him." As I said the words that I hoped were not true, the look of guilt on her face told me otherwise. She had known all along and did nothing to protect me. "I'm going to tell everyone how you pretended to be asleep at night so that your husband could fuck me!"

Willie's head flopped down, and she rushed at me. Her hands moved a thousand miles a minute, landing on me like lethal weapons.

"You are evil! Evil!" She reared back and whacked me across the face with a blow that almost made me tumble backward. I felt like she had knocked my teeth loose.

My mother grabbed me with a force I didn't see coming. Her arms clasped around my throat as she attempted to choke the life out of me. I started to feel lightheaded, but there was no way I would let her kill me. Not after all I had done to live. So, I wrestled myself out of her grip.

"How could you do this to me? I was a child! Your fucking child!" I shouted, my head buzzing with rage. I slammed her against the wall, taking her head in between my hands. I kept pounding it into the wall. "I would never do that to a child. Never! Never!" I screamed, slamming her head until she went limp and her body slipped from my hands onto the floor in a heap.

I don't know how long I stood there shaking, but I knew something inside of me had died. I felt nothing after what I had done.

Everything felt mechanical, as if I were having an out of body experience. I walked into the kitchen and sat down at the table. I didn't know what to do, but I did know someone who would, so I picked up the phone and dialed zero.

"Operator, I would like a number in Waycross, Georgia. Duncan Brothers Service Station," I asked.

She gave me the number and I dialed it robotically.

"Duncan Brothers, this is NeeNee speaking." Her bubbly voice sounded like it was coming from a television screen.

"NeeNee," I mumbled, not recognizing the sound of my own voice.

"Chippy? What's wrong?" she asked, obviously hearing my terror.

"I need your help. I've done something horrible."

Instead of losing her cool or even hanging up on me, she said, "Okay, stay calm. Where are you?"

LC

34

I pulled off I-95 and followed the signs to Fayetteville at about three in the morning. She didn't look like much, but the old tow truck had made a six-hour trip in less than four and half hours. I'd put the pedal to the metal because when NeeNee came frantically knocking on my hotel room door, she made it sound like Chippy was in a life or death situation. I hoped that wasn't the case, but I also hoped Donna would still be speaking to me when this was all over. I would just have to deal with that when I got home, but for now I concentrated on finding Jones Street.

"Hey, my man!" I waved at a brother wearing an army uniform in a souped-up VW that pulled up next to me at a light. He turned his head and rolled down his window. "You know where Jones Street is?"

"Yeah, 'bout three miles down the road by Food Lion. You can't miss it, but if you pass McDonalds, you went too far." I thanked him, and he took off when the light turned green.

I finally pulled up to the address ten minutes later and studied the house. *So this is where Chippy grew up, huh?* I thought, staring at the modest home as I stepped out of the tow truck. Considering all the abuse she'd suffered in there, it wasn't what I expected. Just goes to show that you never really know what's going on behind closed doors, no matter how normal a place looks on the outside.

I tapped gently on the door, not sure what the heck I'd find.

When she opened the door, Chippy stared up at me. She didn't look like her normal, feisty self. To tell the truth, she didn't look good at all, although she did look relieved to see me. I reached out to hug her, and that's when I saw the blood. It was dried up, but it was everywhere. She was totally covered in it.

Shit. What the fuck has she done?

"You all right?" I asked.

She shook her head as she pulled me inside and shut the door. In spite of the gory mess that covered her, I pulled her in and hugged her tight. "What happened?"

"Come with me." She motioned for me to follow her through the living room and down the hall to a small door off to the side, away from the main rooms. She opened the door, and I had to take a breath to stop from throwing up all over the floor.

"Holy Shit!" I shouted. It looked like a massacre had taken place. An older man lay on the floor, naked and bloody, while an older woman was sprawled across the room, dried blood from her head caked on the hardwood.

"I couldn't let him do that to me again," she mumbled. When our eyes met, the pain in hers jarred me, but it was also mixed with something else—relief? I wasn't sure, but I knew that she wasn't the same person I had met a few months ago on the porch. That was the first time I really thought of why she had wound up turning tricks for Big Sam. She was just too smart. Clearly, she had to be leaving something a whole lot worse to wind up in a place like that—so bad that it had ended in the death of her parents. From the position of the male body and the lack of clothing, the situation pretty much explained itself, but the mother, well, that was a bit harder to figure out.

"I'd do it again," she started before breaking down and crying. "My mother," she said, turning back to the bodies. "I didn't mean to . . ." She seemed to be in a state of shock. "She just pushed me too far."

"Who else knows that you're here?" I asked her.

"Nobody. I got a ride, and my mother wasn't exactly calling people to throw me a party to celebrate my return." Her voice cracked as she finished that thought. "What are we going to do?"

"Let me think for a second." I looked around the room. "Does anybody else live here besides them two?"

"No," she whimpered. "He just showed up. They aren't— weren't big on company." She stepped away from me, turning away from the two dead bodies. "And I'm an only child."

"We got four hours to clean this up," I told her, because we had to get back to Waycross. I couldn't make it look like I'd skipped town. "I just read this thing about DNA and how all the cops are starting to use it to solve cases. Okay, so, first things first: I want you to grab some clothes and go take a shower. Can you do that?" I asked, hoping she could keep it together to help me.

"Yes, I can." Her eyes were brimming with tears of both pain and gratitude. For the first time since arriving, I was glad that it was me who had shown up and not Larry and NeeNee. There was no way he'd be able to deal with this and comfort her. Sure, this was more than I had expected, but I couldn't risk leaving and having anything happen to her.

With her in the shower, I headed out to the truck and grabbed two five-gallon gas cans, being careful not to be seen. I spread the gas from one can throughout the house then moved the two bodies into her mother's room. I poured half the remaining can on their bodies, leaving a trail of gas toward the front door.

"What are you doing?" Chippy asked. I was thankful that she looked more like herself. She wasn't wearing any makeup, but she was dressed, and the blood was washed away.

"Getting rid of evidence. Is there anything in this house you need?"

She shook her head. "No, nothing."

"Then when I light this match, you run like hell out that door to the truck, and don't look back, you hear?"

"Yes. And LC?" She stopped as if she were trying to figure out what to say next.

"Yeah?"

"Thank you. I'll never forget this as long as I live." She leaned over and kissed me. It wasn't the most passionate kiss I'd ever had, but it was by far the most meaningful.

"Neither will I." I struck the match then watched her exit the house. I gave the place a quick once over then threw the match to the floor and sprinted out the door behind her. I didn't look back until I was in the truck, pulling away. The house was smoking, and I could already see the curtains go up in flames. Within minutes, the entire place would be gone.

I glanced over at Chippy, who was facing front, looking straight ahead. I knew I had told her not to, but I don't think I could have resisted a final look back.

"You okay?" I asked.

She sighed deeply, reaching over and taking my hand. "Yeah, I think I'm going to make it."

Chippy

35

About two hours down the road, I was still in another world, but I could see LC was getting sleepy, so I asked him to let me drive. He protested a little bit but finally conceded after we stopped for gas and breakfast somewhere in South Carolina. With his belly full, poor LC fell asleep less than ten minutes after we hit the highway. This gave me some time to think about my next move.

"Damn, we home already?" a groggy LC asked two hours later. He stretched, still slouched over in his seat as he looked out the window.

"Yeah, almost home," I said sadly then turned off McDonald Avenue onto the strip on Oak Street. I pulled up to the curb and sighed, leaning over to kiss his cheek. "Bye."

"Bye? What do you mean, bye?" He sat up straight, staring at me with the same horrified look he had when he saw my mother and Willie. "And what are we doing at Big Sam's?"

"Not *we*," I replied. "Me. I'm going to work." I reached for the door handle, but he grabbed my wrist.

"No," he said sternly. We locked eyes, and he softened his approach. "Please, please don't do this. I didn't drive all the way up to North Carolina to bring you back to this. You're better than this."

"Am I?" I shrugged, feeling lost. "Maybe I am, but where else do I have to go?"

"You can come home with me. Everybody's expecting you."

I think he really believed that could work.

I shook my head. "Please. You got Donna, and we both know that she won't understand this thing between us. Hell, I barely understand it, and you, you don't have a clue."

He gazed at me, his face softening even more. "You're right. I don't have clue."

"Let's see if I can open your eyes." I looked at him, taking in all that he was, all that he'd done. I already had feelings for him. Shit hadn't even gone all the way and he was still the best lover I'd ever had, so I knew it wouldn't take much to love him for the rest of my life. "You once told me you envied the way I looked at Sam. Well, it took me a while, and maybe you can't see, but that's how I look at you now. I love you LC. I'm in love with you." There, I'd said it. I'd admitted it not only to him, but also to myself.

He looked spellbound, almost shocked by my words. I don't think he expected me to say anything like that. "Oh, wow. Shit, I don't know what to say." He rubbed his hand across his head.

"You were supposed to say I love you too. At least that's what I'd hoped."

He swallowed hard, looking embarrassed, and I raised my hand in protest. "It's okay."

"I care about you. I really do, but I'm engaged. I made a commitment. If I let myself go there—"

I placed my finger over his lips. "Shhhh. I don't expect you to feel or understand what I'm going through. I just want you to know that I love you, and I hope one day you'll learn to love me too. It's her time now, but my time is coming, and when that day comes, I hope you come find me. Until then, I have to live my life too." I stepped out of the truck.

"Chippy!" he called out to me as he slid into the driver's seat. I turned to him, but we both knew that there was nothing he could say to make a difference. Still, he tried. "Please don't do this."

"Don't worry about me. I'm used to taking care of myself. You go back to your life and let me go back to mine," I said, trying to keep any emotion out of my voice. Even though I was being tough, I was sure he could hear the vulnerability behind my words. I leaned into the car and kissed him again. God, his lips were so soft. "Bye, LC. Don't you be a stranger."

I stepped back and waited for him to pull away. The solace in this whole mess, if you can call it solace, was that although he didn't say he loved me, he didn't say he loved her either.

Larry

36

"Where is that boy?" NeeNee was pacing around the convenience store like a mother waiting for a child who missed curfew. She must have peeked outside the door a hundred times looking for LC and that damn tow truck. He had called to let us know he was safe and on his way home about three hours ago. Unless he made a detour, he should have been coming through that door any minute. "When he gets here, I'm gonna kill his ass," she said.

"Kill him? Shit, you're the reason he's in trouble in the first place." Lou spoke up from the table where he was playing chess with John. He was trying to act like he didn't care, but we all knew he'd be a lot happier when LC walked through the door. We all would. "I don't know what the hell possessed you to roust that boy out of a hotel room with Donna when he's finally getting some, just to send him up to Fayetteville behind one of Sam's whores. I'm surprised that wench Donna ain't killed you."

"I don't care what you say. Chippy is all right with me. And truth be told, she's a hell of a lot better for him than that stuck-up Donna. She's the kind of woman, like me, who'd lay down her life for him. That's what he deserves."

I'll be damned if I didn't agree with her, but I wasn't gonna say it out loud. LC was an adult, and I was going to take my cue from him. Whatever one he wanted, that was fine with me.

NeeNee continued, "I just hope we can get through the day without Donna popping up."

"Oh, she's been by here a few times, and that girl was hot as fire." I laughed, knowing baby brother was about to have some real shit on his hands with that one.

"Look, here he comes," Lou announced, a delighted smile covering his face as the tow truck pulled up. We all ran to the door. "But I don't see her."

"Where's she at?" NeeNee's loud voice carried as she reached LC getting out of the truck. She threw her arms around him in a hug. "Where's Chippy?" she asked before she leaned inside the cab as if Chippy might be hiding in there.

"Hey, bro." I waved, coming to stand next to them.

"I dropped her off at Sam's." He sounded defeated. Before he even got another word out, I could see how upset he was. "I still don't know what the fuck happened."

"What? Why did you let her do that?" NeeNee yelled at him like it was his fault, without even knowing the facts.

"I tried to talk some sense into her," he explained, but his words were falling on deaf ears.

NeeNee was insistent. "That's a bunch of bullshit and you know it, LC. That girl don't need to be in that place, so I don't know why the fuck you left her there." NeeNee was losing it.

"Look, NeeNee, she's a grown-ass woman, and we got enough trouble with Sam as it is. I wasn't about to just stroll in there and say I want the woman who just walked in the door."

"Nee, give him a break," I told her, wanting her to give him some breathing room.

But like all women would have done, NeeNee continued, "Something must have happened, because that girl did not want to go back to that place, and certainly not to do what she had been doing."

"Nee?" I pulled her away from him. "I said give him a break."

"Fine. But I still want to know what happened, even if I have to march over to Big Sam's myself and get it out of her."

The two of us just shook our heads as we watched her turn around and strut back into the store.

"You all right?" I checked because I could see the dark cloud swirling around him. LC just shrugged his shoulders like he didn't want to talk about it, so I left it alone as we walked back toward the shop.

Lou, Levi, and John were all waiting with big smiles on their faces. NeeNee joined in, but I could see she really wasn't happy about this Chippy shit.

"Happy birthday!" We all yelled to LC, who looked like he had actually forgotten that today was his twenty-first birthday. Levi rushed at him and grabbed him in a bear hug.

"C'mon back here." Lou motioned to LC as everybody followed him out the back door.

"What?" LC asked, not able to hide the impatience in his voice. I could see that he wasn't in the mood for a whole lot of fanfare, but maybe he'd change his mind.

"Patience," I joked, trying to humor him so he'd lighten up.

"Yeah, p–p–patience." Levi spat out the word and looked so pleased with himself that it made LC smile for the first time since he got there.

"Little brother, we all know how much you love cars," Lou started, proud of what was coming next. Ever the "amen corner," NeeNee chimed in.

"You spend so much time in this place. I'm glad Lou bought it and gave us all jobs, 'cause it's the only way we get to see you," she said.

"What?" LC blushed, trying to play it off like he was normal when it came to cars. "It's no secret that I like cars. Lots of people like cars."

"Like?" I gave him an amused look. "Boy, if you could marry a car, you would." As soon as I said the word *marry* I could tell it dropped LC into another place. Nobody told him to ask that girl to marry him. He was too young, and they hadn't even been together that long. Still, I hated to see him like this.

"You all right?" I went over and took hold of NeeNee's shoulder.

"That boy got female trouble for sure." NeeNee, stated the obvious. "Wouldn't be no competition if it was up to me."

"We know how you feel," I said, hoping she'd stop. LC needed to make up his own mind.

"Well, the only way to get over one woman is to get under another—or in some cases, into a new car, which will get you under another one." Lou laughed at his own joke. "And since that's the reason we're all gathered out here." He pointed to a car sitting underneath a cover.

LC glanced from Lou to the car, not sure what it meant.

"'Bout time you had your own set of wheels that doesn't have a tow attached to it." I couldn't help but laugh.

Levi and I lifted the cover off of the cherry red and white 1957 Corvette convertible roadster. The look on LC's face was love at first sight. Hell, that car was so pretty I would marry it.

"You're fucking joking, right? Isn't that the car I was working on last week? Quincy's car?"

"It sure is," I replied. "Once you got it running right, we sent it over to Ralph's to paint it."

LC ran his hand over the hood and down the side of the car. "Oh my God, she's gorgeous. That's got to be the best paint job I've ever seen."

"It should be, for what it cost," Lou boasted, handing him the keys.

"Happy birthday, little bro!" I shouted.

"Thank you! You guys are the best brothers a man could ever have," LC said, finally smiling. "Now, I guess I'll take my new car for a drive and go see if I still have a girlfriend."

Chippy

37

I stood in front of that place for God knows how long before I finally got up the nerve to step onto the porch. Taking a deep breath, I walked over to the door and opened it. While everything had changed for me, I quickly realized that life in Big Sam's place continued to function the same way, no matter if I left or stayed put. The owner and proprietor himself, Big Sam, in all his glory, sat at the head of a large table filled with his loud, obnoxious gambling buddies. They all aspired to be him, which he loved. And then there was that new bitch was standing over his shoulder like she owned the place. I wondered if the other girls had felt about me the way I felt about her now. She was young, stupid, and naïve if she thought she would be Sam's girl for more than a minute.

All the girls were gussied up in their skin-tight dresses, hot pants, and negligees, their feet stuffed into high heels. They were traipsing around so they could flirt with the customers in the bar, trying to get them to buy something other than the watered down drinks. There was a reason Big Sam made a killing on the bar alone.

As much as I wanted to ignore him, I couldn't help but glance in Sam's direction, mainly because I felt his eyes on me from the moment I entered. When we connected, he nodded to me like everything was everything, and all the bad that had gone down had been overdramatized in my imagination. So I moved my head. I guess you could call it a nod in his direction, and then I continued through the room and up the stairs, the adrenaline shooting through me even as I pretended to play it cool.

There were feet following behind me, which I soon discovered belonged to Tasty, because the moment I stepped into my room, there she was with her two cents. At least that was what I thought she was going to do.

"Don't pay attention to them. You all right?" she asked. I wasn't sure if she cared or if she was just looking for gossip to share with the girls so they could make fun of me behind my back.

"Yeah," I answered, not really in the mood to talk to anyone.

"So you back?" She wanted to know, even though I had placed my bag on top of the bed and had begun to unpack the few things I'd obtained, putting them inside the chest of drawers.

"I guess." Since there was no use in lying, I told her, "Truth is, I didn't have nowhere else to go." You best believe I was ready to hear something out of her mouth to make me feel worse, but it didn't come.

"Yeah, neither did I," she admitted.

I found myself starting to feel some sort of camaraderie with her. When I looked up, Fancy, Jasmine, Little Momma, Sandra, and Tasty were all crowded into my room.

"Chippy, you all right?" Sandra asked with a crazy expression on her face, her fist clenched at her face like she was about to do the rope-a-dope. "Don't let that man hurt you."

"She ain't even that pretty!" Little Momma sucked her teeth, trying to make me feel better.

Then Fancy had to have her say, and for someone who didn't always know how to string two words together, she wound up making the most sense of anybody. "Sam can't help being Sam. Just like we can't help being hoes."

That's when Big Shirley entered the room and shooed the bunch of 'em out of my room. "Let me talk to Chippy alone for a second. We'll see you all downstairs." Then she came over to me.

"You okay, baby?" she asked, wrapping her arms around me the way I imagined a mother—certainly not mine, but one who knew how to be a mother—would have responded in this situation. God, it felt good to have somebody holding me. Try as I might to keep up my tough act, I couldn't stop the tears from flowing, my body wracked with sobs as I let go of everything and just wept.

She patted me on the back. "There, there, baby. It's gonna be all right" I looked up at her scarred face and broke down again.

"I'm sorry, Shirley. I know you must hate me, but I'm sorry," I apologized profusely as I fought to regain my composure. All my life I'd kept my promise not to become one of those women like my mother, who let a man take away her common sense and dignity, and here I had become damn near worse than her.

"Don't." Shirley admonished me. "Each and every one of us in this house been standing in the same place you in right now, girl. He done it to each and every one of us." Her voice held a bitterness I hadn't heard in her before. I'd seen her get mad, but not at him, not that way.

"That's cause we all stupid to fall for his lies," I told her, the hurt stinging my throat.

Shirley took me by the shoulders and held me at arms' length so she could look straight into my eyes. "Ain't nothing stupid about falling in love and wanting to believe the man you care about is who he says he is, and not a lying, no-good pimp. That's a hard thing to see, and Big Sam, to his credit, is good at making you feel like you the most important thing in the world—till you're not." She had a sadness about her at that moment. I nodded, but still it didn't make sense.

"If you knew he was doing that to me or to the others, how come you didn't try to talk some sense into us? You been here the longest." I challenged her.

"I did, and this is what I got for it, remember?" She pointed at her face. Big Shirley looked at me, her eyes full of kindness. "Baby girl, nobody ever wants to believe it. I didn't."

Her words still didn't comfort me. "But I'm not them!" I yelled, trying to get her to see that I was different.

When her eyes met mine, they were filled with the most love I'd ever seen from anybody who wasn't trying to shove his dick into one of my holes. "We all loved him at one time or another. Hell, some of us still do." I knew that she didn't say this to hurt me, but to inform me so that I would see we weren't that different. Here I was, a newer, younger model, and not as young as the newest one that had just walked in the door.

"But I'm so sad," I cried, not knowing how I was going to be able to survive this kind of hurt.

"And soon you won't be. This is business, but now instead of handing over all your money, you need to get smart and sock some of it away. One day you'll be able to go off and see the world and do some of those big things you got in your head to do. Don't you let that man kill your dreams, Chippy. Don't become me. Don't you waste your years away. You're something better than the rest of us. We can all see it. That's why some of us hate you so much," Shirley said.

I knew that she meant it, and well, that made me feel hopeful in some way.

"Okay," I whispered, going over to take the last of my things out of the suitcase.

She came behind me. "You a ho now, 'cept you a ho with a plan. Get yourself pretty and let's get you back to work."

"Shirley?" I stopped her before she left. "You deserve better than this too. I hope you have a plan."

Even though she didn't answer, I could see her smiling as she left, and I knew she did have one.

After she was gone, I freshened up and got myself together. This time, instead of worrying about making Sam happy, I was thinking about myself and what would make me happy. That's when I heard a knock on the door.

"So you're back?" Sam walked in the room without waiting for me to invite him in.

I shrugged. "Well, that all depends."

He raised an eyebrow, speaking more definitively. "Depends on what?"

"Depends on how this conversation ends," I said matter-of-factly. "Have a seat."

Sam sat down on the chair next to my bed.

"How's the new girl?"

"She's working out just fine." He sat back in the chair, looking a little annoyed. I knew I had to make my point quickly, before he lost his patience and left.

"But she's not me, is she? She's not bringing in Chippy type of money, is she?"

He folded his arms. "What's the point?"

I leaned forward. "The point is, you never had a ho work these sorry asses like I do." He didn't deny my statement, so I continued. "I'll come back to work for you, but I want thirty percent of what I bring in, and in six months I'm out of here to take what's mine, no strings attached." I leaned back and folded my arms defiantly.

It took him a moment to comprehend what I had said. Then he sat up and laughed at me. "Bitch, are you crazy? Why the hell would I give you thirty percent?"

I was not backing down. I stared boldly in his eyes. "Because I make twice what these other girls make, and if I'm motivated, I can probably make three times what they make. More importantly, seventy percent of what I make is a hell of a lot more than any of these other hoes make."

Sam sat back in his chair. "Chippy, Chippy, Chippy, you was always smarter than the rest. Figure you'll get you a little nest egg then hightail cross country, huh? See the world, fulfill your dreams."

"Something like that. You know what they say: make lemons into lemonade."

"What if I say no?" Sam asked, biting one of his nails.

"Then I'll go see Bobcat over at the lighthouse. I'm sure he'd love for my regulars to start coming there. But for the record, I'd rather not, 'cause I don't want to work in that dump. I want to work here."

"So you got this all planned out, don't you?"

"A friend of mine told me I should be a ho with a plan, and we both know you love money too much to say no," I said.

Sam nodded his head. "Okay, but twenty percent, not thirty, and if you tell any one of these bitches about our agreement, I'll cut your fucking throat. I don't care how much money you make. Oh, and fifty bucks comes off the top each week for your room and board."

"Deal." I stuck out my hand and he shook it.

"One last thing," he said. "Tomorrow I need your ass to take a ride with me. Don't ask me why, but your ass has been requested."

I nodded in agreement, and he left.

When I went downstairs, I walked slowly and methodically, with a big smile on my face. I walked to Sam, nudging past that new bitch to kiss his cheek. A middle-aged guy had just come inside the house and caught my eye.

"Hey there, handsome, you looking to have yourself some fun?" I asked him. I was ready to put my new financial plan into motion, but all I could think about was LC Duncan.

38

I'd driven down to Jekyll Island to see if I could find Donna. The crazy thing about it was that the entire ride, all I could think about was Chippy and the fact that she'd told me she was in love with me. I had to admit to myself there was something there. The question was whether it was love or just some crazy infatuation. My hope was that going to see Donna would make my thoughts of Chippy vanish.

Once I got down to the Washingtons' summer place, Donna was nowhere to be found; however, I did run into her father, who couldn't help but talk shit about me working in a garage, belittling me in front of his tennis buddies. The man was pushing me to the point of whipping his ass, so I got in my car and headed north. There was someone I had to see, someone I could always talk to no matter what, who could put this whole Donna/Chippy thing into the proper perspective.

Five hours later, I called Lou and told him I'd checked into a small hotel in West Virginia and that I wouldn't be back for at least a day.

He surprised me when he said, "I wish you would have told me. I would have loved to take that trip myself."

"I understand," I replied. "It was a last-minute decision, otherwise I would have told you. Next time I'll be sure to let you know."

The next morning, I was standing in front of the prison gates, handing a guard my driver's license so I could get in. A few minutes later, I was in a group of twenty people who were frisked then ushered down several corridors, until we arrived at the visiting room.

I sat there for a good five minutes before a stocky, dark brown–skinned woman in an orange jump suit walked around the corner. She stopped and glared at me. It was clear from her features that she had been very pretty when she was young, but prison life and Father Time had caught up with her. She sat in the chair in front of me.

"Hey, Ma. It's been a long time," I said, swallowing hard and waiting for a response. My mother made it clear that she didn't want us seeing her in this place, but once she understood my reason for coming, I knew she'd lighten up. There were some problems that could only be fixed with a mother's help.

"LC, what are you doing here?" she scolded, but I could tell that she was happy to see me.

"I don't know. I wanted to see you. I missed you, Ma."

She took a breath then looked up at the ceiling. Her eyes were starting to fill up with tears, which caused mine to sting as well, as I fought to hold back tears of my own.

"I missed you too," she said, placing a hand on the glass. I placed mine on the opposite side to match it. I looked at her for a few seconds, just taking in the woman who had birthed me. My mother was in prison because she'd done the unthinkable in the state of Georgia. She'd killed a white man, the same white man who had gunned down my father five minutes before for loaning a poor black sharecropper enough money to pay his bill so that very same white man couldn't take his land.

"Look at you, all handsome and fine. I bet them women can't keep their hands off you." She laughed for a moment but then became serious. "My God, you have become such a man. You taking care of your brothers?"

I nodded and smiled. In all my years on earth, my mother had never asked me about taking care of Lou or Larry or even Levi, for that matter. She'd always told them to take care of me. I guess the tide had changed.

"Okay, boy, enough of the bullshit. Why are you here? Are your brothers all right?"

"Yeah, Ma, everybody's fine. I just needed to talk to you."

"LC, what's wrong?"

I hesitated, not sure what to say or do. I'd come there for a reason, and now it seemed ridiculous. Here she was locked up behind bars, and I had come to bother her over some bullshit woman troubles.

"Well, spit it out, boy. What's wrong?" she asked sternly.

"I think I'm in love with two women." I was suddenly feeling sick now that I'd admitted it out loud.

"Oh, that's all? I thought you were going to tell me something really bad. In love with two women, huh? That's an interesting turn of events. How'd this happen?" she prodded me to continue. I could tell she was holding back laughter. Had I been Lou, or even Larry, she would have been teasing me about the mess I was in, but she knew I was the serious one and wouldn't take kindly to being made fun of. I had never treated women the way my brothers did, so this was a serious situation to me.

"I wrote you about Donna," I reminded her.

"Yeah, Doctor Washington's daughter, the one who goes to school with you."

"Yes, that's right. Well, the other woman I met at Big Sam's," I told her and inwardly groaned, waiting for all hell to break loose. When my mother nodded as if she understood, I was surprised by her reaction. Her face was neutral; she didn't look surprised or amused or anything.

"Chippy—that's her nickname, but her real name is Charlotte. She's from North Carolina, and she's different. She's strong and a real reader, but she left a bad home situation and wound up working for Sam. But she doesn't belong there." My voice rose with emotion at the thought of her in that house again.

"Keep your voice down, son," she said, looking around to see if I had drawn the guard's attention. Then she continued, suggesting, "Maybe it's just the sex. You wouldn't be the first man whose head got turned around by it."

I shook my head. "It's not that. We haven't had sex yet. Chippy tells me how she feels and what is going on. I never have to guess or wonder if she's playing games. And we just have this connection that makes me feel so much better when I'm with her," I explained.

"And Donna?" my mother questioned. Suddenly I felt guilty for making it seem like Donna wasn't a good person.

"She's great. I care a lot about her, but Donna's had everything handed to her, and she doesn't always appreciate things, where Chippy and I have both been through hard times and could get through more if we needed to. It's like we speak the same language. If Chippy had the opportunities that Donna did, she would never be doing what she's doing."

Explaining things to my mother was definitely helping me put my thoughts in order. It was the first time I was really thinking deeply about the differences between the two women, and speaking them out loud made me realize just how much I cared about Chippy.

"I don't know," I continued, "I guess I just feel like Chippy would be there for me no matter what, and with Donna I'd have to be a certain way and make choices I might not really want to make in order to keep her."

My mother thought for a long time before she responded, "LC, ever since you were little, you've always been the one to make the right choices and to do the right thing. That might mean something different in this case. The right choice here means following your heart. It will never steer you wrong."

"But what if that means breaking Donna's heart?" I asked, admitting to myself for the first time who I truly wanted to be with.

"Girls like Donna are always going to be okay. You don't have to worry about her. Heck, I'm way more worried about you showing up here on your birthday." She smiled at me and reached up to touch my face.

"Momma, I've missed you so much," I told her, and suddenly I was overwhelmed by the realization that even though she was trapped in here, she had always been a good mother to me. If Chippy had someone like her, she would be all right, and I wanted to be that person. My mother may not have been able to be with me, but the one thing I never doubted was her love for my brothers and me. Chippy deserved to have someone who she knew loved her no matter what.

"LC, I want you to be happy."

I took a deep breath and relaxed, my mind finally made up. "I want that too."

Chippy

39

"Sam, this is so nice." Crystal, the new girl, who I seriously doubted could be over eighteen, started rubbing on his arm like it was some goddamn genie in a bottle ready to grant her wish. Poor thing had learned the hard way to stay off my bad side after the ass-kicking I gave her. I did feel sorry for her, though. It wasn't her fault she had been bamboozled by Sam. Just like I once had, she believed he walked on water and would one day sweep her off her feet into wedded bliss. I still couldn't believe I'd just graduated from that place myself. She'd learn the truth soon enough, and then I'd have to console her, same as others had done for me.

"I ain't never been to these parts," she kept on. Boy, did I want her to shut her mouth with that 'bama accent.

"You do good today and I'll take you to a whole lot of places," Big Sam lied, not even bothering to change up his lines with me sitting in the back seat. She was up front, in the seat where I'd once been riding. From what Shirley explained, Sam always took the new girl on his mysterious road trips. It was probably because it was easier to turn them out that way, which made me wonder why he'd brought me along this time.

"I just love the feel of the air on my face. I ain't never been in a Cadillac before, except yours," she kept gushing.

"Nah, and neither had Chippy 'fore I rescued her neither," he boasted like he had actually saved me from something instead of taking me out of the frying pan and into the fire, having me sell the pussy I used to barter for food and necessities. He certainly was in the best mood I'd ever seen him in, which made me grow slightly curious about our destination.

I'd never say it out loud, but it did feel good to be out in the fresh air, even if I had to tie my headscarf down tighter so the wind didn't wreck my curls. All Big Sam had told me was that I was requested and to look real nice. He even promised us a good meal and a shopping trip if we made him proud.

"Wow!" Crystal swooned, which caused me to look up from my book and see that we had entered the main drag of Jacksonville. I shoved my head back in my book, desperately trying to finish the last couple of pages of the chapter before we got to wherever we were going. The car stopped, but I kept on reading, wanting to get to the end.

"We're here!" Sam announced excitedly, but instead of jumping up and taking Crystal's lead, I kept pushing to get to the end of the chapter. They were about to reveal the benefactor of the heroine, and I really hoped it was the man she loved and not the one that only saw her as a prize.

"This is pretty!" Crystal's voice rang out in the background as the car doors opened and closed, leaving me alone in the car.

"Chippy!" I heard Big Sam bark impatiently, but I couldn't pull myself away from the drama in my book even if I wanted to—which I didn't.

"I'm coming," I lied, hoping to buy myself a few minutes. That's when the door flew open. Next thing I knew, he had snatched the book out of my hand and held it out of my reach.

"You might be getting a cut, but you still work for me. Now get your ass out the car."

"I said I was coming!" I snarled at him, more upset about him taking my reading material away than anything.

Rrrrrrriiiiip! He tore my book in two then threw both parts onto the ground and gave me a look, daring me to pick them up. Ignoring his implied threat, I leapt out of the car, intent on rescuing my book, but his big hands stopped me.

"You really wanna go there? You are here for one reason and one reason only, and that is to work. You lucky I let you read that book in the car, but don't push your luck," Sam hissed, checking his watch. "Now let's go. That Spanish motherfucker hates when I'm late."

"We going to see Mr. Alejandro?" I asked excitedly.

"Damn right, and whatever you did last time, I want you to do it again, because he requested you special. I ain't never seen him do that before."

I straightened up and followed the two of them into the Marriott, trying to forget about my book. I guess if I had to go see a trick, Alejandro was the one to see. He'd given me a $300 tip last time, although I'd given it all to Sam. This time I wouldn't be so stupid.

"Alejandro, my main man," Sam shouted when Alejandro answered the door to his suite.

"Are these two for me?" Alejandro asked, motioning to me and Crystal, who was looking a little too damn happy. I guess when you're forced to fuck poor men with dirt under their nails who haven't had a proper bath in their lifetime, a man who cleans up this well is a real prize.

"That's right. I brought you some fresh new pussy, just the way you like it. You can have one or both," Sam generously offered. He pushed Crystal out front and center, and Alejandro eyed her from head to toe.

"I'll take her," Alejandro said in a firm voice. Crystal was already looking past him into the open bedroom when he pointed to me. I guess he knew exactly what he wanted. And why shouldn't he want me? After all, I was good at my job. I hid a smirk.

"The other one you can bring down to the other room so my men can fuck her. There are only about nine or ten of them. She should be fine." Crystal quickly turned in Sam's direction, looking confused and concerned. Before she could speak, Sam silenced her with a glare that warned, *Don't say a word, bitch.*

"Now while you and your men play, I'd like to pick up my shit, if you know what I mean." Sam laughed, but I could hear the tinge of aggression in his voice that meant he was really serious.

"Very well, Sam." Alejandro tossed him a set of keys. "Take a look in the trunk of the Cadillac El Dorado downstairs. I think you'll find what you're looking for. Oh, and Sam, this is the biggest order you've ever taken from us. My employers expect payment in five days promptly."

"Don't worry, my man. I got you." Sam gave Alejandro a big smile as he led Crystal out of the room.

Instead of reaching for me like I was used to customers doing, Alejandro walked toward the bar and opened up a bottle of Cognac. He poured two glasses, locking his eyes on mine as he approached and handed me a glass. He held out his glass to make a toast. I liked that. I took a nice, long sip of the expensive liquor. It went down smooth, not like that corn liquor Sam sold.

"Thank you," I told him as I set down the glass and began to undress. To my surprise, he stopped me.

He patted the seat next to him. "Come sit. There is plenty of time for that. First we must decide what we should have for lunch. I'm thinking maybe lobster, or perhaps surf and turf."

I settled in next to him and smiled. "Surf and turf would be nice."

"No!" he yelled a little too forcefully. "When I leave Waycross, that car's coming with me."

He must have seen how surprised I was by the strength of his reaction to my simple suggestion, because he tried to clean it up by explaining calmly, "It's very sentimental to me."

Now, I was the first person to understand having an attachment to a car, but a piece of junk like his car didn't seem like anything a person would feel so strongly about. Still, there was no doubt that he was frustrated, so I apologized once again. "I know, and I'm sorry, I'm doing the best I can." I said then nearly lost it myself when I noticed a car parked over near the side of the building. "When'd that car get here?"

"I don't know." He shrugged. "Maybe half an hour ago. The guy's in the back, talking to your brothers."

The car, a 300D Mercedes-Benz, belonged to Donna's father. I closed my eyes and took a deep breath. *Here we go again,* I thought, certain Dr. Washington had come to put me in my place one more time. There wasn't much more of this I could take. I wasn't going to keep allowing him to treat me like some child he could order around or threaten to stay away from his daughter.

I went around back to see if he was bothering Lou, which would not be smart.

As I entered the title loan office, the first thing I saw was Donna's father, but he wasn't puffed up and blowing hot air around as he usually did. Actually, he reminded me of a balloon someone had deflated. Lou and Larry were sitting there with big smiles on their faces when I walked in.

"Well, speak of the devil. LC, come on in here and join us. We're having a little sit down with Dr. Washington. You two know each other, don't you?" Lou said with a sly smile on his face.

"Sure they do. LC here's going to marry his daughter Donna. Ain't that right, LC?" Larry's tone was louder and even more sarcastic than normal.

I turned to see Donna's father's response as I took a seat. That's when I realized he didn't look deflated. This man was distraught. I wondered if there was something wrong with his wife or Donna.

40

I spent two days in West Virginia then headed back to Waycross, arriving at the shop just as John and Harold were closing. I sat there for a while in my new car with the top down, looking at my shop and realizing just how blessed I was. The crazy part was, I didn't just see the shop. I saw the beginning of an empire.

Tap, tap, tap

I looked to my left, and there was John. "Any word on the part?" he asked.

"The guy promised me I'd have it by the end of the week, so hopefully Friday afternoon." I felt bad for John, although I think he was starting to like Waycross. The part I had ordered had come in almost a week ago, but unfortunately for John, they had sent me the wrong part and had to reship it, which meant another seven to ten days.

"Look, LC, I like you, but that is totally unacceptable. I need to get New Jersey, and I needed to be there two fucking weeks ago," he said angrily. It seemed like his reaction was getting more volatile each day. I understood that it was a long time for someone to have to wait around to get his car fixed, but he had been pretty over the top as of late. One minute he'd be fine, helping out around the place, and then it was like he'd remember that he was supposed to be somewhere else, and he'd started yelling and sweating, pacing around like a maniac. I swear, a few times I was worried that he was going to have a heart attack.

"John, I'm sorry, man. If you need to get to New Jersey, I'll drive you myself, and then Lou can bring your car to you on his next run to New York."

"You all right, Dr. Washington?" I questioned, growing worried by this current situation. "What's wrong?"

He shook his head and refused to meet my eyes. "Nothing," he grumbled under his breath, glaring over at Lou. "Can we conclude our business? I have somewhere to be."

"Sure, sure." Lou, ever the host, explained, "Donna's father is our new customer. He just came in to get a title loan. Only we're not comfortable loaning out the amount he's looking for, so we're buying his car."

My head spun around from Lou to Dr. Washington, who was still looking away from me.

"That doesn't make sense," I insisted, until I caught Larry's raised eyebrow, which told me everything I needed to know. He always accused me of giving people's character more credit than they deserved. "They're all capable of the same shit," was his favorite comeback.

Lou continued to needle Dr. Washington mercilessly. "Seems your future father-in-law has run into a little cash flow problem." He smiled like the cat that ate the canary before delivering his next line. "I'll look real good in that Benz. Fuck, I'm a fan of the Germans, making a car like that."

"Why are you selling your car?" I asked, needing to hear some kind of answer that made sense.

Dr. Washington's head swiveled in my direction, and he looked me straight in the eye, his rage boiling over. "Look, you little punk, this is none of your fucking business!"

Lou stood up. "Tsk, tsk, tsk." He was staring down at Donna's father.

"Can I get my money now? I got a plane to catch." He spoke to Lou in a shaky voice, devoid of the nasty tone he had just used with me.

Lou looked ready to laugh when he answered. "You can't get shit from me. Not until you apologize to my brother. Who the fuck do you think you are?"

"It's fine, Lou!" I blurted out. It was obvious the man was having a hard time. His words didn't matter to me right now.

"The fuck it is. He came to us to borrow money; we didn't come to him." He glared over at Dr. Washington.

"Okay, I'm sorry. I apologize for speaking to you in a less than respectful way, LC." Dr. Washington rushed his words, his foot tapping the floor nervously.

Lou motioned to Larry, who began to count out the money for him. Dr. Washington couldn't get up and get it in his hands quick enough. He didn't even bother to confirm the amount before he was out the door.

I turned to Lou for answers. "What the hell was that about?"

"Well, it seems the good doctor is about to go on the run. The feds raided his office and his house this morning and placed liens on all his property and accounts. Hell, the only thing they didn't put liens on were his car, his wife's car, and his daughter's car—and now they belong to us." Lou laughed hard.

I was shocked and bewildered. I couldn't imagine the uptight, seemingly perfect doctor breaking so much as a minor traffic law. "What did he do?"

"Medicaid fraud," Larry replied. "That son of a bitch has been bilking the government for years to the tune of almost a million bucks. I told you, just because somebody has a fancy degree don't make them any less criminal."

"The feds plan on locking his ass up for a long time; that is, if they catch him," Lou added.

"Wait, so he's broke? Like, totally broke?" I grilled him, still feeling like this was some kind of bad dream and it couldn't be real.

"Broke as a joke, except for that money we just gave him."

"You need to go check on your girl. I'm sure she's just about fucked up right now." Larry motioned to the door, and as much as I wanted answers, I knew he was right. I had to go check on Donna.

Lou

41

"Man, you try'na tell me you gonna loan me five hundred dollars but then I have to give you six fifty back?" Pookie Blake, a one-time Waycross High all-star basketball player, shouted as he threw his hands in the air for emphasis. "Man, that shit sounds insane."

Larry shot me a look to see if he should step in, but I gave him the slightest head motion, letting him know he could chill.

I gave Pookie a cold, hard stare. "Yeah, this is a title loan business, just in case you don't understand the shit."

"Yeah, but it's like you stealing from me!" he announced, clutching the title to his four-year-old, bright blue Dodge Challenger.

"Then don't take the money. Matter of fact, you can go on into town and hit up Dr. Petrie, the bank manager, as long as you have some collateral—like a house or a *job*." I emphasized the last word to remind him that his lazy ass didn't seem to be in any rush to locate employment. I wouldn't risk loaning unsecured money to a guy like him even if we were related.

"C'mon, the bank wouldn't be try'na fleece me like this, Lou." He was whining like a little bitch, but I knew it was only a matter of time before he caved. Wasn't like anybody with his spotty work record had options. A business like ours was the last house on the block for people like Pookie, and we both knew it.

"Banks have plenty of insurance," I explained, "but all I have is the word of my customers, and that's a sure way to go broke."

"A'ight, what if you charge me fifty dollars and I promise to pay you back in a month?" he begged. He must have thought my ass was as stupid as he was, 'cause only a fool would take that offer from him.

"Look, you could be out of here with a pocket full of cash in five minutes, but my terms are non-negotiable." I wanted him to understand that I was serious about this business. I would never bend on my terms. This new hustle was a legit way for the Duncans to make some real money without the threat of the big house. A brother was starting to really appreciate the investment in this gas station. Smartest damn thing we'd ever done.

"So that's it?" he asked, not able to stop himself from trying to work me, like his little hurt feelings were somehow going to influence me.

"Look, you came to me for a loan. It wasn't the other way around. Take it or leave it," I snapped at him, because frankly, he had exhausted my patience with this bullshit.

"Fine." He finally relented and handed me his title.

"Take this title and go on over to that office, and the lady will take it from you and have you fill out the paperwork."

"And the money?" He held out his greedy little hand, already starting to itch for the promised cash.

"You'll get that from me," Larry informed him.

Pookie was ready to leave, but I had one final thing to say. "And, brother? You don't pay me back in sixty days, then on day sixty-one I own your ride."

"You don't have to worry about me," he promised dramatically, like his word was something I'd ever believe. "I'll be back with your money, 'cause I love that car more than I love my wife or kids," he swore before stepping into the office where NeeNee was waiting.

Larry shook his head. "Negroes!" he exclaimed, sending us both doubled over in a fit of laughter. It didn't matter that all the rules and regulations were printed out and hung on the wall. People were always asking for something extra, like a discount or more time. Every last customer we'd had since opening had tried the exact same lines and had been shot down just like big, dumb Pookie.

The ringing phone stopped our laugher. I turned to pick up the receiver.

"Duncan Brothers Title Loan," I answered and was met by silence on the line. "Hello?"

"Lou." I recognized the voice right away, although Sam didn't quite sound like himself. We hadn't spoken since the night of the grand opening, when he had a gun to my head. I didn't have to be a rocket scientist to know that he wasn't happy about our taking over Waycross's numbers racket or snubbing his offer for partnership.

"Sam? What's happening, man?" I asked, trying to keep my tone neutral, even though I was suspicious about the reason for his call. Sam Bradford was one of the most conniving people I knew, so I wasn't taking anything at face value. "You ain't looking for a title loan now, are you?" I joked. I tried to imagine Big Sam's flashy ass having to come to me for a loan, begging like all my other customers.

"Funny," he answered bitterly and then changed his tone. "Lou, if we were ever friends, I need you, man. I need you and Larry."

"Sam, you know we're trying to do our own thing right now," I reminded him. As much as I enjoyed the extra money we picked up from hustling for Sam, I realized that LC was right. We needed to separate from him and make our own money.

"Come on, man. This is serious!" His brash voice was ripe with impatience. "My life's on the line. I got these two cats after me that I need you to handle."

"Sam, I'm sor—"

He cut me off. "Look, I know we haven't seen things eye-to-eye lately, but I'm begging you, man. These dudes mean to kill me." I could hear desperation in his voice, and although Sam had been known to be full of shit, something told me this was genuine. "How about I give you your free pussy card back?" he offered.

He had my attention. It would be nice to get access to all that pussy again. "How much you paying?" I asked.

"Ten grand if you get them tonight. Another five if you bring them to me alive."

"Fifteen grand! You serious?" This price wasn't just double, it was damn near triple the going rate, which meant he was more than desperate. To pay that kind of cash, this must have been important. "Hip me to the situation."

"There are two guys up here from D.C. aiming to make sure your man Sam isn't above ground for long. One is the brother of that new Puerto Rican girl from Valdosta I got working for me. The other is her cousin. Guess she couldn't wait to call home and tell her family she was in love. Ain't that a bitch?" It sure as hell was. Any time one of those girls thought Sam loved her, she found out soon enough that the only thing Sam's ass loved was money. It looked like this time Sam was the one who might be learning a lesson, though, if we didn't help him out.

"You got anything else on them?" I asked.

"She's supposed to meet them at that roadside diner on Route 38 at seven o'clock. They two big, well-dressed, high yella brothers that could almost pass."

Their meeting was less than two hours from now. I glanced over at Larry, who had heard enough to understand the situation without me having to explain it. Truthfully, he probably didn't care about the details. I had no doubt that he had decided he was in as soon as he heard me mention the $15,000 payout. Larry nodded his head.

"We'll take care of it," I told Sam. "But I want the money up front." I knew that if Sam agreed to give us the money up front, then he wasn't playing a game, and he was desperate as fuck.

"Sure, sure, Lou, you can send someone over to get the ten grand right now. And I'll give you the other five on delivery."

"Okay, Harold will be over there in fifteen minutes." I was about to hang up the phone when he made another request.

"I want them alive—to prove a point to the girls."

"Whatever you say, Sam," I said before hanging up. Shit, delivering them alive meant I didn't have to do the work of disposing of any bodies. For the kind of money he was paying, I'd be happy to do less work.

"That what I think it is?" Larry was already at my side by the time I lowered the phone to its base.

"Yeah. Come on. We don't have a lot of time, so we need to get moving," I said as I began to put on my shoulder holster and slip my gun in.

Larry laughed, snatching up his sawed-off. "Translation: Let's get outta here and make that fifteen grand before LC gets back and talks us out of it."

I patted him on the back. "Exactly."

LC

42

"Who's that in the cab?" NeeNee, always the busy body with one eye looking out the window, commented on the taxi stopping outside the front door of the station.

Larry stood close by, peering out over her shoulder. I'd just come out front from the garage to grab a bite from the makeshift café that NeeNee had set up in a corner of the room, before getting back under the hood of a Ford I was fixing.

"Humph! Nobody I want to see," Larry snipped and walked over to where Lou and John were engaged in a heated game of chess. It looked like he was trying to get away from the door.

NeeNee leaned forward to get a better look at whoever was outside. "It's certainly taking them long enough."

"That's where you gonna move?" Lou laughed confidently.

John leaned back in his chair, looking unfazed. "I don't know how long you've been playing this game, but I've been playing too long to let you fool me. Checkmate in two."

"LC?" The door opened and Donna sashayed in, a little too overdressed to be visiting a gas station. I hadn't seen her in more than a week. I'd gone to her house after her dad skipped town, even rode down to Jekyll Island again to see if she was there, but she and her mother had gone missing in action. Larry and Lou had me convinced that she was probably somewhere with her old man.

"I need you to pay this cab driver," she said casually, as if the past few weeks had never happened. "I swear he was trying to get over on me, so I told him that my fiancé would be out to handle it." She batted her eyelashes at me in that way that used to send my heart thumping into overdrive.

"Sure," I answered awkwardly and hurried out to settle up with the driver.

"This color is too drab. I can't imagine that it would make anyone want to spend their money here." I heard Donna as I returned to the shop. "I read an article that certain colors make people more relaxed and willing to spend—like blue. And what's this?" she said to no one in particular as she reached for one of the sandwiches wrapped in twine on top of NeeNee's counter, where she displayed her food.

Speaking of NeeNee, she snapped back at Donna, "What does it look like?"

"That's why I asked," Donna huffed. "I mean, do people even buy this stuff?"

"Of course they do. We sell out every day," NeeNee answered, her voice filled to overflowing with pride—and why not? Her food helped to make this place a destination for more than gas and car repairs.

"Well, I guess if people are hungry they will eat anything," Donna shot back, being plain ole mean.

"Donna!" I raised my voice to stop her reign of terror, but also because I was afraid that NeeNee would kick her ass for insulting her food.

Lou burst out laughing at the scene taking place with me in the middle of it. I knew I had to get Donna out of there before she said or did something else that I would never live down with my brothers. They loved to tease me over Donna's prissy ways.

Unfortunately, Donna wasn't done. "This place needs somebody with class to bring it up a notch. Now, once we change the color and add some curtains, that will help, but it's still just a start."

"You got a lot of opinions for someone who ain't never really been up in here and don't get a vote," NeeNee snapped at Donna. She was staring at her like she'd lost her mind.

Donna put her hand on her hip and stared right back at NeeNee. "Last I checked, this was LC's shop, and his name is the one on the bill of sale, so since I'm going to be his wife, I do get a vote," Donna bragged, attempting to put NeeNee in her place.

"Larry, we need to get out of here before I'm facing homicide charges," NeeNee announced, gathering her things. "Somebody handle the food."

"I got it," John volunteered.

When the door slammed shut after Larry and NeeNee, I turned to Donna, who was checking out the place with a real intensity. It didn't make any sense to me, especially since she had told me in no uncertain terms how much she hated this place. I found that I had little patience for this brand new attitude of hers, and I didn't feel like holding back.

"What exactly is this about? Since I got this place you haven't given a damn, and now you wanna make all kinds of changes?" I said.

"Look," she said, not dialing down the attitude one bit. "No husband of mine is going to be running a second rate business. I've had time to do some soul searching, and if this place is important to you, then it's important to me too."

"Is that so?" I asked, more than a little skeptical because I couldn't believe the one-eighty she had just done.

"LC, if this place has the potential to make us money to support our family, then we need to make sure it can make as much as possible."

I grabbed her arm and led her outside, embarrassed that both Lou and John were listening to her come in there like a boss, showing a sudden interest only because of the financial gain.

"Is this about your father?" I asked when we were outside. I knew that Donna had just been through a lot, and I wanted to be supportive, but her attitude was challenging.

"No. Look, what Daddy is going through is temporary. He's gone off to figure out who set him up and made him look like a criminal, but he will be back and everything will return to normal. It may take a little time, but Daddy always comes through," she said, sounding absolutely convinced of her father's innocence. It was a shame the local authorities didn't feel the same way.

I attempted to reason with her. "Donna, I saw your father, and I'm telling you that he went on the run. He's not coming back."

She gave me a look like I was the crazy one. "Sure he is, and he's going to walk me down the aisle. LC, I know my daddy, and he would never do that to me."

"Donna?" I tried to figure out how to talk some sense into her.

She dismissed my concern with a wave of her hand. "We have more important things to think about. How much money do you have toward our wedding? I'm thinking two weeks from Saturday will be a good date. Does that work for you?"

Big Shirley

43

"Sh–Sh–Shirley, you are beautif–f–ful! And you-you g–g–got g–g–g–good pu–pu–pussy t–too." Levi handed me the daffodil he'd just picked from a patch of grass. He was walking me back to Big Sam's after we'd spent the day together at the Duncan farm, half of it in bed and the other half on a picnic by the creek that ran through their property. What most people didn't understand about Levi was that while he was slow with some things, he wasn't no joke with the things that he knew. Not to mention, he was very sweet.

I hated that the wonderful day I'd spent with him was coming to an end, but Sam made it clear that he wanted me back for the Saturday night crowd, despite the fact that I'd already made my quota.

"Levi, you are the nicest man I ever met," I told him when we approached Big Sam's and the end of our time together. I meant it, too.

"Ca–ca–can I see y–you again W–W–Wednesd–d–day?" He stuttered out his request, which I never thought would sound so good to my ears.

The crazy thing was that I liked being with him so much that I hated to charge him for our time together. Anybody who made me feel as good as he did should have gotten the goods for free. It wasn't just that he was sweet and constantly complimenting me, either. He was pretty damn good in the sack, and he took direction real well too.

"I'd really like that, Levi."

His face lit up with real joy. I raised my hand to his face and stroked it lovingly. He did the same, running his fingers down my scar. I gasped, feeling embarrassed. For the first time that day, I'd remembered all the scars on what used to be my pride and joy.

"Y–y–you are s–s–sooo pr–pr–pretty."

"Well, I don't feel that way anymore—'cept when I'm with you," I admitted, turning away so that he didn't see how true that statement really was. Instead of responding, he pulled me into a hug, running his hand soothingly along my back. I almost wanted to cry because it felt so good to have someone genuinely care about me.

Finally remembering Big Sam, I pulled away. "I better go in here so I'm not late." I planted a long, deep kiss on his lips. Normally I would never allow a man to kiss me on the lips, but with him I made an exception. I patted his ass affectionately then bounded up the stairs, thinking about the fact that if anyone had told me I'd fall for a guy like him, I would have called them a bald-faced liar. I'd always gone for the flashy, Super Fly types like Sam and Lou, who made me feel like I was lucky just to be with them. They made me feel worthless.

"B–b–bye, Sh–Sh–Shirley," Levi shouted after me as I stepped through the front entrance.

Of course, all the girls perked up hopefully when the door opened, but once they realized it was me and not a paying customer, they deflated and went back to talking shit and joking with each other. Sam had scared the crap out of us to the point that no one was able to relax, for fear that he'd accuse of us of intentionally trying not to make him money. I kept moving to Sam's office so he wouldn't berate me for being late. I pulled the money Levi had paid me out of my pocket and knocked on Sam's door, knowing that the only thing that made him remotely happy these days was cold, hard cash.

I heard Sam grunt something from the other side of the door, so I pushed it open. When I walked in, I found Sam sitting at his desk, holding the head of some bitch that was on her knees, sucking the hell out of his dick. Sam had his head thrown back in rapture and his ass six inches off the seat, with his eyes rolled back in his head.

"Oooooh, shit, baby. That's it. Don't stop. Don't stop. You about to make me cum!"

Now, I'd seen Sam get his dick sucked more times than I want to remember, but I'd never seen anyone turn him out like that. He was jumping around like a bucking bronco.

"Fuuuuck! Can't nobody suck a dick like you!" he shouted before collapsing in his chair. He was so spent that I don't think he even realized I was in the room, and neither did his companion, until Sam released his head. I could barely breathe when I realized who the giver of his tongue bath had been.

"Jefferson?" My insides shook when I saw the accountant's guilty face pop above the desk, staring back at me. What the hell! You know the phrase "Don't believe your lying eyes"? Well, that's exactly how I felt.

"Oh, crap!" Jefferson blurted out, shaking Sam back into the real world. "I thought you said you locked the door."

"I did. . . . Oh, fuck!" Sam's eyes opened, and it didn't take long for his satisfied expression to disappear, replaced with a grim frown.

"Uh, sorry. I didn't mean to interrupt." I stumbled backward out of the room in a state of total shock. The last thing I wanted was to be standing there with that image in my head. Hell, I still couldn't believe what I'd just seen.

"Shit, Shirley, what the fuck are you doing in here?" Sam called after me, sounding worried—which he should have been after what I'd seen. Now on his feet, Sam came toward me as he zipped his pants, but by now I had crossed the threshold and was moving fast.

"Get your ass back in here!"

I started heading for the front door, but I could hear Sam behind me. All of a sudden, someone grabbed me by the shoulders, and the next thing I knew, I felt a fist come down on the side of my head. "Noooooo!" I cried out as I went down, landing on the floor.

"Don't you fuckin' open your mouth! Do you hear me?" Sam bellowed. I looked up at Sam as he began to kick me, his boots landing deep in my side. "Keep your fucking mouth shut."

"I will! I will, Sam. You ain't got to worry about me," I swore, but he just kept kicking me. "Help me! Please, somebody help me!" I hollered, trying to avoid Sam's fists as they rained down on me.

"Ain't nobody going to help you. This is my fucking world. Bitch, you think you special or something? I ought to kill you dead right now! And I will if you don't keep your mouth shut." The way he was beating the shit out of me, I thought that he would make good on his words and end my life right there.

I might have lost consciousness for a minute, and the next thing I knew, Levi was holding Sam up by his neck, dangling his feet off the floor. Levi hit him one time, and he went flying across the room.

"Levi!" I breathed, relieved to see this man coming to my rescue. All I wanted was to get out and go anywhere but there. I rolled over, grabbed the wall, and then I raised myself up in time to see two of Sam's henchmen swinging baseball bats at Levi's body.

"Make that motherfucker pay! Bitch, you will learn about putting your hands on me." Sam ordered them, like the no good dogs they were, to do his dirty work. These guys were always a step or two away, ready to punish whoever had wronged their boss.

I ran toward them, trying to grab one of the bats, only to have it come down on me. Seeing me get hit must have given Levi strength, because all of a sudden he let out a roar.

"Sh–Shirley!" Levi threw both men at least six feet away then began beating them with his fists. He had this almost barbaric look on his face as they fell to the ground. He turned and headed toward Sam.

Unfortunately, he'd barely gotten his hands on Sam before the twins came out of the crowd, picking up the bats. Levi was a bad-ass man, but even he couldn't stand up to the twins swinging bats, so it didn't take long for him to fall to the ground.

"Move out the way!" Sam hollered at them, pointing a gun at Levi. "I'm gonna kill this son of a bitch."

John

44

I picked up my shot of tequila and downed it. The alcohol hitting the back of my throat had a mind-numbing effect on me, and I certainly needed it, considering the fact that I was still stuck in Waycross worrying about my family, not knowing what type of danger they were in. I glanced around the bar to distract me from my thoughts. Everywhere I looked, beautiful, half-naked black women of every shade were prancing around in stilettos. It almost reminded me of Tijuana, Mexico. The two sexy women seated on either side of me were certainly reminding me of how lucky I was to be a man.

"Another round!" I told the bartender, who poured three more shots and slid them in front of us.

"I like this!" I said as we clinked glasses and downed the dark liquor. Lou Duncan had suggested I come here after I'd punched my hand through a sheet rock wall.

"You ready to go upstairs?" the one who told me her name was Little Momma whispered in my ear.

Not to be outdone, Destiny, the one who looked to be a mixture of black and white, slipped her hand into mine as we got to our feet. They stood on either side of me as we moved to the staircase and headed up. These two women had made me a world of promises, and I wanted nothing more than for them to prove to me they weren't liars.

"Make him pay! Motherfucker, you will learn about putting your hands on me!" a man shouted from across the room. There was some type of altercation, and a crowd had gathered, but I couldn't see anything, and I wasn't that interested. My mind was focused on one thing, and that was these two. As I ascended the stairs, the altercation grew louder. I heard a loud thud, like something striking a slab of meat.

When I reached the top of the stairs, I turned and looked out over the crowd. I wasn't sure if it was the alcohol causing me to hallucinate, but I had to take a second look, because the large man being beaten with baseball bats looked very familiar.

"I know that man," I said to both the women, who were also riveted, watching two burly goons wielding baseball bats repeatedly striking the man's body. "That's one of the Duncans?"

Little Momma gasped. "Yeah, that's Lou's brother Levi Duncan."

Destiny mumbled her response. "Damn, I ain't never seen him get his ass beat."

"That is a very simple man," I said, adding my observation. "And very kind. He doesn't deserve that."

"Whoa! Oh, shit! He's got a gun! Run!" People started to scream and scramble, and that's when I saw the man everyone called Big Sam holding a gun on both Levi and a woman I hadn't noticed before, cowering over him on the floor.

"Move out the way," Big Sam shouted. "I'm gonna kill this son of a bitch, and I dare somebody to go to the police."

"Don't!" Destiny's voice squeaked as I took a step down the stairs. "Don't get involved. Sam will kill you too."

"That man and his family are my friends. I would only hope they would do the same for me and my family members," I said before racing down the stairs and across the room. With all the commotion, it was easy for me to creep up behind Sam, pulling both of my guns out of their holsters under my sports jacket.

"I'd put that down if I were you," I said, pulling back the hammer on both pistols. The two guys stopped attacking Levi and seemed to wait for Sam's orders.

He eased his head around so he could see both my guns. "Obviously you don't know who I am, friend. My name's Big Sam Bradford. I own this place, and this man here attacked me. Now, if anyone should put their gun down, it should be you. That is, if you know what's good for you."

"I don't think so," I replied, standing my ground, "and to be honest, I don't give a shit who you are." I leaned down, and together with the woman on the floor, we helped Levi to his feet. I still kept my gun on Big Sam. Levi could barely stand up on his own, but he seemed to recognize me. "Levi, me and you and this lady are going to back out of here."

"Listen, why don't you go upstairs and help yourself to some of the best pussy east of the Mississippi?" Sam said, ignoring what I had just told Levi.

"No, I don't think pussy is going to be on the agenda today. Not anymore at least," I said. I looked at the woman as she tried to help Levi steady himself. "You got him?"

She nodded. Now I had the guns trained on Sam and his bouncers.

"You better put that gun down, friend. Things are not going to end well for you if you get involved. Listen to me when I say, go and get some pussy and stay out of this," he warned me.

"Haven't you figured it out yet? I am involved." I gestured to Levi. "His family has been really good to me. If I believe in one thing, it is loyalty."

"The only person you need to be loyal to is yourself. This is your chance to do that."

"Sorry, but I'm not a play-it-safe kind of guy. My friends and family come first," I said.

The woman turned to me, her voice shaky with emotion as we hurried out of the building. "Mister, I don't know who you are, but I appreciate what you're doing. I want you to understand, though, that Big Sam is going to find you and kill you." She looked sad when she told me, like it was an absolute certainty that my life was now worthless.

"I'm not worried about a punk like that. But we do need to get away from here," I told her as we emerged from the building and hurried down the steps with Levi barely holding on between us.

"Help!" the woman hollered as we came down the stairs. The commotion sent a couple of guys from the business next door rushing out.

"We need a ride!" I shouted, and just like that, one of the men opened a car near the curb and they helped us get Levi inside.

When we got to the gas station, the woman, who had told me her name was Shirley, hopped out of the car. "LC, Lou, Larry! Come quick!" she shouted.

The door flung open, and the three brothers came running. Both Lou and Larry were brandishing guns. I stepped out of the car on the other side as they helped get Levi out.

"Who did this?" Lou yelled.

"Sam," was all Shirley needed to say

Lou turned to LC. "I guess you was right. We are at war."

"I'm going to get that motherfucker!" Larry swore as the three brothers stared helplessly at Levi, beaten to a pulp but luckily still alive.

The looks on their faces told me that I would not want to be Sam. Shirley turned from Levi, remembering that I was there. "He saved Levi's life," she told them, pointing to me. LC stood up and came toward me, his hand outstretched. I accepted his sign of gratitude, but I knew at that moment that I had just witnessed the beginning of a war.

Lou

45

"We got to get him to a hospital!" Shirley yelled in a panic. She was slowly coming apart at the seams as I sped down Route 38 toward the swamp.

Once we had gotten Levi into my car, Larry and I took off with Shirley, who wouldn't leave his side. I guess she felt guilty about what had happened. I didn't know all the details about what had started the altercation, but I could only assume it was all her fault.

We'd left LC, Harold, and John to secure the shop and meet us later, while NeeNee was right on our heels in Larry's Duster.

"Levi, you all right, bro?" Larry shook him but got no response. "He's out cold, Lou. I think he's bleeding internally."

I nodded but didn't say anything as I smashed down on the accelerator hard. It took a lot for me to get riled up and lose my cool, but after what he'd done to Levi, Sam Bradford was a dead man walking.

"What about LC? You sure he's going to be all right?" Shirley asked, still in a panic.

"He's got Harold with him, and that guy John knows his way around guns," Larry replied, turning to Shirley in the back seat. "He saved your ass, didn't he?"

I made a sudden turn down a dirt road.

"What are you doing? This ain't the way to the hospital. Levi's dying! We've got to get him to the hospital!" Shirley shouted like she was the only one concerned about him.

"I know what I'm doing, Shirley. You're just going to have to trust me," I told her as different options raced through my head. The last thing I wanted was to park my brother somewhere like a public hospital, where Sam could send his men to finish the job. Most people didn't know it, but Sam had about fifty guys on his payroll doing different things throughout Ware County. None of them were as good at handling their business as the Duncans, but you got enough guys pointing guns at you and sooner or later someone was going to hit the target.

"What do you mean? You can't just dump him in the swamp and let him die!" she hollered, getting even more worked up.

Larry once again turned to the back of the car, but this time he grabbed Shirley by the shoulder. "Calm the fuck down! We ain't gonna let nothing happen to Levi, and we damn sure not gonna dump him in no swamp. There are people and places much safer than that white man's hospital."

"Oh yeah? Like what?" Shirley's tone challenged.

"Like here." I brought the car to a screeching halt then jumped out, running to the door of the old shack I'd pulled in front of. I banged on the door repeatedly until a woman answered. Before she could speak, I pointed at the car, trying to get my own words together.

"Ms. Emma, it's Levi. They beat him up real bad with baseball bats. He's bleeding inside, and I don't know if he's gonna make it."

"So what you waiting on, boy? Bring him in," Ms. Emma told me hurriedly before she went inside to get things ready for him. I ran back to the car, where Shirley and NeeNee were already helping Larry carry Levi to the house.

It wasn't a secret that Levi was a big man, but I never knew just how heavy he was until we carried him into that house where Ms. Emma's kids sat quietly on the sofa. Not one of them made a peep as we carried him into the back room and laid him on the bed.

"Okay, now y'all go on outside and let me do my work." Ms. Emma waved us all out except for NeeNee.

Larry and I did as we were told, but a weeping Shirley hesitated until NeeNee approached her. "It's all right, Shirley. Ms. Emma knows what she's doing. If anything changes, I'll come get you right away. I promise." NeeNee's words seemed to be enough. Shirley nodded then followed us out to the porch, where we all sat on homemade rocking chairs.

Shirley stopped her chair from rocking and spoke to Larry and me. "You know Sam's not going to stop until he kills all of you, don't you?"

"He can try," Larry responded, pulling out his guns to check them. "But he better pray he sees me before I see him."

Just as Larry finished his sentence, lights in the distance told us a car was coming down the road toward us. I immediately sent Shirley inside, drawing my .38s.

"Get those kids to lie on the floor, Shirley," I shouted.

"How you wanna handle this?" Larry asked, shotgun in hand.

"If anyone gets out that car without giving us the signal, shoot first and ask questions later," I replied as the car pulled up beside mine with its high beams on. We couldn't see a thing because of the bright lights, but we had our guns pointed directly at the windshield, waiting for them to make the next move. If they opened a car door, we were going to blow them away; it was just that simple. Although it seemed like forever, the car lights finally flashed three times and turned off, allowing me and my brother to relax.

"Hey, don't shoot! It's me!" LC hollered.

"It took you long enough to give the signal," Larry chastised as LC and Harold hopped out of the car. "I almost blew your fucking head off."

"Yeah, well, it's not my head you should be blowing off," LC replied. I could hear the agitation in his voice. "How's Levi?"

"We don't know yet. Ms. Emma's still working on him," I replied.

LC sat down on the porch just as Shirley came back out of the house. "So, big brother, what do we do from here?" he asked.

"It's simple. Once I find out how Levi's doing, I'm going to walk into Sam's place and put a bullet in his fucking head." My words were clear, calm, and serious as hell.

"No, you're not," LC answered without hesitation. "You go down there and you're not going to make it ten feet onto Oak Street without one of Sam's goons putting a bullet in your head."

"If you know so much, then tell me, what the fuck are we supposed to do? You got a better idea? 'Cause we can't let what happened to Levi go unanswered," I growled, pulling out a half-smoked cigar.

"We wait. Sam's not crazy enough to attack us head-on. Not yet at least. By now Sam's probably got Big Sam's and half of Oak Street swarming with men. I'm sure he thinks we're going to just rush in on his ass, guns blazing. He's probably waiting on us to come right into an ambush. But what happens if we don't?

"Sam's not a very patient man. You know that, Lou. Waiting will make him crazy, and while he's going crazy, we start recruiting. There's a lot of Vietnam vets out there outta work, isn't there, Larry? I'm sure they'd like a nice fat paycheck."

"Uh-huh, I'm sure they would," Larry replied.

"Lou, we give Larry a week and I bet he could put together a pretty damn good team. A team already trained by the U.S. military."

"He's right, Lou," Larry replied. "We sit back and wait, and Sam's ass will go fucking crazy trying to figure out what we're up to."

"And when he comes to find out, I'll personally put a bullet in his head," LC said sternly.

Larry, LC, and Shirley stared at me, but it didn't take long for me to make my decision. "Okay, little brother, we'll do it your way. We'll wait, because you're right—Sam's his own worst enemy." The smirk on my face said it all, but it dropped when the door opened and Ms. Emma and NeeNee came outside. Neither of their expressions looked encouraging.

"Is he all right?" LC asked.

She lowered her head with a sigh. "He's still unconscious, but he's alive. Your brother's in pretty bad shape. He was bleeding inside, but I think I stopped it for now. He does, however, have a punctured lung, and at least five of his ribs are cracked. You do know whoever did this was trying to kill him, don't you?"

"But will he make it?" I asked.

Ms. Emma looked me straight in the eye. "I'm not sure. It's a miracle he's alive at all with the beating he took. All we can do now is pray and hope he wakes up soon."

Big Shirley

46

After four hours of waiting around to see if Levi would wake up, Larry and NeeNee headed home to bathe, get some rest, and feed Levi's animals. LC and Harold had left to check on John back at the gas station, so that left Lou and me, sitting on the porch talking about our good friend Sam and why and how all of this had all happened. I had to wait for him to pick his jaw off the ground after I told him about the compromising position I'd caught Sam and Jefferson in.

"What are you trying to say? Sam's a sissy?" Lou shook his head, still in disbelief. "No way. I've seen that man fuck a hundred women."

"And I've seen him fuck two hundred, including me, but that don't change what I saw, Lou. Jefferson was sucking Sam's dick. That's the reason he went after me in the first place. Levi was just trying to protect me," I said, wiping away tears. "So in a nutshell, Levi's lying in there because of me. This is all my fault."

"No, it's not. This thing between us and Sam has been a long time coming. No matter how much I tried to play peacemaker, Sam and LC weren't going to get along. If it wasn't Levi, sooner or later it would have been LC—and no way can our family afford to lose him. He's our future."

"You really think LC is something special, don't you?"

Lou turned to me and nodded. "Don't you?"

"Yeah, I guess I do." I yawned, covering my mouth.

"Come on, Shirley. You look tired. Let's go inside and get a little shuteye. Ms. Emma's got a pallet set up for us in the back bedroom." Lou stood up and stretched. "Hell, a little pussy'll put my ass right to sleep."

I didn't respond at first. I just stared at him, shaking my head. "Sorry, Lou. We're not at Sam's place anymore."

"Oh, damn. I hear you." He reached in his pocket and pulled out a roll of money, peeling off a few bills. "Hell, guess you might as well make a few bucks in the process." He tried to hand them to me, but I refused to take them.

"Are you serious? You just don't get it, do you?

"Get what?" He scrunched up his face in confusion. "Shirley, you're making this entirely too complicated."

"Well, let me simplify it for you." I sighed, sitting up in the rocker and pointing at my scarred face. "You haven't so much as looked at me once since I got this on my face, so yes, I'm going inside, but not to fuck you or anyone else. I'm going in there to nurse Levi back to health, and if he'll have me, he's the only person gonna get between these legs." I spoke emphatically so he would know I meant every word I'd said.

Lou chuckled. "You and Levi. Girl, you barely know my brother. He's different. Let's call him special."

"What I know is that he's a good man. Sure, he's not as smart or as smooth as you or your other brothers, but Levi is kind and good. My whole life I ain't never been treated the way he treats me, and I like it. I like it a lot." I folded my arms with determination.

He stared at me for a whole minute. "Wait, so you want to be with Levi? Like boyfriend and girlfriend?"

"Boyfriend and girlfriend, husband and wife . . . I'll take whatever I can get. And I'll take care of him, Lou. I won't let anybody take advantage of him. I promise."

Lou was skeptical. "And why should I believe you're not just looking to use my brother to better your own situation? I mean, now that you and Sam on the outs, you ain't got nowhere to go."

"Because I love him," I stated simply. "I know you think I'm nothing but a whore, but hoes can fall in love, and I love your brother. I can make him happy, Lou. Really happy."

I was seconds from breaking out in tears before he shocked me with his response. "Well, I guess he could do a whole hell of a lot worse than you."

Chippy

47

"I'll do that and some other things you never even thought of, because a man like you deserves a special treat," I promised Ben, a wealthy trick, leaning over and stroking his thigh suggestively while he downed his gin and tonic. He'd been one of my regulars since my first day, and even though I couldn't stand the way he smelled or his raunchy breath, like he had some kind of allergy to water or something, I was happy for the business—especially my twenty percent. Besides, he came quick and always tipped a few extra bucks that I could add to my stash, so I'd deal with the smell. I had to admit that this job had become a lot easier since I started to look at it as a job and not some grand gesture of love for a man who turned out to be playing me.

"Chippy?" Little Momma hollered at me.

"Yeah?" I answered, my hand now massaging the bald spot on Ben's head.

"Big Sam wants to see you in his office right away."

"Tell him I'm with a customer," I said.

"After the shit that went down with Shirley and Levi last night, I wouldn't play with him, girl. He's snapping at the slightest thing. He even beat that new girl Crystal's ass for no reason." She gave me a stern look, and I nodded my understanding.

I'd tried to sneak over to the gas station earlier, but Sam had all the girls on lockdown. We couldn't even make a phone call. I didn't see it because I was with a customer at the time, but some of the girls said Levi was beat up so bad they didn't think he was going to make it. I'd been working my ass off all day, trying to distract myself from thinking about what LC must be going through with his brother all beat up like that.

I leaned in to Ben and whispered in his ear, taking the opportunity to nibble on his lobe the way he liked before hoping off the stool to get this over with. "I'll be right back."

He reached for my arm. "Baby, don't make me wait too long."

I turned and gave him my best seductive smile. "It'll be worth it," I told him as I sashayed off, knowing damn well his eyes were still on me. I made sure to give him a good preview of what I had to offer him, to give him a reason to wait. Otherwise, I knew that the way those bitches worked, I'd be gone for less than a minute before they were in there competing to take my spot and my money.

Sam's office door was slightly ajar, so I pushed it open. "You wanted to see me, Sam?"

"Come in and close the door." Big Sam's booming voice, heavy on politeness, made me immediately suspicious as I entered the room. There were too big gorillas standing against the wall to the right, but what sparked my curiosity was the person wearing the white-brimmed hat seated opposite Sam. I'd gotten used to the extra security since the incident with Levi, but this mystery person was another thing.

"Is this important? 'Cause I've got a customer," I informed him, knowing money trumped everything for his greedy ass.

"Not anymore. One of the other girls will handle him. You got someone that really wants to see you." I walked over to get a look at the man in the hat, who was obviously the person he was talking about.

He turned in my direction, and the sight of him brought a genuine smile to my face. Smiles like that definitely weren't easy for me anymore.

"Alejandro!" I gushed. The last time I saw him, he'd shown me the time of my life. Yep, if you had to be with a trick, he was the trick to be with.

"Hello to you too, Miss Charlotte." He smiled up at me.

"I didn't know you were coming to town." I lifted his hat and started to run my fingers through his thick black mane as Sam watched. He took my free hand and kissed it as if it were the most precious thing in the world.

"Neither did I, but since I'm here, I was hoping to add business with pleasure."

"Knowing how you get down, that sounds like a lot of fun." *And a lot of money,* I thought.

"So, Alejandro, my man, you said you were here on business. I guess that means you're here for this?" Sam reached down beside his desk, and I could feel everyone in the room stiffen up, until he plopped a briefcase on his desk.

"What is this?" Alejandro asked, eyeing the case suspiciously.

"It's your money," Sam replied nonchalantly. "Thirty-five grand, just as I promised. You said to make sure I paid promptly. I figured that's why you're here, since your boys didn't pick it up earlier this week."

Alejandro let go of my hand and reached for the briefcase. He opened it, and I sighed when I saw all the money.

"We good?" Sam asked.

"Yes, this part of our business is concluded, but there is one other piece of business that we must discuss." Alejandro glanced at his men, and all of a sudden the gorillas pulled out pistols, pointing them at Sam. "Do you want me to kill you, Sam Bradford?"

"No!" Sam's eyes grew wide with fear. I recognized that look. I'd seen it the night Big Shirley came at him with a knife. "And if you don't mind me asking, why exactly would you want to kill a man who just gave you thirty-five *G*s?"

"Because we have two missing men, one of whom just happens to be my employer's nephew. Two men you were supposed to meet and give this money to on Monday."

Sam sat up in his chair and started talking fast. "Look, man, I'm not sure what you trying to insinuate here, but I called you about those boys not showing. Why the hell would I just take out two of your boys then give you the money? You're a smart man. Does that make sense?"

Alejandro stared at Sam as if trying to read his mind. He finally gestured to his men, who lowered their guns. "My men were in this town. We found their car at a truck stop on Route

Thirty-eight. This is supposed to be your town, Sam Bradford. If you want to do business with my people, then I want some answers."

"You want answers, I'll get you answers, but I'm going to need a little time. Why don't you take Chippy on upstairs and let her entertain you until we come up with something?"

Alejandro reached for my hand. "Yes, I think I'll do that, but I will take her to the hotel, and my men will work with you directly. You have no objections to this, do you?"

Alejandro's head was between my legs, doing something most tricks never did. He was good at it—just not as good as someone else I knew. So, I laid back trying to enjoy myself. Of course, every time I closed my eyes my mind went to LC. As the old people would say, I had it bad for that man.

Alejandro and I hadn't been doing it but so long when there was a knock on the door. He sat up and reached for his gun, gesturing for me to go to the door. I wrapped myself in a robe and went to the door. I tried to look through peephole, but I couldn't see anything.

"Who is it?" I asked

"It's me, Sam. Open the goddamn door."

I opened the door and in walked Sam with Henry, the head of his security team, and three of Alejandro's men. "Chippy, you need to leave!" Sam barked at me, but Alejandro took my hand to stop me from leaving. Since Alejandro was the one about to butter my bread, I decided to take my marching orders from him and froze on the spot.

"She can stay. What is it?" he snapped at Sam.

Sam glanced from Alejandro to me. I could tell he still didn't appreciate my presence in the room, but he wasn't about to defy Alejandro. "There is something we need to go check out. My man Henry here thinks he's found what you were looking for."

Alejandro stood up. He placed his hand on the small of my back in a motion meant to keep me at his side. "Let's go, then," he said. "We'll be dressed in five minutes."

"She can't come," Sam protested.

Alejandro clearly didn't like taking orders, so he upped his stance. "She's with me. While I'm in this town, she goes where I go."

Sam tried again. "Chippy can wait right here until we get back. Nothing will happen to her."

Alejandro shook his head. "I'd like to keep her with me. Would you deny me the hospitality of this beautiful woman?" He reached in his pocket and threw some money on the bed, putting Sam on the spot. He offered Alejandro a big, fake-ass smile.

"You're the boss. You want a whore to come, then fine with me."

I could feel Alejandro tense up when he called me a whore. Interesting.

Alejandro and I, were in a car following behind Sam and his men, to wherever they were taking us. Alejandro spent the entire ride asking me questions about Sam's organization. I didn't disclose nearly as much as I could have, although I gathered he was sharp enough to understand exactly what I was not saying, especially about Sam. By the time we headed down a darkened dirt road in the swamp, I was starting to get worried. Sam and his henchmen were in the car ahead of us, and something just didn't feel right about anything that was going down. This wasn't the kind of place I'd assumed we were going when we left. I'd been so happy that somebody had put Sam in his place that I hadn't thought about anything else.

About a two miles down the road, both cars stopped. Alejandro and his men got out but kept the car headlights on. Not that they needed it with the bright moonlight. Sam and his men approached, and they all walked a few feet. I rolled down the window so that I could see and hear.

"*Pinche pendejo!*" Alejandro's angry voice spat out words I didn't understand, although I recognized immediately that they had to be curses of some kind. "*El coño de tu madre!*"

The look on their faces was one of horror. Whatever the hell Alejandro was upset about sure must have been bad.

"These your guys?" Henry asked in a way that was more of a statement than a question. The look on Alejandro's face was pure evil as he paced back and forth, nodding.

"I'm sorry, Alejandro," Sam added.

"I don't want your sorrow!" he roared. "I want to know who the fuck did this!"

I creeped out of the car and walked over to where they were standing. Curiosity had gotten the best of me, and I just wanted to see what they were seeing. Well, I saw all right, and it took everything I had not to throw up. "Jesus Christ, what the hell happened to them?" I blurted out.

There were two men lying on the ground with their eyes, ears, and noses cut off, along with their dicks, which were shoved in their mouths. It was a pretty gruesome sight, especially with all the maggots and flies that had found the body.

Alejandro's voice was pure acid when he answered. "This is crazy. I don't know what kind of person would do this."

That's when I saw Sam bend down and pick up something off the ground. He stared at it and started shaking his head.

"Oh, shit. Fuck, no. No!" He raised his voice before handing Alejandro something I couldn't see.

"This is a Cuban? They are not easy to come by," Alejandro said.

"Yeah, I know." Sam sounded strange. Something was in his tone that I couldn't quite recognize, which was saying a lot. I'd spent a month and a half studying his every inflection to make sure I wasn't upsetting him or allowing him to become bored with me. I could tell you in a second what kind of mood he was in from the tone of his voice. "I can't fucking believe he would do this."

"What do you mean?" Alejandro questioned. "You know who smokes this?"

Sam took a dramatic breath before continuing, almost like he was consciously putting on a show. "Yeah, it's one of my closest friends. Although we're not so close right now."

"You know the animal who would commit such a heinous offense? Who? Who would do something like this?" Alejandro shouted at Sam.

"His name is Lou Duncan. But, Alejandro, he ain't nobody to be fucking with. He and his brothers are some bad mother-fuckers." He sounded like his voice was about to break.

For the briefest moment, Alejandro and I locked eyes.

"I don't care how bad a motherfucker he is. This Lou Duncan and his brothers are dead men," he proclaimed, and I swear I saw a smirk on Sam's face.

The only thing that I could think was, *Damn, what the hell has Lou gotten my LC into?*

48

After two and half weeks of waiting—not to mention listening to John rant and rave about how long it was taking—I'd finally gotten the part for his car. I couldn't wait to fix his ride so that he could finally get on the road. I hadn't noticed when the part was delivered yesterday because of everything with Levi going down, but I decided to surprise John and have his car ready by the time he got up in the morning. The way he stepped up and saved Levi made me certain that Sam and his cronies had added his name to their hit list, and they'd be coming after him, which made me more anxious to get him out of town. There weren't many people who would do what he did to save my brother, so I had to make sure I didn't get him killed.

As I worked on the car, I was starting to think maybe I should have gone to see Levi first, because the work should have taken an hour tops, but here I was finishing three hours later, only to find a new problem.

"What the hell?" I yelled after I banged my hand against something unfamiliar wedged into the undercarriage of the car. I reached my hand up into the cavity, already dreading another issue, when something wrapped in plastic and duct tape fell to the floor. Before I could pick it up, another one joined it. Then I stuck my flashlight up under the hood, and down came another one. From what I could see, there were even more of the same object up there.

"What the fuck?"

Click! The unmistakable sound of the hammer on a gun caused me to drop the plastic-wrapped package from my hand. Then I heard John's voice.

"LC, I wish you hadn't found that, my friend. This is not what I would have wanted to happen." His voice was menacing, but there was a hint of sorrow at the same time.

"John, what's going on, man?" I asked, looking from the items on the ground to John, who was holding a gun to my head. He reached around and took out the holstered gun I'd been carrying since the incident with Levi and Sam. "You in some kind of trouble?" I asked.

"I was in trouble the day I met you," John admitted, sounding sad. He glanced around the garage then motioned to the rope we used to tie things down to the roof of the truck. "Pick that up."

I wasn't sure where this was going, but I knew it wasn't any direction I wanted. "Hey, John, talk to me, man. This is me, LC. I'm your friend, remember?"

"Don't make this any harder than it already is. Just pick up the damn rope!" he shouted, waving the gun at me.

I leaned down and grabbed the rope, holding it out to him. John pushed a chair over to me. "Sit!" he commanded.

My first thought was to fight, but with him holding a gun to my head, I was pretty much out of options. Besides, I preferred to fight my battles with words. Larry would have known how to turn this around in a second, but I wasn't violent.

"John?" I tried to use a calming voice to persuade him to lower his gun, but he had something else in mind as he tied my hands and feet to the chair. "Talk to me. Tell me what's going on. Maybe I can help," I pleaded, hoping to stop this.

He started to pick up the bundles that had fallen to the floor. "Yes, you're that type of man, aren't you? Unfortunately, I am way beyond yours or anyone else's help, my friend. That is, unless you have a hundred thousand dollars."

"John, what is that?" I asked, looking at the bundle he was holding.

"Marijuana," he answered. "Some of the best in the world, grown from the coffee fields of Colombia. And while I'm being honest, my name is not John. It's Juan. Juan Rodriguez."

"I don't understand," I said. "How did you—"

He interrupted my question and gave me some more details. "Three weeks ago, the guy I work for took my sisters and my mother. He's holding them hostage until I sell this to some guy in New York and come back with their money. But now the buyer's gone, and I have less than a week to come up with their money."

Now it all made sense to me, the way he had been acting while he waited for the part to be delivered. Now I understood why he had been so inordinately angry every time there was another delay in getting the part. Every day of delay meant another day of captivity for his family members. I also understood why he didn't want that car out of his sight. Shit, if I was carrying a hundred thousand dollars' worth of weed, I'd want to keep an eye on it at all times too. Of course, that left me with the question of how he had gotten wrapped up in that business in the first place. John had not struck me as that type of guy, but now was not the time to be asking him about the how and why of his choice of work, because he was still holding a gun, and he still looked determined to follow through on the same path he'd started down.

"Look, don't do this. We can help you," I said, growing insistent, but he ignored me.

"Is the car ready?"

"Yes, but you don't have to leave. Let us help you. Lou has contacts. He knows a whole bunch of people up in New York, the kind of people who would be interested in what's in that car." I was pleading with him. John had become a friend, and despite this moment, I didn't want anything to happen to him or his family.

"LC, you don't want this kind of trouble. You can barely handle Big Sam. Now, how do I lower my car so I can get out of here?" he asked. As much as I wanted to change his mind, I knew that I couldn't.

Once I told him how, John picked up the rest of his bricks and placed them back in the compartment under the car before lowering it.

"You sure they're not going to fall out onto the highway?" I was still trying in my own subtle way to change his mind. "You need to think this through."

"I no longer have time to think, LC." He opened the garage door then slipped into the car, pulling it out into the parking lot. He got out of the car and then walked back in to the garage. He placed a piece of duct tape over my mouth.

"You're a good man, LC Duncan. It saddens me that we will not be seeing each other again. You have proven to be a good friend. I wish you luck, and I hope you make the right choice and go after that woman Chippy."

Juan

49

"Fuck! Fuck! Fuck!" I screamed repeatedly, banging my fist against the steering wheel of the car in frustration as I headed east toward Brunswick and I-95. If I was lucky I'd be in South Carolina before Lou and Larry opened the shop and found LC. There weren't many men who put fear in my heart, but Larry was one of them, and I wanted to be as far away from him as possible when he found out about my betrayal. To make matters worse, I was sorry I had to leave in the manner I had, because I'd actually begun to like Waycross, Georgia, and honestly considered LC a friend.

Speaking of friends, there was one person I had to see before I left town, so I pulled into the Waycross Diner and parked. I'd been going there at least once a day, not for their food or their stale coffee, but because of the beautiful waitress, Lola, who worked in the morning. Like LC, she had made quite an impression on me. Seeing her would be my final memento and memory of this little place, so it might as well be a good one.

"Hey! I see you're finally mobile." Lola smiled as I walked in the door.

"Yeah, it's time to go," I said, trying to appear normal and not to think about my friend tied up back at the garage.

"So what are you having for your last meal?" Then she stopped and gave me a playful warning. "Don't say sweet tea." She couldn't help but laugh, because I'd had it every day, even for breakfast.

"Yes, but I'll also have fried eggs, home fries, and bacon. To go," I told her as I took a seat at the counter to wait. Lola brought me an iced tea and shoved a slice of pecan pie toward me. "I say you only live once, so try something new before you leave. It's on me, as a going away present."

When she walked away, I heard something that sounded so familiar yet completely out of place. It had been almost three weeks since I'd heard anybody speaking in my native tongue, and even though the inflection was different, not as regional as the Spanish we spoke in Texas, it was still Spanish.

"Sí." I heard a voice behind me clear as day.

"I want all four of them dead. Do you understand me? Dead." Another one of the men sitting in the booth behind me also spoke in Spanish. That's when I stole a quick glance in their direction. The "all four of them dead" comment had my attention. The one talking was a well-dressed man about thirty, seated against the window. With him were four younger men, who all appeared to be armed, waiting for him to continue. Everything about his manner made it clear that he was the one in charge—and probably the most dangerous.

"Don't worry. These niggers will all be dead within twenty-four hours," I heard another one of the younger men say definitively in Spanish. The fact that they assumed no one in the diner spoke Spanish had made them careless enough to be discussing murder publicly.

"Just because they are black, do not think this will be easy. These men took out Santos and José, two very capable men," the boss warned them, getting up from his seat. "The one they call Larry is a trained military man. He has knowledge the others do not have and will not be so easy to kill."

Shit! I thought with alarm. This was definitely about the Duncans. These dudes were sitting in the diner calmly discussing the murder of all four Duncan brothers. My first instinct was to jump up and do something to prevent it, but then I remembered I had my own problems to worry about. My family needed me.

Not my business, not my business, I kept telling myself.

"Here you go." Lola smiled down at me as she placed my food in a paper bag in front of me. "I put my number on the receipt just in case you wanted to call me."

"I will definitely call you," I said distractedly. My attention was focused on the five Spanish-speaking men who were now exiting the restaurant.

"You do that," she said to my back as I picked up my food and hurried to the door.

Outside, I could see the boss getting into the back of a limousine with two of the four men. The other two got into a Ford that looked like it could pass for an unmarked police car.

My mind was racing. I realized there was a ticking clock and they were about to go after my friends. Worst of all, thanks to me, LC was a sitting duck.

I got into my car and slammed my hand against the steering wheel. "Dammit, Juan, this is not your problem," I told myself as I started the car. "Your problem is in Texas and figuring out how to get rid of this marijuana." I pulled the car out onto the road, thinking about LC lying in the garage, all tied up, and what he was about to be up against. "Sorry, my friend, but this is not my problem." I put my foot on the accelerator and sped off into the night.

Larry

50

It had taken everything I had not to go over to the whore-house and blow Sam's pretty little head right off. Believe me when I said I hated that he was still breathing. It wasn't really a secret that I didn't trust him no way, but LC had said to be patient, and I swear to God I was trying, though it certainly went against my nature.

When I woke up early and LC still hadn't shown up, NeeNee prodded me to go down to the gas station and check up on him. I swear she treated him like he was her child, even if she wasn't old enough to be his mother. NeeNee, Lou, Shirley, and I had taken turns sitting vigil with Levi, who wasn't entirely out of the woods yet, but had woken up. LC, however, had been a no-show at Ms. Emma's yesterday, which seemed strange considering I'd personally told him Levi had woken up, and was asking for him.

"You know we wouldn't have to do this shit if Ms. Emma's ass wasn't too cheap to get a phone," I complained to NeeNee.

"Larry, stop. That woman can barely afford groceries." NeeNee pointed to LC's new ride as we pulled into the station. "I told you he was probably working and fell asleep on the sofa or something. That boy might as well live here."

I reached for my car door handle and she took hold of my hand. "Hey, before we go in, I have something I need to tell you."

I'd figured something was wrong, because she'd been acting kind of funny the past few days. Sure, she was upset over Levi, but she also seemed preoccupied with something else. "What's up?" I asked.

240 Carl Weber with Eric Pete

She opened her mouth to speak, then hesitated, frowning uncertainly.

"Just spit it out already," I said.

"I'm pregnant."

It took a moment to register, but when it did, I couldn't hide my shock. "Shit, I thought you were on the pill."

"I am," she said, offering no further explanation.

There were a million thoughts running through my head, but I didn't say anything because her ass was damn near in tears and I didn't want to make it worse. Talk about being blindsided.

"I'm sorry," she said. "I know you didn't want any kids."

"How far along are you?" I finally asked.

"Ms. Emma told me three months." NeeNee's bottom lip was trembling.

"We'll talk about this when we get inside," I said as I got out of the car, confused and in need of a few minutes to myself.

The front door was locked, so I motioned to NeeNee to stay put and went around to the side entrance to open up for her.

As soon as I entered, something didn't feel right, and it wasn't the fact that my girlfriend had just told me she was pregnant. The lights in the back were on, but there was no sign of my brother—or John, for that matter.

"LC! John!" I shouted out. I walked through the store and into the garage, and that's when I heard a dragging noise coming from the corner. Whipping out my gun, I cocked it, about to shoot. That's when I saw my brother tied to a chair, trying to scream through the tape that covered his mouth.

"What the fuck?" I made a quick check of the room then ran to my brother's side, removing the tape from his mouth and untying the rope that held him down to the chair. "Who did this, LC?"

He answered in one single word: "John."

"John? Why the fuck would John—?" At first LC's answer confused me, and then it hit me. "Did he rob us?"

NeeNee rushed into the garage, and when she saw me untying LC, she flipped out. "What the hell happened?" She started fawning all over him.

"I think that motherfucker John robbed us," I spit out irately.

"No, he didn't." LC stood up, attempting to explain. "I found this stuff in the wheel bed under John's car." Because of his excitement, the words came out in a blur. "Hell, I'm not even sure his real name is John."

"Slow the fuck down," I told him. "You're starting to sound like Levi. I can barely understand anything that you're saying." I needed to hear exactly what had happened so I could decide just how badly I was going to punish that motherfucker John once I found him.

LC took a deep breath to calm himself down before continuing. "John had something in his car that he didn't want us to know about. It looked like some kind of drugs."

"He could have us all locked up with that shit! I'ma kill him!" I bellowed, ready to jump in my car and go after this motherfucker.

LC put out a hand to stop me. "No, Larry," he said. "He's caught up in something that he can't get out of."

I didn't see how my brother could be defending the guy who just tied him up and duct taped his mouth, but it seemed like NeeNee felt the same way. She chimed in with, "He just seemed like such a nice guy. I really wouldn't think John would do anything like this."

"He is a good guy," LC insisted, but I wasn't trying to hear that. You hurt my family then you deserved to be dead, and I was the one who would do it. Just because I couldn't take Sam out yet was no reason I couldn't destroy John.

"He's just caught in a bad situation," LC continued.

"I don't give a shit what y'all say. If I ever see him again, he's a dead man. I'm sick of motherfuckers like Sam and John thinking we're soft. Time to make a few motherfuckers pay."

NeeNee gave me a look meant to calm me down, but it was too late for that. With Levi laid up at Ms. Emma's at the hands of Sam and now this happening to LC, I was ready to hurt somebody.

"Someone's pulling up," NeeNee said as we heard a car outside. It was too damn early for us to be open.

"Probably Lou," I said because I couldn't imagine who else it would be.

"Nah, that don't make sense, 'cause he's got those two hoes with him. I can't imagine he got out of bed willingly," NeeNee commented, making the most sense. I clutched my gun to my side as we walked into the store area and peered outside.

"That's John!" LC looked mystified.

"Son of a bitch." I couldn't believe what I was seeing.

We all took off outside, both LC and I with guns drawn, ready for him as soon as he stepped out of the car—which he did, with his hands raised high in the air.

"Don't you fucking move," I said, handing my gun to NeeNee and instructing her, "Blow his fucking head off if he as much as flinches." I approached him quickly, frisking him before retrieving my weapon from my girl. To my surprise and confusion, he didn't have a weapon on him.

"Why the fuck did you even come back?" LC grilled him. "I thought after what happened you'd be miles from here."

John stared at LC with an expression that had me even more confused. He didn't look angry or hateful or anything else you'd expect from a man who'd pointed a gun at you and tied you up not too long ago. In fact, he was looking at LC with what appeared to be concern.

"That was the plan," he answered simply, "but you're my friend, and I could not stand by and let you be killed."

I didn't know what this motherfucker was up to, but I, for one, was not about to fall for his scheme. "Let's not talk about killing," I growled, "because I'm about two seconds from putting a bullet in your ass!" I pulled back the trigger on my gun, but he didn't seem remotely concerned about it.

"Look, you may not believe me, but I didn't want to see y'all dead."

LC looked as confused as I felt. None of us knew what the hell he was talking about. Maybe this was his way of trying to buy time and save his own ass. In truth, none of it made sense.

"What the fuck are you talking about? You better stop talking nonsense before I put an end to you real quick." I raised my gun to his temple.

"Larry, let's hear him out," LC pleaded calmly. "But John— or Juan, or whatever the fuck your name is—I'd start making sense of this real quick."

"They were coming to kill you," John said.

"Who?" I challenged, expecting—almost hoping—to catch him in a lie so I could blow his head off.

"They're back there," he said, jerking his head slightly in the direction of the back door of the station wagon.

"Show me," I told him, pressing the gun against his temple to push him in that direction.

Through the glass in the back door, I saw two burly, olive-skinned guys on the floor, tied up with the electrical cord from a lamp.

"What the fuck is this?" I yelled, taking the pressure off my trigger finger ever so slightly.

"These men are professional killers sent to hunt you down. But today the hunters became the hunted." He had a proud smirk on his face.

"How did you know they were coming after us?" LC asked, walking over to the car.

John explained how he had overheard them talking in the diner. The more I heard, the more I started to believe this guy's story. I lowered the gun and turned to look at my brother.

"I don't get it," I said. "These aren't Big Sam's men."

"These men are professionals," John suggested. "Cuban, possibly Mexican. Look at their tattoos."

"How the fuck did they get in the mix?" LC looked over at me for answers, but I didn't have any.

"I don't know, but we better find out fast. There's no telling who they'll send next and when," I said with finality.

Lou

51

I raced into the kitchen to answer the ringing telephone, naked as the day I was born and pissed that I had to leave the girls alone in bed. Normally I would have just let the damn thing ring, but these motherfuckers kept ringing my phone. I finally got up after the fifth call because Levi was still not out of the woods over at Ms. Emma's and I couldn't take any chances. Not to mention the fact that Sam was still a serious threat to my family.

"What?" I shouted into the receiver, ready to take somebody's head off for their bad timing. Couldn't they get the fucking hint?

"Lou, Jesus! Thank God. Brother, we thought you were dead." It was LC, and he sounded totally relieved.

"Man, ain't no one getting past these dogs without me knowing it. I'll talk to you later. I got company."

"Get rid of them. We got a problem." LC's tone let me know that my little party had come to an end. When he explained what John had just done for us and that he had two guys still being held hostage in the station wagon, I went ballistic.

"Bring those motherfuckers over here right now." I slammed down the phone and went back into the bedroom, where double the pussy was waiting for double the pleasure.

"Finally!" one of the girls complained as her greedy little hands reached out for my package.

"Sorry, ladies, but I just got a very important call and we have to bring this little social visit to an end." I motioned for them to get to stepping as I slipped into my drawers.

They pouted, still not moving, as if their need to be fucked was the biggest problem in my life right now. "Hey, I'm not fucking playing. Get dressed and get gone, I got a fucking emergency!" I shouted at them, picking up their dresses and tossing them onto the bed.

"You said you was going to take us out for breakfast," one of them whined.

I reached in my pocket and peeled off a couple of bills, tossing them on the bed. "You got money to buy breakfast, lunch, and dinner. Now get the fuck out. I'll call you when I'm done."

They must have finally heard the urgency in my voice, because they scooped up the money like they had caught fire and were dressed and out of there in a flash.

I was standing on the porch sipping a cup of coffee and smoking a cigar when the truck pulled up, driven by LC and followed by John's station wagon. They parked around to the back of the barn and I followed on foot. When John opened the car, I saw these two guys looking salty and resigned at the same time. I'd never seen them before, but there was definitely something about them that seemed familiar.

"Get their asses outta there," I demanded as LC walked over and stood by my side. "What's your thoughts on this, college boy?"

"I'm not sure. This seems way bigger than Sam," LC replied as Larry and John dragged them out of the car. "Larry tried to get them to talk back at the shop, but those are two tough cookies. They weren't saying shit."

"Maybe we need to give then some motivation," I said as Larry paraded them in front of me. "You were planning on killing us?" Both men stayed silent, their bodies stiff as steel, like well-trained soldiers. "All I wanna know is why."

"Fuck 'em. Let's just smoke 'em!" Larry said, pointing his piece at them and looking real eager to pull the trigger. That wouldn't have been smart, though, considering we needed some answers.

"No. That would be too humane for these men," I replied, blowing smoke in their faces as I paced back and forth in front of them. "John, how exactly did you come upon these two?"

His eyes shot over to LC and Larry, then to the two guys, and finally to me. I could tell there was something between him and LC, but whatever it was would have to wait.

"I was at the Waycross Diner when I heard these two talking in Spanish to a man in a white suit," John started. Then he proceeded to tell me about how he had followed these two, who were headed in the direction of our property. When they pulled over, he approached them like he needed to ask for directions. I didn't know the details of how he managed to get both of them tied up and into his car, but one thing I knew for sure: that John was a bad-ass motherfucker.

I turned to the silent men. "Who's your boss and why does he want you to kill us?"

They exchanged looks, still refusing to answer. Larry took it upon himself and kneed one of them in the nuts. Down he went. Then he turned to the other, but I held up my hand to stop him, at least for now.

The other one finally spoke. "You are going to shoot us anyway, so why should we tell you anything?"

"I never said I was going to shoot you. There are a lot of ways to die." I whistled, and all thirty dogs came running. I grabbed the leader of the pack, Busta, a two hundred–pound German Rottweiler, by the collar and let him sniff the men. Busta barked, and all of a sudden the dogs went crazy.

One glance at the thirty ferocious animals baring their teeth made those men look ready to shit on themselves. I took a pull off my cigar, watching them closely. Larry started to laugh at their response. I caught his eye and nodded at him, and he went into the pen on the other side of the yard.

"Gentlemen, I know that you have cockfights in Mexico or wherever the hell you're from, but here, we have dog fights. These dogs you see are the most vicious dogs in all of Georgia, and they do not lose. You want to know how we train them to tear the heads off of other dogs? We deny them food for long periods of time, so that when they get in the ring, they don't see another dog. All they see is food."

"Eat!" Larry timed this perfectly as he returned with a baby pig raised high above his head. In one swift motion, he hurled it overhead and into the open. The dogs went insane, attacking the pig, which squealed out in pain. The noise didn't stop until the entire animal was devoured by the ferocious pack. Everybody was affected by the swiftness of the kill, especially the two men who knew what that little demonstration was meant to say to them.

I turned once more to the men. "So, as you can see, there are many more painful ways to die," I explained in my most rational voice, as Larry picked up one of the men and held him on the fence. The dogs, sensing yet another nibble, raced to the fence, ready for their next meal.

"No! No! Please!" he begged, starting to truly understand his fate as the dogs barked violently right below him.

"You better spill quick, 'cause the beasts will enjoy you way more than that pig," Larry said with a laugh.

"Alejandro!" He cried out his boss's name in a voice filled with terror. "His name is Alejandro Zuniga."

I couldn't blame him for trying to save his miserable life. I nodded to Larry, who looked disappointed as he lowered him to the ground. John and LC held on to his partner, who had just pissed his pants. I looked around and grabbed a barrel and sat down, suddenly enjoying this.

"And who the fuck exactly is Alejandro?"

Our captives were suddenly ready to spill all the details. "He is part of the Mexican Mafia. He was sent here to take control of the drugs in the entire Southeast. He is a very important man."

For the life of me, I had no idea what was going on. This didn't make any sense. "I don't know him, so why would this man want to see me and my brothers dead?"

"Because you killed our men and desecrated their bodies," one of them said, the bitterness apparent in his voice.

Larry shot me a look of concern. I was sure we were both thinking about the same job we'd done recently.

"One of the men was the nephew of a high-ranking member."

"What men? And what do you mean we desecrated their bodies?" I asked, because this was the one kill where we didn't leave the men in the barrels.

"You know what you did. It was despicable. You cut off their dicks and shoved them in their mouths. Why would you do that? It is one thing to kill them, but another to treat them like animals. You should have just fed them to your dogs."

"Whoa! What the hell are you talking about? We can do some sadistic shit, but we have never cut off anyone's dick," Larry protested. I could tell that he hadn't put two and two together yet.

"The two guys from the diner that Sam sent us after," I said, and Larry's face lit up with recognition. I turned and spoke directly to our two captors. "We didn't do that. When we gave them to Sam they were alive."

One of the men spoke up. I don't know if he believed what I'd said, or if he even cared. He seemed stuck on the way the men's bodies had been treated, not necessarily on who did it. "Our boss is not necessarily upset that they are dead. That is a part of this business," he said. "But the desecration is sacrilegious. Their souls cannot go to heaven in pieces. Only a true monster would do that."

"Yeah, a monster named Sam Bradford," LC stated clearly, giving voice to the thoughts that we were all realizing at that exact moment.

Chippy

52

I slipped out of bed quietly, sliding into the silk robe I'd left folded on the night stand. I made way across the room, opening the sliding glass door and taking in the warm, salty sea air just as the sun was beginning to crest over the ocean's horizon. I'd never seen anything so beautiful in my entire life. The only thing that could have made it more special was if LC was there to see it with me. God, I hoped he was still alive. Even if I couldn't have him, I still wished him only the best.

I let out a long sigh then gasped when I felt two hands grab me from behind. I'd been so into my own thoughts that I had completely forgotten Alejandro was in the room until his hands were on my shoulders. He wrapped his arm around my waist, pulling me closer.

"Pretty, isn't it, mi amor?" Alejandro whispered into my ear with that sexy Latin accent of his. He kissed my neck, tickling me with his thick mustache as I continued to gaze at the beautiful blue Atlantic shimmering below the balcony.

"Breathtaking. It's like a postcard. I could stare at it all day," I cooed, turning around in his arms. He stared down at me, smoothing the hair out of my face. I still couldn't believe how much he'd paid Sam for me to spend the weekend with him, only to bring me all the way down here to his new home in St. Augustine, Florida.

"Yes, you are breathtaking," he said.

I giggled, unaccustomed to such compliments, as I turned back toward the water. I just didn't understand him. Not only was he completely gorgeous, but he also had money and knew how to treat a woman. Most men who paid for sex needed to be lord and master over a woman, or at least get her to do the freaky shit they would never expect from their wives, but he did none of that. There had only been one other man in my life to treat me this well, and unfortunately, he was the person I spent most of my time trying to forget. Getting as far away from Waycross as possible should have helped heal my broken heart, but it didn't.

I stared out at the shifting blue water, trying to keep my thoughts in the here and now. I felt a calm taking hold of me as I watched the waves, like ten years of bad luck had finally fallen off of me. From the moment we'd arrived, Alejandro made sure that any and every thing I asked for or wanted had magically appeared. Down in the kitchen, he had a woman whose job was to cook whatever I wanted, and she had talent. She didn't understand how to make soul food, though, so I'd started eating some of Alejandro's native dishes, and man did I like Mexican food. This whole experience had certainly shifted something in me: the expensive clothing, shrimp and lobster meals, boat rides, and the overall comfort felt incredible, like I was finally living my real life.

There was nothing for me to do except make him happy, which, if the smile on his face was any indication of my success, I'd done that well. I felt like this house, this life, this was exactly the way that I deserved to be living. Too bad it was only temporary. I didn't know how I'd deal being back at Big Sam's after having experienced how the other half lived.

I started imagining my life growing as wide and deep as the water in front of me, and I thought, *Why the fuck not?* There was so much more that I wanted out of life. I had been dealt a bad hand in life up until this point, and I was just now realizing that I deserved much better than what had been offered to me thus far.

"My entire life I've wanted to see what's on the other side of the ocean," I said, pointing across the horizon.

"Then why don't we do that?" he responded calmly, his words surprising me.

I laughed, refusing to be made a fool. "Yeah, right."

"I am very serious. Why do you laugh?"

"Because I don't believe you're serious. What about Sam?"

"What about Sam?" he answered, almost like it was a challenge. "Let me deal with him. I will pay him whatever it costs
for him to leave you alone forever."

Now I finally understood his game. I stepped back, facing
him. "So I would go from working for Sam to working for
you?" I asked, and I guess it made sense now that I'd said
it out loud. Sam had roped me in with shopping sprees and
a clean hotel room, and now it seemed that Alejandro had
stepped up using the same tactics. I guess I was supposed to
go from ho to high-class ho.

"No!" he shouted emphatically. "I never once said anything
about work, and I never will. I want you to be my woman."

I gazed up at him, trying to figure out what his angle was,
but he wasn't finished.

"First we will go to my villa in California. If you think
Florida is nice, then my other home will be an oasis. Then we
will go to London, Spain, Greece. . . ."

"Paris?" I asked, letting my guard down for a minute as I
imagined myself finally in the city of love.

"Of course, we will go to Paris first," he insisted in a tone
that sounded so real it threatened to break my heart, because
I knew he was just playing with me.

"I wish I could believe you."

He shook his head. "Chippy, my actions speak louder than
my words. You are here, are you not?"

"Yes, but—"

"I am going to drape you in jewels, trips, clothes . . . everything your heart desires." He took my hands in his and stared
deeply into my eyes.

"But why? Why me?" I questioned. Sure, I was cute and I'd
proven myself to be a great fuck, but no one would be willing
to do this much for sex.

"Because I have fallen madly in love with you." His words
took my breath away.

"You love me?" I repeated.

"Since the day I laid eyes on you," he said sincerely, which
was more than a little overwhelming. "My only wish is that
one day you will love me half as much as I do you."

I pulled back, walking over to the railing to put some distance between us. "This all sounds good, but . . . but what if I can't love you back?" I confessed, risking everything for the sake of staying true to my heart.

He stared at me. "Yes, I can see that you have held back your emotions from me. There is another man, yes?"

"Yes, and because of him, I could never love you."

"Who is this man? Sam?" He chuckled. "I am not worried about Sam Bradford. He does not love you, or anyone else other than himself."

"I know that. I learned the hard way," I said sadly.

"If not Sam, then who? One of these men who have paid for you?"

I raised an eyebrow and he caught himself.

"I do not mean any disrespect. I am merely curious about my competition."

"If you must know, his name is LC Duncan."

"Why do I know that name?"

I suddenly realized that mentioning LC's name might have angered Alejandro and put LC in more danger. Then again, I realized, he couldn't be in any more danger than he already was. In fact, maybe I could use Alejandro's feelings for me as a way to protect LC.

"You know that name because last night you sent your men to kill him and his brothers. LC is engaged to be married to someone else, so I know he and I will never be together, but I still have strong feelings for him. I would never want to see any harm come to him. So you see, I could never love you if I knew you had brought harm to the Duncan family."

He gazed into my eyes, and I was relieved to see that there was no anger over my admission of love for LC. Instead, he looked at me lovingly and said, "Your honesty is one of the reasons I love you. Most women seeing this life I lead and hearing what I have offered you would never think to be this honest. They would have said yes no matter what they felt."

He stepped closer and took my hand. "You will love me, Chippy, because I will stop my men from killing this LC Duncan."

I wanted to throw my arms around him and kiss him at that moment, until he deflated my joy by finishing with, "But I cannot do the same for his brothers."

A knock at the door saved me from having to thank him for sparing only one life. I was torn up about not being able to help LC's brothers too. I thought about poor NeeNee and what she would do if Larry was killed.

Alejandro crossed the room to answer the door. I knew he'd be back shortly to continue our conversation, so I tried to figure out what I would say. In spite of the fact that he was willing to spare LC's life, I still couldn't promise him my heart. I knew it didn't make sense to be giving up all the luxury and world travel he was promising me. The girls back at Big Sam's would be cursing me out for being stupid if they knew what I was thinking, but giving him my heart would feel like a betrayal, and I just couldn't do it. I didn't know if I'd ever be able to love another man. Alejandro could have my body. That would have to be enough for him.

At the door, Alejandro shouted, "Who is it?" He was obviously annoyed by the interruption.

The man on the other side of the door answered, "It's Luis."

My heart dropped because I knew Luis was one of the men sent to kill LC. From the panicked look Alejandro gave me before he opened the door, I'm sure he was thinking the same thing.

I gasped when the door opened. Luis was standing there, but it was the person next to him that caused my knees to buckle. The man standing next to Luis, holding a gun to his head, was LC.

Lou

53

LC and John shoved the two guys, handcuffed together, into the room with guns to their heads. I puffed up my chest as I entered, sizing up the man who I assumed to be Alejandro Zuniga. I was concerned when I saw that Chippy was there, wrapped in nothing but a bathrobe, wondering how her presence would affect LC and our chances of getting out of there alive. She was staring at LC, which didn't go unnoticed by Alejandro. He looked at LC and smirked, like he knew something we didn't.

I grabbed two chairs, strolling over to where Zuniga stood motionless. I sat down, gesturing for him to sit down as well, which he did. His eyes darted over to his two men, and I saw a flash of anger. No doubt he was furious that they'd botched their job and brought the enemy right to his door.

I took out a cigar, one of my favorites, and cut the tip with the cigar cutter I carried around. I had to give the guy credit; even sitting there in his drawers, he had a presence about him that I'd only seen in a handful of men. This guy was not one to be trifled with. Larry must have sensed it too, because he had his gun aimed directly at Alejandro's head, just in case he got the idea of trying something stupid.

"I take it you're Alejandro."

"And you, I presume, are Lou Duncan." Alejandro looked me up and down.

"Yeah, that's me." I lit my cigar and took a drag while studying the man.

"I'm sure you've come a long way, Mr. Duncan, and as you can see, I am rather preoccupied." He glanced in Chippy's direction. In response, she wrapped the robe tighter around her body. Alejandro turned his attention back to me. "So, how can I help you?" he asked.

"Plain and simple, you can tell me why you have a problem with the Duncan brothers."

Although he didn't lose it, his demeanor seemed to change right before my eyes. There was rage lurking just below the surface. "I have a problem with anyone who kills my men."

I moved my chair closer so that I could look him straight in the eye when I spoke. "That's why I'm here. We did not kill those men."

"I don't believe you," he said simply. "And you need to know that your life is now worthless. I will make sure that there is nowhere you can go and nowhere you can hide from the retribution for what you have done to men I promised to protect. All of you are as good as dead."

Alejandro was calm as he delivered those words, which concerned me. In our line of work, it wasn't the loud ones you worried about; it was the ones who acted like threatening a man's life was a normal, everyday occurrence. LC, who had been busily focused on Chippy, also did a double take when he heard the threat.

I couldn't show any fear, so I replied with a threat of my own. "You do understand that you're sitting here in your boxers, there's a gun to your head, and I could shoot you at any moment, don't you? You're our prisoner. We're the ones in charge."

Alejandro sat back in his chair and laughed heartily. "What you don't realize is that my men are armed and trained. The minute you stepped foot on the grounds, you were being watched and followed." He pointed at my chest. "You see that red dot?"

I looked down and saw a red dot moving around my chest.

"That is a sight combining a reflecting curved mirror and a light-emitting diode, designed by Swedish optics company Aimpoint AB. It is attached to a high-powered rifle. The man holding it is very skilled. You could have been dead five minutes ago if I had wanted you to be." He smiled wide. "If you look at your brothers, you'll see similar red dots. So yes, I'm in my boxers and I have a gun to my head, but I'm the one in charge."

"Oh, shit. He ain't lying, Lou. I heard about sights like this in 'Nam," Larry exclaimed. He tried to move, and the red dot followed him.

I took a long, hard breath to regain my composure. "Well played, but you do understand that if we die, we're going to take you with us?"

"That is quite possible," he answered, "but where I come from, you kill a man and there are two ready to take his place. My satisfaction will be that all four of you are dead, and the deaths of my men will be avenged."

I realized that Alejandro and I could go back and forth all day, debating which one of us was in charge, but it would go nowhere until somebody felt the need to pull a trigger. It was time to take this conversation in another direction. "Look. I have heard that you are a reasonable man," I said, making sure that my voice held steady and even.

"I am reasonable in reasonable circumstances!" he roared, ready to bite my head off. This was the first time he allowed me to see him lose his cool. He was clearly someone used to having all the power.

"We were only doing our job," I said. "And as I said before, we didn't kill those men. They were alive when we delivered them to the man who hired us."

He tilted his head to the side, and although he didn't respond, I knew he was at least considering the possibility that there was someone else involved. I kept pushing forward to strengthen my argument.

"Look, man, think about it. We ain't never crossed paths with you before today. We're small-time money lenders who run a gas station," I said, purposely downplaying our rising status in the criminal circuit. "What reason would we have to go after your men and risk pissing off someone as powerful as you?"

Again, he stayed quiet for a while, apparently considering what I'd said. Then he asked, "And who is this person that you say hired you to kill my men?"

"Someone I know very well, and so do you, considering the company you keep." I glanced at Chippy. "Sam Bradford." His

name dropped out of my mouth like a heavy weight crashing into the middle of the room.

Alejandro glared angrily at me. "That doesn't make sense. Sam was prepared to give those men thirty-five th—" He stopped himself, as if coming to the realization that it was indeed possible for someone to want to get rid of two men coming to take a shitload of money from him.

Alejandro turned to Chippy. "And what do you think of these men and what they have to say about your employer?" I was amazed that he was turning to a whore for advice of any kind, but in this case, I was relieved to know that she was on our side.

"I know these men, and I believe them," she said. "That Sam's a snake that would cross his own fucking mother if the price was right."

Alejandro must have put a lot of stock in her opinion, because he seemed to be accepting the fact that it was true, and he looked disappointed. "I see." He stared off into the corner, asking his next question to no one in particular. "Why would Sam do this?" He obviously didn't understand the person he'd gotten into business with.

I wanted to help him understand. It might be the only way for us to get out of this situation alive. "The way I see it, the whole reason he set this up was 'cause he wanted you to do his dirty work. He wants us dead so that he can control everything in Waycross. See, we have the numbers operation that he thinks should be his. We've gotten a little too big for our britches, and he's a man with a vendetta. Unfortunately, your men became pawns in his scheme."

"I see. You are starting to make some sense." Alejandro rubbed his face as he considered what he'd just been told. "Sam Bradford."

LC spoke to Alejandro, further detailing the scenario. "It would explain why Sam was able to lead you to the exact location of the bodies. That's a whole lot of luck for someone who didn't have anything to do with it."

Alejandro and LC locked eyes, and I could see Chippy's body tighten up. The tension in the room was sky high. None of us knew what would happen next. Did Alejandro finally believe that we hadn't killed his men?

I breathed a sigh of relief when he announced, "You men still owe me a debt for delivering my men to Sam. The families—I will have to comfort them and compensate them."

"I understand," I agreed, knowing that this job came with its own unique code of ethics that we had to abide by.

"But . . . I will wipe that debt away as long as you bring me the head of Sam Bradford. He will not get away with killing my men—or with treating me like a fool."

My face lit into a smile. "That will be a pleasure. Hell, we were going to kill him anyway."

"In addition, you will also be responsible for his end of my drug business. Two kilos a month."

"But we're not drug dealers," LC chimed in. I glanced at him and shook my head, ordering him to remain quiet. We were so close to walking out of there with no bloodshed, and I couldn't let my brother's mouth derail the progress we'd made.

"You are now, and that is nonnegotiable," Alejandro said.

"Fine by me," I said, reaching out to shake his hand.

We were two powerful men, suddenly aligned with a common enemy and a new business alliance.

Big Shirley

54

"You gotta be shitting me!" I complained when Ms. Emma threw down her cards, displaying sixteen. She'd won the last seven games of tonk and taken about fifteen dollars from me. I tossed my cards down on the table, mad as hell because I had seventeen. How the hell was this country bumpkin beating me at my own damn game? Where I came from, nobody ever won at cards so long as they were playing against me. Hell, I was half the reason Sam banned the girls from playing in his private game. He couldn't stand losing to one of his whores.

Emma reached out and palmed the three dollars in the pot at the center of the table with a big-ass grin on her face. For a second I was almost happy for her, knowing she had a gang of mouths to feed, but that didn't last long.

"Where you going? I know you ain't quitting with all the money you lost." NeeNee needled me. She knew I hated losing.

"Hell no! I'm going to get another deck of cards, 'cause this shit is incredible. Something's gotta be wrong with these cards. That's the only way Emma been winning all night."

"Nah, she just that good. Matter of fact, I think I'll get out while the getting's good," NeeNee announced, picking up the few dollars she had left.

"Shit, I'll just have to win back all of my money *and* yours then, Nee," I proclaimed, walking into the back bedroom. I shut the door behind me when I saw Levi lying on the bed, smiling. I walked over and gave him a kiss. He was alive; I was thankful for that, but Sam and his goons had broken all his ribs on the right side and fractured his arm in two places, along with his jaw. He was having a real hard time breathing.

"Hey, baby. You okay? You want something to eat?"

He shook his head then looked down at his private parts.

"Boy, you are one horny-ass man. I'm starting to wish I never gave you your first blow job." I laughed, sliding my hands under the covers. Of course I was joking. I'd do anything for that man-mountain of mine. I had started to slide my way down to his privates when I heard a loud crash in the other room.

"What the fuck?" I was about to run out front when I heard a very familiar voice that made me freeze right where I stood. "Well, well, well, what do we have here?" I swear hearing Sam through that door almost made me pee myself.

"Levi, hide. It's Sam," I whispered, pointing to the closet. He shook his head. "Please, baby," I whispered, about two seconds from tears. "Please, if he finds you, he'll kill you; and I can't live without you, so please just go in the closet."

Levi reluctantly did what I asked, moving slowly and wincing with each painful step as I listened and prayed that I'd get him in that closet before they decided to search the room. I'd just gotten him in the closet and jumped on the bed when the door burst open and one of the twins came in, gun first. He looked around quickly but, to my relief, didn't go searching in the closet or under the bed. He pulled me off the bed and jerked me out of the room, slamming the door behind him.

"Well, look what the cat dragged in," Sam said with a sinister grin when he saw me.

"What do you want, Sam?"

He ignored my question. "You know, Shirley, it took a lot of my resources to find you. Anybody that knows me knows how much I hate using my money for bullshit. Course, I fully expect to be compensated in one way or another for my troubles."

"Don't you touch my kids," Ms. Emma shouted, not giving a damn about Big Sam or his vendetta against the Duncans. He shot her an annoyed look like he'd just become aware of her presence and didn't like it one bit.

"I don't care about you or your snot-nosed kids," he assured her then motioned to the twin standing closest to him. "Take her in the back room and shut her up." No sooner had he spoken than the twin hustled her out of the room to where her kids were still sleeping soundly, strangely unaffected by the drama unfolding only feet away from them.

"Don't you hurt her," I said, motioning to NeeNee, who was sitting on the couch with a hand over her stomach.

He ignored me. Clearly he had other things on his mind. "Where are they?" he said.

"Where are who?"

"You know what the fuck I'm talking about! Where are the Duncans?"

"I don't know," I said, scowling at him. Even if I did know, there was no way I would tell Sam and give him the chance to perform a sneak attack on them like the coward he was.

Whack! Sam slapped me across the face, sending me shrinking away, because I suddenly felt overwhelmed by the memory of years of being punished by Sam. NeeNee roared to my defense, pounding on Sam's chest.

"Don't you hit her again!" she screeched. The other twin cocked his gun and aimed it at her, ready to shoot. I grabbed NeeNee away, because I knew firsthand the kind of masochist Sam could be. The other twin, hearing NeeNee, flew into the room, his gun already raised to protect his boss.

Big Sam's eyes narrowed as he barked his orders at them. "Put them in the car."

"Nooo!" I screamed as one of the twins picked me up and carried me out like a five-pound sack of potatoes. The other did the same to NeeNee, who was not going easily.

"Put me down! Put me the fuck down!" she hollered, kicking and clawing at him to no avail.

When they got us outside, they put us down and tied our hands together before shoving us both into the trunk. My heart thumped against my chest, as everything in me figured this was the end of the road for us. My only regret was that I hadn't been able to spend the rest of my life loving Levi the way that he deserved. I'd spent so much of my life focused on the wrong kind of man, only recently understanding the kind of love Levi had in him.

The car started moving, and we rode for a while before it stopped. When the trunk opened, there was Big Sam, smiling down at us. They hauled us out of the trunk, and when I looked up, I saw that we were in the back of Big Sam's.

"Say one word and I will shoot you both myself," Sam promised, and I had no doubt that he meant it. NeeNee and I shared a look and silently decided we had to ride this out and not test him. Maybe there would still be some way for us to escape.

NeeNee glowered at Sam as she spat out her words. "You do understand that Larry's gonna kill you, and if he doesn't, Lou and LC will."

He laughed as if she had just told him a good joke. "Larry ain't gonna do shit. He's gonna drop to his knees and cry like a little baby when he finds out that I have you. And frankly, I'm not that worried about Lou, 'cause he's always been my bitch. All I have to do is throw a few of those whores up there at him, and he'll be easy to lure into my trap."

"Oh, you think that's it?" Obviously he didn't know that to underestimate LC was a problem.

"I wouldn't even worry about that young buck LC," he said as if he were reading my mind—although he clearly didn't believe in LC's strength like I did. "The college boy ain't got the balls to go up against Sam Bradford."

He barked orders at the twins. "Do it!" One of them opened the cellar door, and they led us down the stairs as his voice boomed with confidence. "Besides, I got something that will bring that little punk to his knees."

All my years living in this place, I'd never once been in the basement, where the biggest surprise since we'd entered the house awaited us. Standing there alone, looking scared to death, was Donna.

Lou

55

Even though it was just after noon, I was mentally and physically exhausted from being up all night as we approached Ms. Emma's house. Thanks to Larry, we'd broken all kinds of speed laws, but luckily we weren't pulled over once. As much as I wanted to stop and get breakfast, Larry kept complaining that he didn't like to be away from Levi this long, especially since Ms. Emma had refused to get a phone installed, even after I offered to pay for it.

My personal opinion was that Larry's impatience had something to do with NeeNee. The two of them had been acting mighty strange the last day or two. NeeNee had been moody as hell, and Larry had been short-tempered with everyone.

"Looks awfully quiet," Larry commented as we pulled up in the yard. There wasn't one of Ms. Emma's wild children in sight, which did seem strange to me.

"Yeah, those kids are always around." LC, who sat next to me in the passenger seat, chimed in. He and Chippy had been avoiding each other during the entire trip, probably because of the fact that he'd found her half-naked in the room with a man who put a hit out on us, so LC rode up front, and she sat in back with Larry and Juan. I really didn't want to take her, but Alejandro insisted that she be the one to call him when either Sam was dead or we were.

Just as we started to get out of the car, the front door flew open and Ms. Emma came running toward us like a bat out of hell.

"They done got 'em!" she hollered, breathing heavy and darting around like a chicken with its head cut off.

"Slow down. What are you talking about?" I asked her, trying to get clarity. The more emotional people got, the calmer I became.

"They took 'em! They took 'em both! They took NeeNee and Shirley."

The color drained out of Larry's face as he grabbed her by the shoulders. "Who took them?"

"Big Sam. He and his men came and took 'em. I couldn't do nothing to stop 'em," she said as tears rolled down her cheeks.

"Damn it!" Chippy cried out, a look of horror covering her face, probably because she knew Sam better than any of us. "This is not good."

"We gotta go get them. If he laid one hand on NeeNee, I will kill him." Larry's voice was shaking with rage as he started to climb back in the car.

"Wait." I stopped him. "What about Levi?" I asked Ms. Emma right before he shuffled out the door, still not one hundred percent yet, and took a seat on the porch. I felt grateful that at least he was still there.

Ms. Emma pointed to him. "Shirley hid him in the back room closet. She knew Sam might have finished the job just to prove his point. If it wasn't for her, they would have killed Levi."

"That was good thinking on her part. So just everybody, let's figure this out. We're not going to go off half-cocked and get ourselves and the women killed. Emma, tell me from the beginning everything that happened."

Ms. Emma took a deep breath then started to explain. "Last night, Sam and his men, those twins who work for him, busted in here and took NeeNee and Shirley. They said you would come looking for them."

"And they just left you here?" Larry questioned, looking at her with suspicion.

She shook her head. "They didn't have no use for me. They told me to go in the other room with my kids, and when I heard the door slam shut, I came out and they were gone. I didn't know how to get in touch with you," she admitted. "Lou, y'all got to get those girls back. That Sam is a motherfucker, and I don't trust that they're safe."

I saw how hard her words hit Larry, who usually only showed one emotion—anger—but right now all I saw was the fear of a broken man.

"I know, Ms. Emma, but that's how he's planning on trapping us," I said.

"Get in the car!" Larry shouted. His eyes were filled up with tears, and I could tell from his expression he was close to losing it. "Everyone get in the fucking car!"

"Larry, calm down, bro. We're going to get them, but we need a plan." LC was trying to defuse Larry's rage to no avail. Larry snatched him up by the collar, and I swear it looked like he was going to punch him.

"Larry, Larry, let him go!" I shouted.

"I don't wanna hear it, Lou. Just get the fuck in the car! I don't got time for no plan. I ain't got time to be talking. Just get in the car, 'cause that bastard's got my woman and my unborn child."

"Oh, shit! Nee's pregnant?" LC blurted out, and just like that, Larry broke down, falling in a heap of tears into our little brother's arms.

"We gotta get her, LC." Larry wept. "I didn't even get a chance to tell her I loved her or that I wanted the baby. We gotta go to Sam and get her."

LC held him. "Larry, we can't just walk into Big Sam's. Lou's right; it would be a trap. We don't even know if he's holding them there."

"Maybe that's not a bad idea." Chippy, who'd been relatively quiet, surprised me with that. She seemed pretty smart for a woman who made her living on her back, but what she had just said made no sense.

"How the hell we gonna do that?" I asked. I couldn't see any way to just walk into Big Sam's that didn't end with us all dead.

Chippy's face broke into a devilish smile before she answered. "I say we walk right up to the front door—or to be clear, I walk right up to the front door."

LC, who clearly didn't like the sound of that, stepped in front of her. "No, that would be too dangerous."

But Chippy had already made up her mind. "Sometimes you gotta do what you gotta do. NeeNee's my friend, LC, and so is Shirley. If I can help them, I'm gonna help. You know what I'm capable of when I'm mad. I ain't afraid of Sam. In fact, he should be afraid of me."

Chippy

56

"Chippy! Girl, you back." Little Momma shouted out as I stepped into Big Sam's, looking fly as hell in the new clothes Alejandro had bought when he took me shopping. I'd left most of the other clothing behind, though. I knew better than to bring all my new goodies up in this house, 'cause my future plans had nothing to do with me staying longer than I needed.

"Yep, I'm back." I smiled and went right to Little Momma. She was just the right person to give me the lowdown on everything that was happening. Nothing—and I mean nothing—went down at Big Sam's without her knowing about it. Of course, it never took much to get information out of her, 'cause that girl lived to hear and spread gossip. She was our very own Rona Barrett, and nobody could be mad at her, because it was just her nature.

"Sam's been gone all day, but I know he'll be glad to see you," she gushed, checking out my suede hot pants, matching fringe jacket, and knee-high boots.

"Let's get a drink," I suggested, knowing that all it would take was one rum and Coke to help loosen those lips. Looking around, I noticed there were a few new faces, mostly men, the big muscle-types who you could tell were packing guns underneath their jackets, 'cause it was too hot to have them on inside for any other reason. I pretended not to notice them, but their presence told me one thing immediately: Sam was worried about retaliation, or else he was trying to hide something—or both.

"Dennis, could we have two rum and Cokes?" I asked my favorite bartender, who slid two drinks across the bar. We clinked glasses, and before I could even get halfway through mine, she had downed her whole drink and was looking for a second.

"So, where were you? And that guy musta been a big deal, 'cause that's the only way Sam would've let you go. Hell, you make more money than two or three of us combined, so you know his greedy ass must've made that guy pay big."

"Yeah, he had a whole lot of green, and he didn't mind spending some of it on me." I laughed. "Wasn't bad in bed either."

Little Momma licked her lips. I swear she actually enjoyed the sex she had with most of the johns who came through there. "That's what I'm talking about. Just 'cause they paying don't mean they shouldn't know what the hell they're doing. Did he put your needs first?"

"Hell yeah, and he treated me like a princess," I admitted, thinking about Alejandro for the first time since I'd left him.

"Then why the hell you come back here? I woulda made his dick so desperate for me that he kept my ass. You would have never seen my black ass again. All you'd know was that I was somewhere riding that dick to the bank." She laughed, slapping herself on the knee. I figured she was good and sauced when Dennis placed the third drink in front of her and she downed it.

"So, what the hell has been going on around here? Besides the obvious," I said, motioning to the bodyguards.

Just like I'd hoped, she took the bait and leaned in close. "After what Sam done to Levi Duncan, he's treating this place like Fort fucking Knox."

"Really? You mean the bodyguards?"

She shook her head. "Nah, I'm talking everything. Some of the customers are being patted down when they come in here if we don't recognize them . . . and there's something else." She glanced around, all suspicious, like she didn't want anybody to hear, then leaned in close to whisper to me. "There's something happening in that cellar."

"Like what?" I asked, acting like this was just regular old gossip, but my reasons were way less pure.

"I don't know, but Sam's been going down there a lot. Those bodyguards been taking food and other stuff when they don't think nobody is looking, but my ass sees everything."

"You think maybe they're just having meetings?" I questioned her innocently.

"Uh-uh. You know Sam takes all his meetings in his office. He likes people to see his fancy desk and shit. I tried to find out firsthand what was going on," she said then lifted her sleeve to reveal a bright reddish mark on her arm. "Sam damn near took my arm off just for trying to get a peek." She stopped suddenly when the front door opened.

"Ooh, I got to go get that money. My quota is so low today, and I ain't try'na catch his temper." She downed the rest of the drink and sped over to the door to meet a new customer.

Our little chat had definitely proved to be enlightening, just like I thought it would be.

"Dennis?" I motioned for the bartender.

He grabbed the rum and came toward me. "You want me to top you off?"

"Nah, I just wanted to ask you something."

"What is it?" he asked.

"You keep all the liquor down in the cellar, right?"

He shook his head. "Not lately. Sam moved it to a hall closet and put a lock on it. That cellar is off limits."

"When did that happen?" I asked, growing more convinced that NeeNee and Shirley were being held downstairs.

"'Bout four or five days ago. I was trying to restock, but he told me the new guys would bring whatever I needed upstairs, and then next thing I knew, he had the entire liquor locker put up here."

Bingo! I thought.

"No telling why Sam does the things he does, right?" I said innocently to Dennis.

He smiled at me. "You know that's right."

That night, or should I say early the next morning, I tied a scarf to the window to give the Duncans the signal that the girls were being kept in the house. I couldn't take a chance on calling them or leaving the house, so I figured I'd wait until noon and make some excuse to go into town. In the meantime, I wanted to see for myself. I opened the door and crept into the hallway and down the stairs. The house was dead silent, just as I'd figured it would be. Nobody rose before noon, so the coast was clear. When I saw one of the bodyguards sleeping on the sofa in the living room, I tiptoed past him into the kitchen and through the small hallway, where I could reach the door to the cellar.

"What you looking for?" Big Sam's voice stopped me in my tracks. I pulled my hand away from the doorknob like it was flaming hot. He was glaring at me, his anger starting to boil over. I hated that I knew him so well.

"Nothing, Sam," I said as sweetly as possible, trying to put him at ease.

"It wouldn't have anything to do with what's in the cellar, would it?" he asked, not taking his eyes off of me.

I went over and started rubbing on his leg, willing to fuck him if that was what it took to calm him down and distract him. "I was looking for you. Alejandro told me to let you know that he had taken care of the Duncans."

"Oh, is that so?" he said, and I couldn't read his tone to know if he believed me. I had no choice but to continue trying to seduce him. Hell, if I could get him into bed, I could probably slit his throat in his sleep and end this whole thing.

"Yeah, that's half the reason I'm back." I gave him a big smile.

"Half the reason? What's the other half?" he asked as I felt his dick growing hard beneath my touch.

"I kind of missed you."

"I thought it was just business between us," he said with a hint of suspicion in his tone, although he didn't stop me from stroking him through the fabric of his pants.

"It is, but when a girl wants some really good dick, Big Sam Bradford is always the one to call. And I'm horny as hell." I could see him puff out his chest a little after that comment. No one had a bigger ego than Sam.

"Is that right?" He chuckled and allowed me to keep giving him a hand job while he went back to our original conversation. "So, Alejandro's guys killed the Duncans, huh?"

"That's what he said."

Suddenly, Sam grabbed me by the hair with one hand and used the other one to open the door to the cellar.

"You a bald-faced liar, bitch! My men already told me the Duncans are back in town and that you were with them. I don't know what's going on, but I know your ass is part of it."

In one swift movement, he tossed me down the stairs like a sack of dirty laundry.

57

"I see three, four, five men out front," Juan said as we drove past Big Sam's in an old van, wearing baseball hats and sunglasses, hoping to get some type of reconnaissance and see a signal from Chippy. Larry had wanted to go, but Lou and I thought he was too wound up and might do something stupid. Sure enough, flapping in the upper window was a bright purple scarf, just like Chippy had promised she would leave if NeeNee and Shirley were in the house. I briefly wished that I could get her out of there first, before she got caught in the crossfire, but I had to I remind myself that she could take care of herself.

"You all right?" Juan asked, noticing the expression on my face.

"Yeah, I'm okay," I said, loosening the grip on my .45 as we exited the Oak Street strip.

"Man, you're usually the most honest guy I know, but right now I can tell you're lying through your teeth. It's Chippy, isn't it?" Damn guy must have been reading my mind or something, because I hadn't stopped worrying about her ever since she left Ms. Emma's house to go back to Sam's.

"Chippy and I are just friends. I'm worried about her. That's all," I lied, hoping he would leave it at that.

Juan turned to me with a big smile on his face. "I've seen the way you look at her. I also saw the way you looked when Alejandro kissed her good-bye. You've got it bad, my friend."

"Hey, I said that I care about her, and I do, but it's not an easy situation I'm in, either."

"Of course. It's difficult when you're in love with one woman and engaged to another," he said. "You don't look at

Donna the way you do Chippy. Why is it that everyone sees this but you?"

"I see. I just don't know what to do about it." I shook my head to clear my thoughts. "Look, I can't concentrate on that right now. We got a real problem that needs to be solved, and it's bigger than my love life."

I pulled up at the spot Lou had gotten these two girls he messed with to lend us for the day, so that we could get all locked and loaded. Larry had hired three of his military buddies, who came strapped for battle and were ready when we walked in.

"It's there!" I announced as I entered the room.

Larry was pacing the floor like a madman. "C'mon, let's go!" he yelled.

I shot a look to Lou. It was our job to calm him down before we did anything.

"Relax, man. You got to relax, Larry," Lou ordered, but Larry was past being able to reel it back in. He just wanted his woman back.

"Man, that motherfucker is dead. You hear me? You can take my money, my car—hell, even my life, but you take my woman? Are you fucking serious? You might as well rip my heart out with your bare hands. If he harmed one hair on her head, I will kill him and burn that place to the ground," Larry ranted, still pacing frantically.

"If there wasn't so much good pussy in that place, I'd have to agree. Hoes need a roof over their heads too." Lou, ever the protector of women, chimed in. We may have been going on a rescue mission, but I knew that if there was a way for Lou to wind up with his dick deep inside one or two of Sam's girls by the end of the night, that would happen. If Lou was one thing, it was consistent. Even at a time like this, when the pressure was sky high, he was still thinking with his little head.

I could see that Larry wasn't feeling Lou's humor, so I stepped in to keep everyone's minds on the mission. "Larry, we need you to have your men ready."

"We stay ready!" He looked to his men for their agreement, and everybody nodded, clutching their weapons and looking eager to go shoot somebody. Larry snatched up two guns with enough artillery to start a war—which was good, since that was what we were doing. Technically, Sam had thrown down the gauntlet when he took the women, but the Duncans were putting an end to his bullshit.

"Then let's go!" Lou stood up calmly, as if he were going to the diner to get a bite and not into battle.

Larry faced his men. "Once NeeNee and Shirley are safe and out of there, you can do whatever the fuck you want to those motherfuckers. But until my lady is back with me, we need to be careful. You understand?"

"As long as I get the second half of my ten grand, I'll do anything you say," one of the men, a white guy with red hair, said.

"Okay, then it's time to ride." Larry was the first one out the door, with the rest of us following, each loaded with at least one firearm. When we got into the van, my heart was pounding. Even though I knew we were going to rescue NeeNee and Shirley, I wasn't leaving that place without Chippy.

Chippy

58

"Oh my God! Chippy!" Through the fog and the pain of my fall, I heard Big Shirley's voice not far from me.

"Is she dead?" NeeNee rushed over and grabbed me up in her arms. When I opened my eyes and blinked, it made her jump damn near across the room. Even with the physical pain and the messed-up situation we were in, I couldn't help but burst out in laughter at her reaction.

"Um, guess she's alive." Donna spat the words out, sounding like the bitter, jealous bitch I knew she was.

"How'd they get you?" I asked Donna, shocked to see her there along with NeeNee and Shirley as I sat up. "Ouch!"

"Same way they got all of us. The element of surprise—unless you don't know what that is," she answered, all salty.

I stared her down, ready to take her on. "Oh, I know what it is, and I use it when I want to whip somebody's ass without them expecting it coming." I almost laughed again when she took a few steps back, just in case.

"How'd they get you?" Big Shirley asked. "Hell, I thought you had left this place. At least that's what the girls told me last week when they stopped by the shop."

"Well, I came back with LC." I stopped there, just wanting to stick it to Donna. I was happy to see from her sour expression that it bothered her to hear that LC and I had been together. "And Lou, Larry, and Juan."

"Who's Juan?" Shirley asked.

"It's John. Now he's Juan," I answered. When she gave me a puzzled expression, I said, "I'll explain later."

NeeNee jumped in, bringing the conversation back to the important details. "So they know we're here? Does Larry know that Sam took us? I swear Larry will kill him."

"Yeah, and believe me, when he found out that Big Sam had taken you, he was insane with rage. But we needed to be smart and not have them walk into a trap. They sent me in here to find out if you were in the house before they came in."

"So did you tell them?" Donna snapped. She was getting on my last nerve. "Or did you mess that up?"

I nodded, refusing to let that bitch make me feel like I was less than her. "Yeah, I told them. We had a signal that if I found you—meaning NeeNee and Shirley—then I'd leave a scarf tied to my window. Of course, none of us knew that you were even here," I said, hoping it made her feel like the outsider I viewed her to be. Just to add salt to the wound, I said, "So, I guess LC hasn't tried to go see you yet, 'cause otherwise he would've known you were missing."

She rolled her eyes at me. "He will. I know you got your eyes on my man, but you can forget it. He'd never leave me to be with anyone like you."

"Hey! Hey!" Big Shirley interrupted. "I'm too busy worrying if that Negro upstairs is going to kill us 'fore we can get out of here alive, so I'm not that interested in you two arguing over a man. Besides, neither of you will be alive to ever see him again if we don't get out of here."

She had a good point, so I would leave the bitch alone for now. I glanced around the cellar. There were no windows, and just a tiny bathroom.

"So how come none of you tried to get out? You ain't tied up, and if you bang on the door real hard, somebody is bound to find you," I said.

Donna took a step toward me. "We tried that, genius, but those twins came down here with guns and said the next time we knocked on the door or tried to alert anybody that we were here, they would blow our brains away. So, you can see how having a gun shoved in your mouth can stop any stupid plan."

"Yeah, and they were serious," Big Shirley added, ignoring Donna. "You know they don't have any regard for human life. It's like they're waiting to kill somebody just for the hell of it."

"What they want is for all the Duncan brothers to come in here, guns blazing, to try to rescue us, so that they can kill them. I swear, if one of 'em hurts Larry, I will kill them with my bare hands," NeeNee promised, and I believed her.

"They won't get the chance," I said, trying to restore her hope.

"So, you seen him lately. Is he okay?" NeeNee said, sounding anxious and worried, which was the female equivalent to a man who was angry and homicidal.

"He's good," I answered. "He's worried about you and the baby."

"He said that?" She looked like she was about to cry.

"Yeah, he did. He really loves you, NeeNee, but right now let's concentrate on coming up with some kind of plan to get out of here."

"Yeah, before Sam runs out of patience." Big Shirley shuddered.

I had an idea. "What we need is a gun."

Donna sighed impatiently. "Where we gonna get a gun from, genius?"

"That girl is stuck on stupid. Don't mind her." Big Shirley sneered at Donna and paid close attention, waiting to hear what I said next.

I glanced around in the cellar, looking for things that we could use to help us get out of there. Unfortunately, all I saw were a couple of cots, chairs, a table, and a couple of lamps, which were our only source of light.

I looked again, and suddenly a smile covered my face. "Ladies, I think I have a plan."

Big Shirley

59

We'd been sitting in the dark for at least two hours, maybe three, waiting for someone to come through the door.

"This is taking too long," Donna complained for the umpteenth time, even though she wasn't the one holding her position in case someone showed up. No, the princess was resting comfortably on a cot pushed against the wall, while NeeNee, Chippy, and I did all the proverbial heavy lifting. That damn girl had been getting on everybody's nerves, and I just hoped she shut up before one of us put a hurting on her.

"Shhhh!" Chippy hissed as we finally heard the door unlocking.

Then someone spoke. "Fucking light's out!" a male voice grunted, obviously annoyed at the inconvenience. "Shit, are they gone?" he said to himself, or that's what we were thinking as we waited to hear if someone was going to answer him. When there were no other voices, I felt the collective sigh of relief. For a second, I felt panicked, 'cause the plan Chippy had put in place could only work if there was one man, and Lord, if Big Sam was with him, it would definitely be the end of us.

"Hey!" he hollered out down the stairs. "You bitches down there?"

Just like we'd planned, Chippy answered. "Yeah, but NeeNee is hurt. She's pregnant. We need you to come quick. It's serious!"

"Let me get a flashlight first," he answered, saying the one thing that would torpedo our scheme.

"Oooh! Help me. Please, help me," NeeNee cried out dramatically, writhing like she was really hurting. That damn woman should've been an actress, because she had me about to help her, and I knew she was fine.

"Dammit!" He complained. "You whores better not try no funny business."

"Who you calling a whore?" Donna snapped at him, forgetting that her dumb ass was supposed to stay quiet. That bitch was about to get us all killed.

"Shut up!" I hissed at her, soft enough so that the guard couldn't hear. What if her smart mouth made him change his mind and he ran to get a flashlight or get some backup?

Luckily, NeeNee knew the score and cried out again, this time louder. "Help me! Please, help me!" I had to give her props. She sounded desperate.

That's when we heard him coming down the stairs, his heavy feet landing like bricks as he took each step. It gave us all the information we needed to put our plan into motion. Chippy and NeeNee were each standing on chairs on opposite sides of the stairway. Stretched across the stairs was the cord from the lamp, held taut in their hands. With every step, I could feel myself growing more terrified. In my head, I could hear Chippy's voice egging him forward. Just as he took the next step, they tightened that cord. He tripped over it and went flying forward, until his ass hit the ground.

"Let me get the light," I said and raced over to turn on the one lamp we had left. It was one of those twins lying there. I swear, I hated them both for what they did to Levi and me. I picked up a two-by-four leaning against the wall and started whooping his ass the way he had done to my man.

Thwack! Thwack! Thwack! I hit him as hard as I could, and I would have kept on doing it if it weren't for Chippy.

"Shirley!" Chippy whispered to me. "It's all right. It's all right." She took the two-by-four out of my hand and dropped it to the floor. "I need to get his gun." Then she reached down and removed the weapon from his hand.

NeeNee came over and stood next to us, putting an arm around me to offer some comfort. "Okay, you got the gun. Now what we gonna do?"

"You know there's like twenty men up there with guns. Now they're gonna kill us for what you just did." Donna glared at Chippy accusingly.

"Shut up, Donna!" I snapped. "I'm 'bout sick of you," I told her and gave her a look that dared her to try me.

NeeNee sneaked up the stairs and held the door open. Then Chippy and I followed along with Donna, who kept her distance.

"Close the door!" Chippy whispered, because NeeNee had opened it wide enough for anybody walking past to spot us. NeeNee did as she was told, leaving it open just a tiny bit, so that no one would even know we were there.

"I don't see anything!" Donna whined.

Chippy

60

When I first heard all the shooting and carrying on going down on the first level, I thought Sam's security was shooting at us. After all, NeeNee had opened the damn door up wide enough for anyone to have spotted us. I was not sure I had told her to close it soon enough before we'd been spotted by someone. All I knew was that the sound of gunshots rang out and had our asses running back down those steps.

"You hear that?" Big Shirley said. "Sounds like it's more than just somebody being shot. Sounds like an all-out war."

I had mixed emotions. A part of me was excited. I knew my signal had worked and that LC and his brothers had come to our rescue—at least NeeNee's and Big Shirley's rescue. I'd already established that LC had no idea that Donna had gone missing, and how would he have had any idea that I'd been thrown in the dungeon with them?

So, even though relief surged through my body, riding the waves of anticipation to get the hell out of this basement, I was afraid. Sam had a great deal of added security, men that the Duncans knew nothing about. I think this was that "element of surprise" shit Donna was tooting her horn about. The Duncans had a reputation as the baddest brothers in town, definitely not to be fucked with, but Sam had upped the ante with the men he had securing the place. Would the Duncans be prepared for this? If only I'd had a way of communicating with them. But it was too late for all that now. They would find out soon enough.

"The hell with this," NeeNee finally said. "I'm not about to sit down here and wait until the dust settles." She headed for the steps. "My man is up there, and I'm going to see about him."

"But wait!" Big Shirley said, still trying to whisper. I guess she figured maybe if we stayed quiet, everybody upstairs would kill each other, and then the last man standing would go on about his business, leaving us alone. "How do you know Larry is up there? You know how many enemies Sam got? It could be anybody up there trying to take him out, and you think they gon' give a shit about you? Hell, you just gon' be another ho to them."

NeeNee turned around slowly, glaring at Big Shirley with the look of death. "I know my man, and my man ain't gon' leave me here to die. He'd die first before he ever let that happen. I know my man," she repeated, "and he's come for me." NeeNee paused, giving Big Shirley a chance to respond, although her eyes said that if she even though about it, the other side of her face would get fucked up, along with the side that was still healing.

Big Shirley turned to look at me. She bucked her eyes and then nodded her head toward NeeNee as if I was supposed to say something to her. So, I did.

"You are a woman who knows your man," was all I could say.

NeeNee half-smiled at me with her eyes before she turned to go up the steps.

"So, you just gon' let her jump in the line of fire for her man?" Big Shirley said to me.

"You mean kind of like you did when they were beating Levi senseless." I wasn't usually an I-told-you-so kind of girl, but how quickly Big Shirley had forgotten about the time she risked her own life for the sake of the man she loved.

The way her eyes mirrored the look NeeNee had just shot me before going up the steps let me know that she'd needed that reminder. She watched NeeNee climb the steps and then took off after her.

"Where you going?" I asked Big Shirley.

"With her. Where you think? If I'm getting taken out, it ain't gon' be down here in this shitty basement with you two." She pointed to Donna. "Especially her. I'm with NeeNee. If I'm going down, I'm going down fighting." Big Shirley turned around and resumed her climb.

It was just Donna and me standing there. I knew that dog's bark was way worse than her bite and that she wasn't going anywhere, but before the thought even left my mind, she was heading for the steps too. "Now where you going?" I asked.

She stopped and looked me up and down like I was a bag of trash. "With them. I sure as hell ain't going to be caught dead with you. Hell, I don't even want to be caught alive with you. I want to die with dignity, not with hoes." She turned her stuck-up nose in the air and then marched up the steps, where NeeNee had once again cracked the door to get a feel for what was going on upstairs. Big Shirley was hovering over her, trying to get a peek.

If it weren't for the fact that I was busy worrying about whether I was going to get out of that place alive, I'd have snatched Donna's ass up and mopped the floor with her. I'd been wanting to beat that highfalutin' heifer's tail, but on the off chance that we made it out of there, I didn't want to get free only to be turned over to the authorities for killing her ass. I'd already gotten away with murder before, and lightning doesn't strike twice. Who knows, though—if we did escape from this basement, I might consider myself lucky enough to tempt fate and commit another murder. Then I'd kill her dead and check it off my bucket list.

"Bitch," I mumbled under my breath.

"I heard that," she said, twitching her ass as she walked up the steps.

"I meant for you to," I lied. Well, I actually didn't give a shit one way or the other.

"This could be our last breathing moments, and you two wanna cat fight?" Big Shirley shot over her shoulder in a hard whisper. "Well, more power to you, but do you mind shutting the fuck up, at least until the two of us, who want our chance in hell of surviving, get out of here?"

"Shhhh." NeeNee turned to all of us with her index finger over her lips.

All of a sudden, the rapid gunfire and thumping and bumping that had been taking place over our heads came to a halt. An eerie feeling rested in the air. No one spoke, but from the looks on our faces and the way our eyes darted back and forth,

we were all thinking the same thing. If the Duncan boys had come for us, it didn't sound as though all of them had survived.

But just then, we heard a loud thump, and we all instinctively ducked. If I had to guess, it sounded like a body dropping to the ground and then the sound of doors being kicked in. There was more screaming that sounded like it was from both men and women.

"I can't take this anymore," NeeNee said, placing her trembling hands on her temples. I imagined that not knowing whether Larry was a casualty of the violence we heard taking place above our heads had taken its toll on NeeNee. She grabbed the doorknob and pushed it open.

I held my breath, waiting to see what would happen next. Big Shirley might have climbed those steps right behind NeeNee, but she didn't go out that door right behind her. She had good sense. She was going to wait for NeeNee to get shot dead at best. She sure wasn't going to run out there haphazardly amidst bullets with no names on them flying around.

"What's going on? What do you see?" I asked Big Shirley as I walked up a few steps.

Donna's scary ass had backpedaled a step or two. She almost backed right into me and knocked me down the steps. She didn't say a word; just shifted her head from left to right as if she was trying to figure something out.

"Well, blow me over, but I think . . ." Big Shirley peeked out a little further, and then her facial expression turned to excitement. "She was right. It's Larry." Big Shirley was next to dodge out the door.

"Wait Bi—" I started, but her big tail had moved like a skinny chick. I was worried about her. Just because she saw Larry didn't mean it was safe to go running. I could still hear lots of commotion, but that hadn't stopped Big Shirley, as Donna and I stood there eating her dust.

Next, Donna tiptoed to the top of the steps and decided to try her luck. She peeked and then ran out as well.

And then there was one. What was I waiting on? What did I expect to happen next? Perhaps deep down inside I was expecting what NeeNee had expected, and apparently gotten,

out of Larry. He had come for her. I wanted that same thing from LC.

Even though LC had no idea that I was being held down in the basement with NeeNee and Big Shirley, I think a part of me had just wanted him to come for me period; come take me away from Sam, this house, this life. I shook my head, releasing the thoughts of the happy ending that belonged to someone else. That was not the story of my life. Things never ended up good for me.

With that being said, what did I have to lose? The same way the other girls had gone up the steps and out the door to freedom, risking being hit by a bullet, I did the same. Without contemplating any further, I went up the steps and walked out the door.

Around the room was mayhem, though. There was blood, and there were bodies, and there was still commotion going on overhead. I decided I needed to get while the getting was good. I took one step toward the door before I felt a strong hand grab my hair and pull me back. When I looked up, there was Sam's angry face.

"Where you think you going, bitch?"

Larry

61

The van came to a screeching halt as we pulled up to Sam's with one of my guys tied to the roof. His job was to take out anyone standing in front of the building before we even stepped out of the van. All I can say is that he was very good at his job.

Even though LC had already told us it was there, it was a relief to see Chippy's scarf tied to the window with my own eyes. Knowing that my baby was inside that place somewhere and I was there to rescue her had me riled up even more than I had been. Once I entered, I'd be able to kill two birds with one stone. I'd take care of Sam and rescue NeeNee all in one stop. I couldn't wait to put a bullet in his head.

"Let's move," I told the guys, who stepped out of the van just a half a second after I did. We were definitely in sync, just like back in 'Nam.

We stormed the door, and our timing couldn't have been more perfect. I almost felt sorry for the poor bastards Sam had hired, because for three army rangers, this was like shooting fish in a barrel. Of course, you know the first to go was one of the twins, running at us with guns in both hands like it was the wild, wild West. I took him out personally. Once the room was cleared, Lou and Juan came through the door, while my buddy on the van's roof cut himself free to protect our rear at the door.

"I'm going to find Sam," Lou said as he and Juan headed to my right, toward Sam's office. I pointed to the staircase, and my two guys moved toward it as I headed for the back. I heard shots and women screaming upstairs, and I knew my guys had found someone armed to take out.

It looked like Sam had tripled his protection team. I was a little bit overwhelmed at first by all these new cats coming out of the woodwork, but it shouldn't have surprised me. The dude who ran all the pussy in town turned out to be the biggest pussy of them all.

As I moved down a hallway, it was time to try door number one. I wasn't sure if it was a closet or a basement, but it didn't matter. I went to grab the doorknob, my gun raised, but just as I went to open it, it flung open and I cocked the gun, set on pulling the trigger next no matter who it was. If a ho and her john had been turning a trick, at least one of them might die happy.

"Larry!" she screamed. "Don't shoot, baby! It's me." I pulled back my gun instinctively, and NeeNee wrapped her arms around my neck, holding on so tight she nearly choked me. Her tears soaked my face. "Oh, baby, I knew you was coming for me."

Staring into NeeNee's eyes, I could see that she had never doubted me. I wished I could have stood there and held her forever, but Sam was still in that house somewhere. The fellas were still handling some resistance throughout the house. I could hear the commotion of doors being kicked in, shots being fired, and terrified screams. But there was still some unfinished business I needed to tend to.

Just then, I saw Shirley come out of the same place NeeNee had exited. "You get out of here," I told NeeNee. Shirley was already headed for the door. "I'll meet you back at the house."

"Fuck that!" NeeNee said, throwing her hands on her hips. "I ain't leaving you in here. If you die, we die together, because I sure as hell can't live without you."

She was safe and sound, and I needed her to get out of there so that we could keep it that way. "Look, Nee, I don't have time to argue with you."

"And I don't have time to lose you." She placed her hands on my cheeks and looked deep into my eyes. "I believe in you. I trust you, but if you stay, I'm staying. If you want me out of here and able to live to see another day, then I want the same in return. We've got a baby to raise."

I tried to push her away from me toward the exit, but she refused to budge.

"So, what's it going to be?" she asked.

I knew that no matter what I said, she was not going to leave Sam's place unless I did. As badly as I wanted to hang his head above a mantel as a trophy, I would have to let one of my comrades have the honor of killing Sam. I took NeeNee by one hand, keeping my gun raised with the other, until I could get her out of there safely. This bird in the hand was worth two in the bush.

62

I was the last one in Big Sam's, because I was driving and had to help the guy on the roof cut himself down, which, I was starting to think, had been my brothers' plan all along. As I entered, gun in hand, I saw that the floor was riddled with bodies, and I was just glad that none of them were my brothers or our men.

"LC!" Larry shouted as he and NeeNee headed toward the door behind me. "It's pretty much over. All Sam's guys are dead or on the run."

"NeeNee, girl, you are a sight for sore eyes." I gave her a quick hug. "Y'all seen Lou?"

"He and Juan were headed toward Sam's office."

"What about Chippy?"

"Last I saw her, she was still in the cellar." NeeNee pointed in the direction they had come from.

Larry tugged on her arm. "Come on. I'm getting you outta here," he told her.

"Y'all go 'head. I'm gonna find Lou and Chippy." Before they left, I grabbed Larry and looked him dead in the face. "What about Sam? Is he taken care of?"

He turned and looked into NeeNee's eyes while he spoke to me. "I'm gonna let Lou or the boys take care of him. I can't be getting all crazy like I used to. I got a family to look out for now."

A huge grin covered NeeNee's face as they walked out of the building. I could tell right then and there that my brother was a changed man. Back in the day—hell, just yesterday—Larry wouldn't have left until he split Sam's wig.

As I stood inside the front room of Sam's place and surveyed the scene, it looked like Larry's boys had truly handled their business. Unfortunately, all those dead men meant nothing if, as I was soon to find out, the main reason for our surprise visit was still breathing.

I walked in the direction that NeeNee had pointed, and I ran right smack into Big Sam. Even worse, he had Chippy pulled tightly against him, with a fist full of her hair. His other hand gripped a twelve-inch hunting knife, which was pressed against her throat. From the way her face was scrunched up, I could see she was in pain.

"Let her go, Sam," I demanded, aiming my gun right between his eyes.

"Motherfucker, how you gon' tell me to let go of my own bitch?" Sam spat.

I had to play this thing out right, so I tried to remain cool. As good a shot as I was when hitting cans and bottles, I wasn't sure if I could hit him without taking a chance of hitting her. "Sam, you don't want to do this," I said. "Look around. Does it look like you are going to make it out alive? Your friends down here didn't."

Sam eyeballed the room, noticing his dead security detail strewn about the place. No matter how much he had beefed it up, his guards had been no match for the Duncan brothers. Just then, two of Larry's ex-army buddies appeared from upstairs, their eyes gleaming with the pride of victory.

"And it doesn't look like your friends upstairs fared any better." I shook my head.

As it sank into Sam's consciousness that he was alone—no bodyguards, no twins—and his fate was pretty much sealed, anger rose in his eyes.

"Ugh!" Chippy cried out as he twisted her hair tightly, probably pulling it from her scalp. He was taking out his anger on her.

"Just let her go and you and I can handle this like men," I said.

"Why you keep trying to tell me what to do with my bitches?" Sam said, spittle flying from his mouth. He was trying his best not to show his fear. "Come on, tell me. What is it about this particular ho that got you in here actin' like some hostage negotiator?" He tried to laugh, but it was weak and hollow.

I looked at Chippy, who was trying to pry Sam's hands off of her hair.

"Because I love her," were the words that escaped my mouth.

For one hot second, it seemed as though my words had healed all of Chippy's pain—not just the pain being inflicted on her by Sam, but a lifetime of pain.

"Aw, you looooove her," Sam taunted.

I ignored his menacing laugh and continued staring at Chippy. I spoke directly to her. "Because I love you. I realize that now."

"Ain't that sweet. Now drop the fucking gun or I'll cut her fucking head off." He pressed the knife against her neck just enough to draw a few drops of blood. "Do I look like I'm playing? Drop the fucking gun, or you going to be in love with a headless woman!"

"Okay, okay." I laid down my weapon.

Sam grinned like a motherfucker. "Now, for the record, I own this pussy. I own all the pussy in this fucking state," he shouted and drooled at the same time. He had this King Kong demeanor, as if he was the biggest and baddest around. It was time for me to break his ass down.

"From what I hear, you *are* the biggest pussy in town too. Or was that sissy?" I laughed derisively.

The look in Sam's eyes was priceless. It was like he'd seen a ghost. It might not have been a ghost, but something was definitely coming back to haunt him.

"That's right, Sam. Your little perverted secret is out," I said.

"You motherfucker!" I guess Sam wanted to hurt me the same way I'd just hurt him. He raised the knife in the air to bring it down on Chippy's chest. Before he could do so, I charged his ass. I could have gone for my gun, but I didn't want to take any chances of not getting to him in time.

Right before his hand came down, I grabbed his arm with both of my hands. Chippy managed to slip away from him as we struggled. Sam gripped the knife tightly, trying not to lose hold of it. I used my body weight to push him down to the floor, and the two of us tussled. Finally, the knife found flesh to puncture, and within seconds, blood was covering my shirt and Sam's as it exited the deep wound.

"Jesus!" Chippy cried out and turned her head away. I'd seen what her mama's place looked like when she got finished with her stepfather and mother, so I didn't think it was the blood that had her turning her head as much as it was the reminder of the scene she'd left back in the house she was raised in.

I lay there on my side, face-to-face with Sam. He reached his hand out to wrap around my throat in one last attempt to take out a Duncan, but he didn't have the strength to do me any harm. It wasn't long before he succumbed to the wound in his chest. He spit up a mouthful of blood, and then his eyes rolled into the back of his head.

When I knew it was over, I got up off the ground. I felt something inside of me shut down and go cold. I think I was in shock after what I had done. Looking down at the body that used to belong to that evil son of a bitch but was now just a corpse with puddles of blood oozing out of it, I felt strangely removed. There had been so many times over the last few years that I imagined killing him, but I never really thought it would come to this. I would find a way to make peace with my actions, though, because after what he did to Levi—and then to kidnap NeeNee, Shirley, and Chippy—I had more than enough reason to end his life. Hell, he deserved to be dead just for the way he had taken advantage of Chippy, the woman I loved, turning her into a prostitute with his lies.

"LC." I heard Lou calling me, but I couldn't get past the fog to get to him. Then I felt him grab my hand, trying to shake me out of it. Until he took the knife from me, I had forgotten that I was still holding it. "Relax," his calm voice advised me.

I glanced up at Lou, and that's when I saw her moving toward me like a bright light in the storm. Since we'd sent her back into this house, I hadn't stopped worrying about her safety. I felt my entire body begin to relax as her eyes held mine.

"Oh, baby, you're all right!" Donna's voice jarred me, and suddenly her hands were on me, trying to pull me into an embrace.

"Don't—" I called out to Chippy, but she had already switched gears and was moving into the other room. I glanced over at the bar and saw her take a seat and pick up a bottle of liquor. I wanted so much to join her.

"Oh God, LC, I was so worried," Donna said, burying her head into my chest. "But I knew you were going to rescue us. I told them."

"Yeah," I mumbled, still not getting my head around the last ten minutes. Nor could I understand why this was the woman in my arms and not Chippy. But of course, she wouldn't understand that.

That's when Larry and NeeNee walked in. "Give the man some room," he chastised Donna. "You all right? Bet you feel like a real Duncan now, bro."

Donna shot Larry a dirty look. "I'm making sure he's all right. After all, LC is the real hero."

"Go somewhere!" Larry snapped back at her. "We need to check on our brother." He nodded to NeeNee.

"C'mon, girl. Give the men a minute." NeeNee took Donna's arms and hustled her out of the room, even though I could tell NeeNee wanted to stay right there.

"You okay?" Lou asked, and then he did the damndest thing: he threw his arms around me and hugged me in a way he hadn't since Mom got carted off to prison. I swear I wanted to break down, but I knew that Larry would never let me live it down. Besides, that's not the way a Duncan behaved, and I was a Duncan.

I pulled away, glaring down at the corpse. "He fucking deserved it!"

Larry laughed. "Damn if you didn't just earn your stripes, little brother. Guess all those years of teaching you how to use a knife finally paid off."

"Leave him alone!" Lou barked at him.

"Hey, I'm good. I am," I insisted, finally starting to feel like myself—but different. That was the moment when I knew that I was going to be okay . . . eventually. At this moment, though, what I really wanted was to check on Chippy, but she was nowhere to be found.

"You all right?" Donna had appeared at my side once again.

I stared at her, feeling guilty that she wasn't the one I wanted by my side after having had this life-changing experience. And now there was absolutely no chance.

"Yeah," I answered, allowing her to hug me. "I'm good."

63

Standing there with my heart in my throat, I glanced over at Lou and Larry positioned next to me. They didn't look too comfortable either. It was one of those moments when I would have done anything to have my mother here to give me guidance.

I suppose to anyone who knew us, today seemed inevitable, but I found it hard to believe that it had finally arrived. I was even more on edge once the music started and the ceremony was about to begin. There in the front pew was Levi, looking a whole lot better, sitting right next to Shirley. Seated next to him on his other side was NeeNee, who I'm sure wished it was her and Larry walking down the aisle. And then there was my friend Juan, who, believe it or not, was seated next to his mother and sister, thanks to Lou's connection in New York, who paid a handsome amount for the weed. The rest of my side and a good portion of the bride's side were filled with my friends and family, including most of the whores from Big Shirley's place.

The back door of the church swung open, and there she stood. She held on to her uncle's arm, looking absolutely stunning, and I was humbled. I couldn't get over how beautiful she was and that she was doing me the honor of becoming my wife. I was certain that every man in the room envied me. She looked even more beautiful as she came closer.

When she reached the front, her uncle placed her hand into mine, kissed her on the cheek, and then he took his seat in the front row, along with what was left of her family now that her mother and father were gone.

The pastor started to recite the vows, but instead of relaxing, I felt even more out of sync. My nerves were definitely getting the better of me. I looked toward Lou and Larry, my two best men, and instead of butterflies, I felt like I had bats in my stomach.

"We are gathered here today to join this man and this woman together in the bonds of holy matrimony. If anyone has just cause why these two shall not be joined, speak now or forever hold your peace." Pastor Simmons paused as if he was expecting someone to object. I looked around, my eyes locking with NeeNee, who didn't say a peep, as hard as it must have been for her.

"Humph!" Lou snickered, no doubt surprised.

The pastor turned to her, looking sort of relieved. "Donna Marie Washington, will you take this man, Lavernius Charles Duncan, to be your lawfully wedded husband? Do you promise to love, honor, and obey him, in sickness and in health, from this day forward, as long as you both shall live?"

She smiled up at me with a sweetness I hadn't seen much of lately. "I do."

The pastor's face lit up with joy as he continued.

"And do you, Lavernius Charles Duncan, take Donna Marie Washington to be your lawfully wedded wife? Do you—"

"No!" My voice erupted from deep within, surprising me. I took a step back. "I can't. I can't do it."

"LC, what are you doing?" Donna snapped, flabbergasted. I couldn't have gotten a better reaction if I had slapped her in the face. "You don't know what you're saying."

"Yeah, I do. Donna, I can't marry you," I said, repeating the words that had been ringing in my mind ever since I took that long walk up there that day. "I'm not in love with you."

"That's ridiculous. It's just cold feet," Donna said dismissively, but I shook my head, growing more resolute.

I took her hand and waited until I had her full attention. "It took me coming all this way to realize that I'm not in love with you," I said finally, feeling relieved.

Donna reached out and whacked me across the face, but it did nothing to lessen my relief. I turned and smiled at Lou; then I nodded, and my two brothers and I stepped off the stage, slowly and intentionally making our way down the aisle.

The guests on one entire side of the church stood up and began to applaud, like they had just witnessed the very thing they had hoped would happen.

"LC Duncan, you can't do this to me!" Donna cried out, but I was too far gone to even pretend to care what she wanted anymore.

"To you? I can't do this to myself," I said with finality.

NeeNee met me as I got to the back of the church. She threw her arms around me in a celebratory motion. "Yay!" She jumped up and down, not giving a damn who knew how happy I had just made her.

Chippy

64

"What you think?" Essie, the best black hairdresser in Las Vegas, careened her neck to gaze in the handheld mirror along with me. I wanted to make sure that I could get a good look at the way she had styled it in the back. Her girl had already done a fantastic job on my nails. They were the perfect shade of fire engine red.

I lowered the mirror, pleased by her work. "Yep, I look good," I bragged. These days I made sure to keep my hair done and my fashion updated on a fairly regular basis. This was the second time I'd been in there that week.

Essie removed the apron covering my outfit and brushed off any remaining hairs from my collar before I stood up. She grinned appreciatively. "Sister, that pantsuit is happening."

"Ain't it, though? I got it over at that new store out on Highway Twenty-three. The one with the big pink awning."

Essie nodded, letting me know she knew exactly what I was talking about. "That place is too rich for my blood. Besides, I would never look as good as you do in it no way. My hips done did too much birthing, and I got the bad-ass children to prove it." She laughed, throwing her head back.

"That means there's more for some lucky stud to get his hands on." I winked at her, opening my purse to pay for her services. I couldn't believe I'd managed to find the one hairdresser within miles who had skills enough to impress me. I pressed an extra ten in her palm before strutting out into the hot sun. I glanced back at my reflection in the window and had to acknowledge again just how fine I really looked.

"Baby, you miss me?" I purred as I opened the door to my brand new burgundy convertible Fiat Spider. When I slid behind the wheel, I felt a wave of jealousy for my own damn self. I had certainly come a long way from the secondhand dresses and beat-up shoes my mother used to make me wear to school.

The car rode like a dream as I zipped down the road, turning off and stopping in front of the only structure for miles around. Nobody showed up here without knowing exactly where they were headed or what they were looking to do once they got here. From the outside of the building, people had no idea how well maintained and impressive the place looked on the inside, or the number of beautiful women in there, anxious to fulfill your every need.

"Hey! Looking good." Cheryl, one of the new girls at the front desk, called out as I came through the heavy wooden door. I acknowledged her and then went straight into the bar area, where I sat in my regular seat and lit a cigarette. Luis, the bartender, brought over a whiskey sour. I'd seen the kind of artillery he kept behind the bar, so I always made sure to treat him right, in case I ever needed more than a drink.

I took one sip. "You sure know how I like it. Thanks, Luis. I'll take care of you later." He gave me a wink and a nod and went back behind the bar.

"Damn, your hair is fly," Nicole, a big-titty waitress from California, exclaimed, placing a box and envelope in front of me. "This was left for you."

I opened up the box and saw that it contained a beautiful diamond ring. I took a deep breath, hesitant to put it on, because I knew what that would mean. I opened up the envelope and removed its contents: five one hundred–dollar bills, a key to one of the suites upstairs, and a first class ticket to Paris in my name, leaving the next night.

"Alejandro." I laughed out loud. Gathering my things, I left a twenty-dollar bill to pay for my drink and gratuity, and then I headed for the elevator with the key to the suite in my hand.

Once everything had gone down at Big Sam's and I saw Donna in LC's arms, I slipped out the door and made my way to the bus station. No way was I dealing with that bullshit when I had a man like Alejandro waiting for me in St. Augustine, willing to devote himself to me. I might never be in love with him, but I sure as hell could learn to love his money.

At least that was what I told myself the first few months I was with him.

Eventually, though, I realized that I couldn't shake my feelings for LC, which wasn't fair to Alejandro, so I told him and then moved out to Vegas. I'd been working for a high-priced escort service run by the hotel's concierge, which was a lot less work and a hell of a lot more money than working at Sam's. I had a few regulars already, and I certainly knew how to keep them coming back once they got a taste.

Alejandro still looked out for me, though, and actually visited every other week now that he was permanently living in L.A. Apparently his little arrangement with the Duncans was even more lucrative than what he'd had going with Sam.

I took the elevator up, checking my makeup in a compact mirror as I looked for the suite. I found it at the end of the hall. When I opened the door, the man on the other side was not at all who I'd been expecting. I had to grab onto the door frame to keep myself from falling down on weak knees. My emotions got caught in my throat.

"What are you doing here, LC? How did you find me?" I tried not to panic at the sight of him. Dammit, I wished I'd had some warning. He looked so good.

He walked over to me and then moved past me to close the door; the whole time his eyes were boring into me. "Alejandro. He said he wanted you to be happy, and he knew you'd never be happy with him." Then he moved so he was standing close enough to touch me.

I felt my heart threatening to beat out of my chest just from his proximity. Why had he come? Just to torture me? I tried to turn away, but he held onto my arm. "I heard you married Donna," I snapped, hating what this was doing to me.

His face lit up, and he had the nerve to smile. I wanted to slap the happiness right off his face, until he corrected my version of events. "You heard wrong. Donna and I are no more. I couldn't go through with it."

I wasn't sure I had heard him correctly. "What? What happened?"

"Kinda hard to marry one woman when you're in love with another." He took the boxed ring out of my hand and dropped to one knee. "Charlotte, I love you. Will you marry me?"

Tears of joy sprang from my eyes. "Yes! LC, I'll marry you."

He slipped the ring on my finger. "Good, because I already paid for the honeymoon," he said, wrapping his arms around me and pulling me close. Then he whispered in my ear. "I'm gonna pay for this one time, and one time only." And then he kissed me. It was long, deep, and exactly the way I'd imagined it would be, before he lifted me up and carried me to the bed.

Discussion Questions

1. Did you feel like you were in the seventies as you read the book?
2. What did you think about Levi's dogs?
3. Do you remember Donna from *Family Business 3*?
4. Would you have thought Chippy was a prostitute at one time before reading this book?
5. What were your feelings about Donna?
6. Did you feel bad for Big Shirley when she got cut?
7. Were you shocked by Big Sam's relationship with his accountant, Jefferson?
8. How much did you hate Big Sam?
9. Did you like NeeNee?
10. Did you feel Larry was crazy?
11. Were you upset about what happened to Levi?
12. Is LC becoming the man you expect him to be?
13. Were you glad Levi and Big Shirley got together?
14. What did you think of the brothers' mother?
15. Were you happy with the ending?
16. What did you think of Chippy and Alejandro's relationship?

If you enjoyed *Grand Opening*,

Please read the teaser for Carl Weber's
next Family Business adventure:

Coming
February 2016

Niles Monroe

1

As the cab exited the Brooklyn-Queens Expressway and traveled through downtown, I couldn't help but stare out the window like some tourist visiting for the first time, instead of a lifelong resident of my favorite borough. It was hard not to be amazed that the neighborhood I last visited five years ago didn't look anything like it had when I left. It had undergone a real transformation, I thought, as we passed the Barclays Center, home of Jay-Z's Brooklyn Nets basketball team. All around the area, businesses like Starbucks had sprung up, revitalizing what used to be a really sketchy area where I grew up watching my back. Now it was definitely on some other, higher end shit.

It wasn't that long ago that rich white folks would never have dreamed of living across the bridge, but now according to my uncle Willie's letters, they were flocking here like shit was free. Made me wonder if the Marcy Projects, where I grew up, would be any different when I got there.

Less than ten minutes later, the cab pulled up in front of my old building, making me nostalgic for the foreign land I had left behind me thirty hours earlier. Time had stood still, and nothing seemed to be different about this low-income projects, one of the most notorious in all of the five boroughs. A lot of things were happening here, and none of them good, as far as I could see. I knew that if I didn't get things poppin' straight out the gate, then like a lot of soldiers returning from the service, I'd wind up never leaving, because this place had the ability to make you sink like quicksand.

Across the concrete walkway up ahead, I spotted a black-and-white pulled over near the entrance to my mom's building. I wish I could say it caught me off guard, but in this neighborhood, the police, ambulance, and fire engines were always showing up to carry someone off to either the hospital, jail, or the morgue. It made me wonder which of the three the cops had come to deal with.

"Pull over here on the right," I instructed the Armenian cab driver, who looked like he wanted to keep moving and get the hell away from this area as quickly as possible. I was surprised he had even stopped for me at JFK once I explained that I was headed to Brooklyn, but then I assumed that it was one of the privileges of wearing a uniform. That was, until he told me about something called Uber that was cutting into his ability to make a living, meaning he could no longer afford to be picky.

"Here?" He glanced out the window at the neighborhood denizens, huddled around in small groups like that was their job or something. There was drinking, drug dealing, and plain old-fashioned unemployables, many who had made peace with the hand they were dealt, hanging out all around us.

"Yep!" I reached into my pocket and paid the man, noticing that he made no motion to get out of the cab to help me with my bags. Damn, this place had him shook up like a scared little girl, but if these guys hanging on the sidewalk made him nervous, then he was damn lucky he'd never been to war and seen real enemies up close. He tried to hand me the change, but I waved it off and didn't bother to react negatively when he popped the trunk for me to get my own bags. Dude was scared, and frankly, if I hadn't grown up in this place, there was no way I'd want to be anywhere near here either.

I grabbed my duffle bag and backpack out of the trunk and headed toward the building. Cabbie didn't wait one second before he bounced out of there like his ride had caught fire or something.

For a long time, I hadn't imagined I would ever wind up back here. My feet hadn't moved ten steps before a couple of guys came rushing at me.

"Hey, soldier, can we spit something at you?" The taller of the two stepped in my path, blocking me from moving forward. He had to be in his late twenties, a couple of years younger than me, but he had that look of weariness that told me he had already squeezed a little too much living into his time on earth, and if he wasn't careful, he'd meet his expiration date shortly. The small guy behind him had a pockmarked face and was missing a front tooth that made him appear like a candidate for the short bus.

"Sure." I leaned my duffle on the ground to relieve myself of the weight while I listened to what they had to say.

"You wanna buy a little party favor? I know shit is harder to get over in those war zones. I got some rocks and some pot." He said it bouncing up and down, like he himself was on something.

"Nah, I'm good." I picked up my bag, suddenly focused on moving past them right now. I had time for a lot of things, but drugs weren't for me. I had never seen anything positive come out of people who got involved. In fact, I had only seen the opposite. No, they could really miss me with that bullshit.

"Brothas and sistas coming home from doing Uncle Sam's work need to get a little high, you hear me?" His sidekick threw in his two cents. "They drop you back here and forget all about what you just been through." He actually sounded a whole lot smarter than he looked.

This shit I'm selling is sweet. Make you forget all your troubles. Now, I know you done seen some things over there you want to forget, so why not let me help you out, my brotha?" He continued to press, even after I had been kind enough to entertain his stupid-ass conversation and told him no.

I don't fuck with drugs, so no thank you!" I said in a tone meant to clarify my position before I had to stop myself from physically removing them from my way. Lucky for them, they took the hint and walked away, but not before throwing in a last word.

You know where to find us when you realize we were try'na be helpful and shit!" the tall one snarled like I had pissed him off. I ignored them and kept moving toward the entrance. I had to walk around the cop car that didn't seem to mind blocking the entrance.

I hit the elevator button and felt a wave of relief when it actually showed up in working order. On the ride up to my mom's apartment, I felt myself getting a little excited. It had been too long since I'd seen her, and I don't care how old I get, I'm always gonna want to see her face. My moms wasn't no saint, but she had done the best she could to raise my sister and me. It made her proud that I had gotten away and built some kind of career, instead of making the streets my business, which almost happened.

I could have done another tour and stayed, but so much had gone down that I knew it was time to come home. I'd only been back to visit twice in almost ten years, and I couldn't help but have guilt about it. That was the main reason I felt so glad to be home.

"Don't touch me!" I heard the screaming voice before I got off the elevator.

"Shit!" I grabbed my things and bolted toward my mother's apartment at the far end of the hall. Her door was wide open.

"Ma'am, please calm down." I entered as two cops were trying to reason with my mother, who held a large kitchen knife in her hands, daring them to come any closer.

"Get out, you devils!" she yelled.

"Lorna, please!" my uncle Willie pleaded with his sister, but she was too far into another realm to be able to comply. Seeing me, his face flooded with relief. "Niles, help her!"

I dropped my bags and held my hands up so that the armed officers understood my passivity as I moved into the room. Last thing I needed was to become another casualty in the ongoing war between the cops and people of color.

"Mama. Mama," I called out to her, my voice calm and coaxing. Unfortunately, seeing my mother in this state wasn't rare; it had just been a long time for me.

She turned to me, her eyes glassy in that way that let me know she hadn't really seen me yet. "Get these devils out of my house. They are trying to poison me!" she shouted, flailing her hands and waving the knife around.

"Mom! Mom!" my voice boomed as I attempted to jar her out of her current state. I turned to the officers, their guns still drawn, and pointed at my mother. "Keep your fingers off the trigger." I waited as they lowered their weapons before turning back to my mother. "It's Niles. I'm home, Mama." I moved toward her, waiting for her to recognize her only son.

"Niles?" she said, lowering the knife, a spark of recognition coming through. "These are devils, and they are going to hurt me real bad."

I pointed at the cops, who were now watching us curiously. "Those aren't devils, Mom. They're angels in disguise." My tone sounded light and sing-songy, nothing like how I felt. "Look closely and you'll see it."

My mother glanced from me to them and back before her face broke out in a sweet smile. She then lowered the knife before collapsing into my arms. "You're home. My baby is home!" she shouted as I removed the knife from her hand.

Notes

Notes

Notes

35674053976313   252 6410